Praise for
HUYSMAN'S PETS

"FASCINATING, AND ELEGANT . . . This book promises a great deal and does not disappoint . . . A GOOD SOLID READ."
—*Science Fiction Review*

"ENGROSSING . . . Kate Wilhelm, winner of science fiction's Hugo and Nebula awards, has come up with a story that is frightening, and given today's scientific capabilities, plausible. SHE KEEPS THE SUSPENSE MOVING!"
—*Marlboro Enterprise/Hudson Daily Sun*

"SKILLFUL . . . believable characters!"
—*Fantasy Review*

"A SUSPENSE THRILLER . . . a well-told blend of mystery and science fiction with Wilhelm's usual finely drawn characters."
—*Science Fiction Chronicle*

"LIVELY . . . a very credible exploration of the bonds between human beings."
—*San Francisco Chronicle*

"WILHELM HAS NEVER BEEN BETTER . . . The combination of the sf theme of genetic manipulation of humans with the political intrigue of government officials' will to do anything to obtain and retain power makes for NON-STOP READING . . . WONDERFUL!"
—*Voice of Youth Advocates*

"COMPLEX AND CHALLENGING . . ."
—*Bil*

"ENJOYABLE!"
—*Ki*

Contin

HUYSMAN'S PETS

KATE WILHELM

ACE BOOKS, NEW YORK

HUYSMAN'S PETS

An Ace Book/published by arrangement with
Bluejay Books Inc.

PRINTING HISTORY
Bluejay edition/January 1986
Ace edition/December 1988

ISBN: 0-441-35441-6

Ace Books are published by The Berkley Publishing Group,
200 Madison Avenue, New York, New York 10016.
The name "ACE" and the "A" logo
are trademarks belonging to Charter Communications, Inc.

PRINTED IN THE UNITED STATES OF AMERICA

10 9 8 7 6 5 4 3 2 1

To Amit Goswami

PROLOGUE

March 14, 1970. Kansas City. Wet snow was melting, making rivulets that joined, became torrents in the gutters. Already, by eight, the air was balmy. Children had their coats open, their mittens in their pockets; their fingers were fiery red and felt hot. The heavy, wet snow was perfect for snowballs. The school bell blared and reluctantly the swarming children moved toward the doors, flinging one last snowball, sliding one last slide. One of the boys dumped a double handful of snow down the sweater of one of the girls, and she chased him around the brick building shrieking. The bell rang again; from now on they would be marked tardy. Lisa Robbins, a sixth grader, had been hanging back, not wanting to play with the smaller children. Now she ran up the wide stairs, but at the top she came to a complete halt. Someone rushed into her from behind and she staggered, caught a railing for support. Her face looked pinched, as if by cold. She turned and went down the stairs, against the current of the last few children hurrying to class. At the bottom of the stairs she started to walk fast, away from the building; she did not look back, and she held herself stiffly, gaze straight ahead, hands clenched. Her lunch box bumped against her leg with each step.

It was only four blocks to her house, one half of a duplex in a development where all the buildings were dun colored and there were no garages, no real yards, only a patch of grass before each building right down to the street where cars were parked as close as they could get to each other—nose to tail to nose. The footsteps she had left in the snow were distorted, each one larger than both feet together, round, black with melted snow and dirty water.

No one was out now; the children were all in school, parents had gone to work or were still getting ready for work, too early for the mailman or deliveries. She had to find her key in her pocket before she could let herself in. Her mother was in the bathroom getting ready to go to her job in the diner. The child did not take off her boots or her jacket. She put the lunch box down on the kitchen table and tapped on the bathroom door.

Judy was out of the shower by then and partly dressed. When she opened the door and saw her daughter, ashen faced, rigid with fear, she drew in her breath sharply.

"Those people are at the school," Lisa said.

"I'll hurry," her mother replied. "Get the box from the closet and the suitcases."

Fifteen minutes later they were in the two-year-old Ford leaving town, heading west. It was almost an hour before the child began to relax.

April 3, 1970. There were six black children in the sixth grade that year in Lincoln Elementary School, and at recess they kept themselves carefully segregated from the other students. Four girls, two boys, playing a game with a ball, the rules of which only they knew. The third graders had their morning recess at the same time, but the bigger children paid no attention to the smaller ones. Their game was too rough for babies. The bell rang, and they started to dart about like a miniswarm, keeping the ball in the air. One of them, Franklin Gillette, suddenly stopped, a listening look on his face. A girl poked him in the ribs and flashed away, but he did not move. "Come on," they yelled at him, running backward, then forward, laughing. He turned and walked away fast, down to the bicycle rack where he unchained a bike and got on and sped away from the school.

He pedaled toward his apartment building, but, nearly there, he swerved and went down an alley instead, then down a side street, and finally the main street that took him to the highway out of town. He pedaled as fast as he could. The fear taste in his mouth reminded him of the pennies they put on the railroad tracks, the same coppery taste that would not go away.

He knew he could not keep riding on the highway. He took the exit that was near the switching yards, and there he dumped the bike and swung aboard a freight car. He never had done this before, but he had seen it in movies and the other kids had talked about it. He huddled as far back in the corner as he could and no one found him until the train was outside Oklahoma City, where he was thrown off.

June 1, 1970. Mrs. Henderson's face was red and her hair was wet with sweat when the sixth graders finally marched into the gymnasium and seated themselves without anyone falling down or tripping anyone else, without any rude noises that made them all break out in wild laughter, without any real pushing or shoving or scrambling for the chairs. It was a mistake, she thought grimly, to let them march in in pairs. She had told everyone it was a mistake, but would anyone believe her? Never! Five times she had been forced to make them start over. Five times!

"Now remember to do it like this tomorrow," she told them sternly. "If you mess it up, I'll . . . I'll . . ."

Someone giggled and she had to smile too. What could she do?

"That was fine," she said then. "It looked really good. Bobby, don't move your chair when you sit down, okay? And Sandra—"

One of the girls—Michelle?—had risen. She looked pale, sick.

"What's wrong, dear?"

The girl shook her head, her eyes too wide open, her color washed out down to her lips.

"The rest of you go back to your rooms now. Go on, and don't make noise in the halls. Remember, other classes are working. Sit down, Michelle. Are you faint?"

A few girls were clustering about Michelle. Some of the boys began to chase each other through the gymnasium; chairs were scattered with rasping noises of wood on wood. The gym teacher would have a fit. . . .

"You girls go on. I'll look after Michelle." Mrs. Henderson took the girl's hand. It was cold, clammy. "Come along, dear. I'll take you down to the office for a rest. I expect you've had too much excitement."

"I have to go home," she whispered.

"We'll see. Maybe if you just put your head down for a minute or two."

"I have to go. I . . . I'm going to throw up."

Mrs. Henderson gently forced her down into a chair. She looked at the three girls who were lingering. "Sandra, please go to the office and ask Mr. Holbein to come here. Now go on, all of you. Out!"

They left with obvious reluctance. Mrs. Henderson sat down next to Michelle, holding her hand. "I'll take you home, but we have to get permission from Mr. Holbein first. Okay? Can you wait for a minute or two?"

She nodded, but it was clear that she was sick, shaking with a chill. Mrs. Henderson sighed. She could not remember ever having a graduation ceremony go off without a hitch of some kind, and every other year she was in charge of the damn thing.

"What is it?" Gregory Holbein demanded as he entered the echoing room. He was the principal.

"I have to take Michelle home. She's not feeling well."

He joined them, peering at the girl, frowning. "Would you step over here a minute, Mrs. Henderson?" He crossed the room to the wall and waited impatiently for Mrs. Henderson to join him.

"You know we have to have full attendance for those tests," he said in a harsh undertone. "This is the first day in a month that we've had perfect attendance. You know how important that is!"

"Look at her. She's going to heave any second."

"Oh, God! I called them and told them to come today! They're waiting, all set. I told them we have perfect attendance!"

"Well, don't tell them otherwise! What can I say? She's sick. I thought she was going to pass out cold. That kid's got to go home. Don't tell them anyone's missing. This isn't one of our tests or the board's; nothing goes on the transcript. Just don't tell them anyone's absent."

He took a deep breath. "Take her out the back door. I won't mention it, and for God's sake, don't you either."

"I'll be at least an hour. They'll be gone by then. Just relax, Greg. See you later."

She did not show her amusement. How he fumed when any of the older teachers told him what to do, called him by his first name as if he were a child. She did not do it often, only enough to keep him in line somewhat. She went back to Michelle. "Can you walk, dear?"

"I think so." She was unsteady. At the outside door, she held on to the frame and looked agonized.

"Just wait here and I'll bring the car around. Can you manage that?"

"Yes. I'll hold on."

Mrs. Henderson hurried, and when she returned with the car, the girl was still clinging there. She helped her get in. Michelle put her head down on her knees as Mrs. Henderson drove through the grounds, out to the street, and toward her home. Blocks away from the school, the child sat upright again; color was returning to her cheeks, but she did not look fully recovered. It was good that she was going home, Mrs. Henderson knew. She probably needed a doctor, a checkup, something.

Michelle's mother was home, a single parent from the look of it. The house was well furnished, clean, but small. There was no sign of a male's presence.

The girl's mother looked frightened, and Mrs. Henderson reassured her that it was nothing serious, that girls this age often became faint with the onset of the menses, excitement . . . She drove slowly when she left the child with her mother; she was in no hurry to return to school, in fact had no intention of returning until after hours. She stopped at a coffee shop and had a cigarette and coffee until it was time to go back. The next day when Michelle was absent, she was surprised; she meant to call and inquire about her, but there was the rehearsal for one last time, and one of the boys knocked a chair off the low stage and for a while everyone thought the boy it hit might have a broken arm, but he was all right, and then the day was over. Michelle did not appear for graduation that evening. Mrs. Henderson never saw her again.

ONE

The road was a wet black snake slithering through the dense forests in upstate New York. The rain had stopped, but the trees dripped, and pools of water gleamed on the serpent's body, treacherous spots that could be smooth and level, or could be potholes. And it was damn cold. July, Clay Moseby kept thinking in disgust. It was July, and it was cold! He slowed from twenty-five to twenty and leaned forward to read names on the mailboxes that had appeared in a cluster. He was looking for Jay Rissel. He had lost faith in Jay Rissel. Just a couple miles after the turn-off, hah! An animal scurried across the road, and he slowed down again. He did not know what it had been. A possum? Woodchuck? Raccoon? Animals belonged in zoos with nameplates in front of their cages, for god's sake. Another bunch of mailboxes stood at attention by the side of the road. The third one said JAY RISSEL. He slowed again, this time looking for the driveway. First one after the boxes. Right. If he didn't find the place soon, he knew, he would not find it at all this day. It would be dark in half an hour. No one could find a thing on a road like this once it got dark. Black trees, black road, rain, wildlife to claim the road as soon as the light failed. Maybe bears and dangerous stuff like that, who knew?

He almost missed the driveway it was so narrow, so hemmed in by trees. People actually lived out here, lived here year-round, in the winter with snow up to their keisters! Sent their kids to school on buses that wound in and out of the trees with hardly enough room to make a turn, and god help them if something bigger than a bike was coming the other way . . . The driveway was gravel and even windier than the road and one car wide. All at once it ended at a log house.

No one responded to his pounding on the door; he tried it and found it unlocked, entered, wandered through the house that was darker than outside, and finally found Drew Lancaster on a deck behind the house overlooking the lake. The lake was so still it looked artificial, a wet painting.

"Hey, Drew, how's it going?"

"Fine, Clay. How'd you find me?" Better, why did you bother?"

"Pat had the address. She said to tell you hello."

"Hello, Pat."

Drew was long; stretched out on a chaise as he was now, he seemed even longer than his six feet plus, and thinner than Clay remembered.

Clay sat down and studied him. Neither spoke for several minutes until Clay asked. "Where's the booze?"

"Kitchen. Help yourself."

"Yeah, right back."

He switched on a light this time, hunted in cabinets, found a glass, and half filled it from a bottle on the counter. It was too cold to add ice.

"What are you doing out here?" he asked when he returned to the deck.

"Watching fish rise."

Clay took a deep drink.

"Look. You see that ring out there, where I'm pointing? Fish. They come up to feed this time of day."

"When you're not watching the fish, what do you do out here?"

"House-sitting for my old friend. Too bad he's not here. I could say, 'Clay, Jay.' "

"Pat said this place is empty nine or ten months each year. Doesn't need a house sitter."

Drew shrugged.

"When are you coming back to the city?"

"What's the date?"

"July ten, nineteen eighty-two."

"Maybe October. Maybe December. Maybe never."

"Did you read that stuff I sent you?"

"About Huysman? Some of it."

"You going to do the book?"

"Probably not."

"Why not?"

"I'm retired."

Clay took another drink, deeper. It was good bourbon. "You can't be retired, for god's sake. You're only forty years old!"

"Two. Forty-two."

"And I'm sixty-two. Huysman was eighty-five when he died!"

"See what working all his life did for him? Killed him finally."

"Not funny. Look, he was a famous man, Nobel Prize, all that. It's a natural for you. His widow says no one else can have the private stuff. Searles wants you to do it. I can get you the biggest advance you've ever seen for it. In fact, it's in the works now. It's a beauty."

"He was a terrible man. I don't like him."

"You don't have to like him. No one liked him, not even his widow, but he will make a hell of a book! No one expects a whitewash, for god's sake."

"You know why I don't like him? Not because he was a fascist, if he really was, or because he was a government toady, and he was. Not for those reasons. Because he was a genius. I hate him for that. I'm not a genius. You're not. Few of us are, but he was, and he knew it and despised everyone else who wasn't. For that I hate him."

"Drew, you may not need the money today or this year, but think of next year, ten years from now. You have to think of the future, and it's damn good money. His widow even called me. You know who's been after her for all the private stuff? Vidal! McPheel! Even Manchester! And she told them all to get lost. She likes the way you write. She liked the Stravinsky book and the Eisenhower book. She wants you to do this one. An authorized biography. No one but you."

"Flattering."

It was getting too dark to see his features; his face was a smudge of paleness in the gloom of the twilight. "You have anything to eat in the house?"

"Steaks in the freezer. Vegetables, lettuce in the crisper. Help yourself."

"I'll make us both something to eat. You stoned?"

Drew laughed, a low rumbling sound that was somehow mirthless. "Funny thing. That's what I came out here for, to get high on something every night, and I haven't done it yet. But I will. I keep forgetting, but one day I'll make it.''

Drew was not aware when Clay left him. The lightning bugs were out now, flickering here, there over the lake, and bats were squealing, swooping. . . . Across the lake, lights had come on in other summer houses, and distant voices were indistinguishable from one another, their words only noises without meaning. He supposed Clay was right; he should think about next year, about the next decade. Clay didn't understand, he decided, nor Pat, anyone. Huysman would understand now, although before his death he would have had the same trouble as everyone else, no doubt, genius or not. But now he would understand. It didn't make a damn bit of difference, that was the secret that Drew had come to the lake to think about, and having thought about it now for how long? six weeks, two months? he knew it was the ultimate secret hardly anyone could acknowledge.

Clay would tell him to get a new woman, if he mentioned this discovery to him. That was Clay's answer to any problem—a new fuck, a new thrill, a new contract. Life is like quicksilver, he sometimes said, speeding here and there, never static. You stop moving, you're dead, pal. Finis. Move! Get with it! Find something new and fun to do. Clay would think this was the result of having Pat leave; he did think that. Most people thought it was too bad how hard he was taking what was, after all, an everyday commonplace any more. No one expected a man and a woman to stay together more than a few years, for goodness' sake! How old-fashioned. He, Drew, did not expect that. And he, Drew, accepted that he had made his discovery long before Pat had cleaned out her things from their apartment, cleaned out Sherry's things, made the move back to Richmond and Washington, a bonafide miracle living in two places at once.

He really did not need the money, he mused, watching the pale green lights, yellow lights in random motion, Brownian motion. His needs were relatively few. That was nice, having a wife with her own fortune, so that when you split, she did not grab alimony or attorney fees. You have yours, I have mine, she had said, and she packed up Sherry, who presumably was hers now except for vacation times and a few holidays and when he could get to Richmond. But he could get to Richmond any time he wanted, Pat had pointed out. He could live where he chose. Not in Richmond, babe, not anywhere in the South, in the land where women are women and men men and the only good black is a dead one and girl children automatically belonged to their mothers.

"Hey, Drew, come on in and eat! God, it's freezing outside!"

They ate in the kitchen. The house was sparsely furnished with throw-away chairs and rickety tables. There were bunks in the two bedrooms, a cot in the living room.

They ate in silence. Clay had sliced a tomato to go with the steaks, and they both drank the bourbon.

"Seriously," Clay said, pushing his plate back, "what do you do in a place like this?"

"Swim. Fish. Hike."

"And think?"

"Hardly ever." He had found that he could walk for hours and not remember a thought afterward. He wondered if his brain had died or was simply on vacation. He did not worry about it.

"Come back, kid. Poke around with the book and then if you really don't want to do it, okay. No hard feelings. Sometimes you just don't. But give it a chance." He stood up. "Got any coffee?"

"In the refrigerator." He drained his glass, examined himself for a sign of drunkenness and failed to find it. He had not been drinking quite enough, he decided. He was not a serious drinker. Pat was right: he was not serious about anything. "Why do you keep working?" he asked Clay.

"For the money. What else?"

"You have more than anyone. How much is enough?"

"There's no such thing, kid. There's never enough. No matter where you are, it's never quite enough."

Drew nodded. That was an open secret. Money. Prime mover. The ultimate cause behind every other cause. The real secret was that it generated itself. Those with, got more, just as the song said. Those without could never count on getting close enough to it to get a good sniff. Simple. He was not certain where he fitted into that spectrum. The South was not for him because he couldn't be a good ol' boy, but neither could he pursue money in the northern way. He needed a third category, he decided: those who didn't give a damn found themselves stumbling over piles of money from time to time with no effort on their part, and it really did not matter or they ended up on Skid Row and that didn't matter either.

The silence was broken by the sound of the coffee pot making its peculiar snuffling noise. It worked in protest every time. He found himself thinking of Stanley Everett Huysman, after all. Why had he kept working right up to the end, or until a stroke stopped him, with death following within the year? That was a mystery. Eighty-five fucking years old! A biblical span. A venerable age, the age our forefathers achieved with dignity and hard work and the assurance of another life hereafter even longer and more venerable and more dignified. He laughed and when Clay looked at him questioningly, he shrugged.

"Why not? Maybe I'll do it. What drove him? Money?"

"Probably. Got any cream?"

"No. And no sugar. I keep forgetting."

Clay sighed, poured coffee for both of them and brought the cups to the table. "Let me tell you about Irma, the widow." He tasted his coffee, made a face, and added a slug of bourbon. "She lives in New Haven part of the time, in Mesa, Arizona, during the winter, and in Princeton a month or two each summer. She's in the process of selling the Princeton house. That's why she's anxious for you to start, she says. His stuff is being boxed now and eventually it'll be donated to the university, but first you get a crack at it. She's donating it with a catch: it can't be examined or used for twenty-five years."

Drew nodded absently, paying little attention. Three houses, how about that! That's what happened when people had more money than they could spend: they bought more houses. So Huysman had not worked up to the end for money. Power? Glory? Prestige? Habit? He grinned. Probably habit. What else was there to do?

"... asked Ed Searles if he thought a biography coming out now would make the other books have more value, and Ed assured her that he thought so. Huysman must have written a dozen popular books over the years, all out in trade paper."

A front had come through that afternoon bringing pounding, driving rain and chill winds, and now the log cabin was damp and cold. He should make a fire, Drew thought, and made no effort to go out and find dry wood under the overhang. Irma was seventy, he remembered. He had read the material Clay had sent him in New York back in June. May, whenever, and there it was, still in his head. She was seventy, sixteen years younger than her husband. She had been twenty-two to his thirty-eight when they married. And then what? What had she done with her life, married to a famous if somewhat mad scientist? Entertain his equally mad friends? Visit him during July and August in Princeton? Come home long enough to dust, put up some preserves, check the curtains for mildew . . . ?

And now she wanted his books to sell more copies, make more money. What for? Why did she need more money? Yet another house? Pat was thirty-eight. She had been twenty-two when they were married, and he had been twenty-six. Pat had lived through the same span of years that had separated Stanley Everett Huysman and his bride Irma, and Pat said that she was no longer the girl she had been, that a new woman had evolved in her place . . . He stifled the laughter that rose, not wanting to try to explain to Clay, knowing he could not explain. It had occurred to him that if he died, Pat might well want to do whatever she could to prolong the life of his books, to insure their continuing sales. Not for the money, she would say, believing it, but because.

Later, Drew stood on the back terrace and watched fog swirling over the lake. The water was warmer than the air now, and pockets of dense fog had formed, but in the middle of the lake it was wraithlike, uncertain of its powers. Through the mists the lights of other houses shimmered, became distorted, grew firm, only to lose coherence again. Ghosts walked the water, spread over the ground, grew bolder and climbed the trees, reached out to other ghosts with ephemeral hands that nevertheless blotted out the sky and finally everything else until there was only the fog ghost in possession of the night.

He would have to go to Washington and read all the articles Huysman had written in all the deadly scientific journals in the Library of Congress. He thought of the wooden seats and scarred tables, the musty air, the foul lights, and he thought of Pat who kept an apartment in Washington. And a home in Richmond. He left the terrace, went to the telephone and called Western Union. His telegram said: HAVE A JOB, GETTING A HAIRCUT, CAN I VISIT? ALL IS FORGIVEN.

"My husband," Irma Huysman said briskly, "will be known as the original thinker of the century. He has been much maligned and even ridiculed by his contemporaries who were as gnats to his genius, but he will be vindicated. He was to physiology and biology and genetics what Einstein was to physics, more than Einstein was to physics." She was tall and straight, heavy through her shoulders and breasts but with thin legs and arms. Her hair was metallic gray, cut short with firm waves that looked painted in place.

"Yes, ma'am," Drew said from time to time when she paused and waited for him to say something.

The Princeton house was three stories, elegantly furnished— French provincial, fine Hepplewhite pieces. A pale blue and gold Chinese rug was inches thick; there were lacquered tables with ornate blue vases of gold and copper-colored dahlias, and a chandelier that sparkled and gleamed as if set with diamonds. Drew was afraid to move.

With him and Irma Huysman in the museum-like setting were Florence Charmody, unknown beyond her name, and an attorney, Malcolm Letterman. Florence was a stocky woman of any age from thirty to fifty; she had red hair and green eyes and wore what people called sensible clothes—a tailored suit, low heels, no makeup, a single gold chain. Her nails were short, no rings; there was just the gleam of a watch from time to time when she moved. Letterman was in his sixties, bored.

"I want to tell you a story about my husband," Irma said. "To explain what kind of a person he was. People called him a racist, and they were wrong. He never gave a thought to purity of the races. All he ever wanted to do was improve the quality of the human mind. That was his goal in life, his dream. His entire life was dedicated to that end. At one of his lectures a man in the audience asked if Stanley's parents were geniuses. Well, of course they were not. They were rather common, I'm afraid. He was a minor government employee, a clerk or something like that. And she . . . Well, I suppose she could cook. Anyway. When Stanley replied that they were ordinary people, the man made a disgusting noise and there was a great deal of laughter. After it stopped, Stanley said, just as if there were a dialogue going on, 'What is more to the point, sir, is that it is quite evident from observing you exactly where your parents rank in the spectrum of intelligence.' ''

Drew glanced at Florence to see if she had got the point, but she was engrossed in her thumbnail. Letterman was stifling a yawn.

"He respected intelligence," Irma continued. "Nothing else. Not wealth, not position, not influence of any sort, only intelligence." She stood up. Drew noticed that she held on to the arm of her chair until she was sure of her footing. "The rules will be, as I explained to Mr. Searles, that nothing is to leave this house until it has been approved either by myself or by Florence here. And I am to have final approval of whatever material you elect to use. Now, if you will excuse me."

Letterman had jumped to his feet and was at her side instantly, his hand hovering near but not quite touching her arm. They left the room together.

"He never laid a finger on her," Drew said when the door closed behind them.

"He never does. No one would dare. I'm actually Dr. Florence Charmody," she said with a sigh. "She always forgets that part. I'm going through his papers just to make sure there isn't something that should be published posthumously."

"Medical doctor?"

She shook her head. "Psychologist. He was my adviser and then I worked for him a few years. I teach at Sarah Lawrence, or will again when this is over."

"Okay, so you're the cop. What are my privileges, hours, rights? Do they feed me on the spot or do I go out?"

She grinned and looked closer to thirty than fifty. "Let's wait for Letterman. He's in a tizzy about all this, by the way. He's afraid someone's going to steal the silver."

"The rug maybe. How much would you say it's worth?"

"Forty thousand? Fifty?"

"I wouldn't want to be the one to spill india ink on it."

"But it does look and feel rollable, doesn't it? Have you actually felt it? Silky through and through."

"Maybe we can roll in it together before our work is done."

She studied him thoughtfully.

"You're not married? Or gay?"

"Neither of the above." She looked past him and he turned

to see Letterman reentering the room. "I was just telling Mr. Lancaster that no food or drink is allowed in this room."

"Good god, no! Look, Lancaster, I'm not at all sure any of this is going to work out. I mean, you'd have to do much of your work here in the house, and we're trying to get appraisals done . . . There's an interested party . . ."

"I won't mention the leaky faucets or the mold in the basement."

"Oh, god! This is not a laughing matter, Mr. Lancaster! Believe me, it is not! We've already had a theft here, and, frankly, I don't at all like the idea of letting people wander in and out."

Drew looked at Florence who raised her eyebrows and lifted her shoulders slightly. "We don't know if anything's been stolen," she said. "Maybe just misplaced. Some of the files aren't where they should be."

"If they're in the house, we'll find them," Drew said stoutly. "I promise you, Mr. Letterman, we will find them."

The attorney closed his eyes for a moment. "I see. Well, hopefully our paths won't have to cross very often. I'll show you the office and a room you may sleep in if you choose." He tone was arctic, his face set.

He led the way from the room with Drew following slowly. On his way out, he whispered to Florence, "I don't think he likes me." He thought he was rewarded by a nearly inaudible chuckle.

He arrived in Washington at midnight and pushed the bell of Pat's apartment with a finger that had gone rubbery. She opened the door.

"You're beautiful," he said, not moving.

"Come in. What a silly telegram. You didn't either get a haircut."

"Got the job, though." He held up his briefcase. "Today a job, tomorrow a trim."

"Are you all right?"

"You're beautiful. Are you alone?"

"Of course. Do you plan to come in or just stand there?"

"Can we go to bed?"

Her eyes widened. He knew they were blue, but with the light behind her, they looked black, bottomless. He wanted to drown in them. He told her that.

"Come in, Drew. Have you eaten anything today?"

"I don't remember."

She took his hand and pulled gently. She was wearing a floor-length housecoat of some light material that clung to her when she moved. Her hair was loose, not curly, not straight, dark brown with a glint of silver when the light was just so. He pushed the door closed with his foot and tightened his grip on her hand. She did not resist but moved with him through the apartment to the master bedroom where a lamp was on, a book on a table by the bed.

Then they were in the bed and his hands were on her, all over her, and he was gliding into her, murmuring, "Slippery, slickety, warm, hot . . ."

"Sh," she said. "Don't talk."

And he didn't.

TWO

He woke up at eight. She was in the kitchen, already dressed, not in sensible clothes at all but in a beautiful pale green linen dress and matching high-heeled sandals. A white linen jacket was draped over a chair, a white leather bag on the chair seat.

"Let's go to the beaches of Rio. Remember the sand like brown sugar, the kids flying their kites? And the bikinis!"

"We never were in Rio. I have to go to the office."

"Paris. We can take our lunches in brown paper bags and spend the next two weeks lost in the Louvre."

"Paris is full of tourists all summer. There are eggs and bacon—"

"Madrid. That brutal white light on the red tiled roofs—"

"There's orange juice in the fridge. I squeezed it yesterday, but it's still good."

"I'll meet you for lunch. Hot dogs and cookies and Kool-Aid in the park."

"I have an engagement. When you leave, just close the door; it'll lock. And the coffee's on a timer, so you don't have to worry about turning it off."

"Are you still going out with the senator?"

"I work for the senator. Not quite the same thing."

"I should hope not. Still on that financial feasibility study for the big muddy dam?" He watched her put on her jacket and run her hand under the collar to release the captured hair, just the way he remembered the gesture. "I thought the senators were all off on junkets this time of year."

"Senator Wiley's staff is hard at work. I'm part of the staff." She picked up her bag. "I don't want to talk to you about the senator or about the dam."

"Why?"

"You know what you said the last time I tried to talk about my job." She glanced at herself in the foyer mirror.

"I forget."

"You said I would do less harm in the world if I just stayed home and counted my money. Good-bye, Drew. I'll be out until awfully late; please don't hang around." She turned at the door. "I almost forgot. Your mail has been forwarded here from New York. Stop it, Drew, or I'll just write Refused on it and send it back." She left.

He drank her orange juice and her coffee, but he did not eat her bacon and eggs. Probably he should not have said that to her, he thought. And not on the day the divorce came through. They had gone to bed that day, and sometime during the long afternoon of celebration and mourning he had said that and made her mad all over again. That was his talent, to make her mad. You love me, he had insisted that day, and she had said, yes, I love you, and I can't stand being with you any longer. He loved her, still loved her, would forever and ever love her, and she would forever and ever love him, but she was seeing the senator and he was going to roll on the rug with Florence Charmody the first chance he got, and the world was as insane as he was, as she was, all insane together.

After he showered, he wrote on the ten-foot-long bathroom mirror with soap: *The big muddy dam is a boondoggle and all the financial feasibility studies, all the cost-effective statements in the world won't make it anything else.* He had to squinch up the last line, but it was impressive, he decided, surveying it.

He gathered up the letters that had been forwarded from his New York apartment. Most of the mail was throwaway junk and bills. He tossed them. The phone rang. For a moment he regarded it; it continued to ring. Finally he lifted the receiver.

"You have reached Ms. Patricia Stevens' residence. This is James the butler speaking. May I be of assistance?"

There was a silence and a throat clearing, then a male voice. "Uh, may I speak with Mr. Drew Lancaster, please?"

"Just a moment, sir. In the event that Mr. Lancaster is on the premises, who shall I say is calling?"

"Leon Lauder. But he doesn't know me. Just tell him—"

Drew hung up. Indeed he did not know a Mr. Leon Lauder, had no desire to meet a Mr. Leon Lauder, and certainly did not wish to speak to Mr. Leon Lauder on the telephone. He left the apartment. Behind him the phone started ringing.

"You really don't have to go to Washington," Florence had said. "Most of the articles are here, and the few that we don't have copies of, we can order."

"I know. But I am thorough and efficient and conscientious. I see it as my duty to make sure personally."

"You're really weird, you know?"

Yes, he knew. He filled out the order for the articles he wanted, checked the catalog for anything not on the list Florence had provided, and was done in Washington. It was bright hot outside and Washington, like Paris, was filled with tourists. They came by bus, by station wagon, on foot, planes . . . And they filled the avenues, all of them carrying cameras. Their sweat was responsible for the famed Washington humidity, he decided.

"Mr. Lancaster?"

He felt a touch on his arm and turned to see a gray-haired man at his side. "I'm Lauder of the Secret Service," the man said, opening his hand, as a magician might, to reveal identification. "Could we have a little talk? Someplace where it's cool."

"A nice dim cool bar?"

"Un-hun. A nice lighted coffee shop. There's one around the corner. God, this weather!"

The coffee shop reminded Drew that he had not eaten breakfast; he ordered corned beef and beer. Lauder had iced coffee with a scoop of vanilla ice cream.

"How convenient that we both happened to be at the same place at the same time," Drew said.

"Your ex-wife doesn't have a butler."

"Fired already? Poor old man turned out into the heat to die like a dog!"

"Yeah, way it goes."

"Lauder was thick in every dimension: thick body, thick neck, thick hands and wrists. Even his gray hair was thick and bushy. He was sunburned. He talked admiringly about the Eisenhower book while Drew ate.

Drew finished his sandwich and beer and wiped his mouth. He reached for the check, but Lauder took it.

"My treat. Nice meeting a famous writer, having lunch. Doesn't happen often."

"My pleasure," Drew said politely.

"You're on a new book? That right? Your ex-wife said you're doing research."

"Yes."

"Must be a nice life. Work when you want, pick your hours, your subject matter, all that. Must be fine."

"Yes."

"And you're not going to ask me a thing, are you?" He laughed. "Man, in your place I'd be dying of curiosity. What's the Secret Service doing on my tail, watching my ex-wife's apartment, running me to ground. I'd be full of questions, if I were you."

"You're doing your job. Following orders."

"I'm the chief of the northeast department."

"Then it has to be duty. Not orders, but duty. You don't get to be chief without knowing and doing your duty in a steadfast manner day after day, year after year."

"That's right, Mr. Lancaster. You know Arnie Sorbies?"

"No."

"Sure you do. Owns a bookstore in New York. Out of Print Bookstore. You're in and out of it a lot."

"Oh, that shop. Is that his name?"

"One of them. We want him, really want him. We've wanted him for a very long time. Has he been in touch with you?"

"When?"

"Recently."

"No."

"We think he has, Mr. Lancaster. In fact, we're sure he has. We think he mailed you a letter a few weeks ago, in fact."

"Really? Maybe my book came in."

"What book's that?"

"The Secret Sex Life of the Native Aleuts Before the Advent of the Russian Fur Traders."

Lauder sighed and waved to the waitress to bring him more coffee. "You want anything else?"

"Coffee. Hot, black."

Lauder waited until they were served. "Look, Mr. Lancaster, it's your duty to help the Secret Service if called up to do so. I know many people dislike informing on others, but sometimes it's a necessity in this life."

"I'm having trouble seeing Sorbies as an assassin," Drew said. He mentally filed duty as another motive for the insane things people did.

"Not that department. The Secret Service is also in charge of tracking down and bringing in counterfeiters, Mr. Lancaster. Your friend Sorbies bought his shop with paper, has lived a rich and comforting life for many years with paper. What did you talk about with him?"

"Counterfeiter? Sorbies? Son of a gun!"

"What did you talk about?"

"Books. My books, books I wanted that he could trace for me, buy for me. He owned a bookstore. I'm a writer."

"Yes. What did he write to you a couple of weeks ago?"

"I didn't get a letter from him to my knowledge. But I've not been to my apartment for a couple of months. God knows what's up there."

"Your mail's been forwarded to your ex-wife."

"So it has. Bills, pleas for money for good and just causes, a few letters."

"Where are the letters?"

"Here, some of them." He opened his briefcase and pulled out the mail, tossed it down on the table. Lauder sorted through the envelopes quickly and extracted one, held it up. "Well, it seems your informant was right," Drew said. "It's from the Out of Print Bookstore!"

"Would you please open it, and then let me have a glance at it, Mr. Lancaster? We can do it this way, or I can get a legal writ . . ."

Drew was already opening the envelope. He pulled out a sheet of paper, looked it over and handed it to Lauder. It was a dot matrix printout of a list of books.

"Catalog," he said. "With my first book listed at fifty dollars. Cheap at half the price."

"Shit!" Lauder said.

"You want it? If he's on the lam, or whatever, I doubt that he'd fill an order anyway."

"Yeah, I'll hang on to it. Do you know where he might have gone? Do you know any friends of his?"

Drew shook his head sympathetically.

"Yeah. If he gets in touch, give us a call, okay? Sorry to trouble you." Lauder stood up. "Your ex-wife asked me to ask you to call, tell her what the hell this is all about. So long, Mr. Lancaster." He left the check on the table.

"For god's sake, Drew!" Pat was white-faced. They were in his car.

"We can't talk in public," he had whispered. "Get in." She had got in. He was driving in very heavy after-work traffic, heading nowhere in particular. It was oven hot in the car. She looked as cool as a lime popsicle.

"What in God's name do you mean *your* counterfeiter?"

"Remember Sorbies in New York? I told you he confessed to me. He wanted me to write his story, remember?"

"I don't remember. I didn't believe a word of it!"

"Examine that statement, Pat. Explore the ramifications of that statement in light of our various personal difficulties—"

"You're driving me crazy! Do you understand that? You are driving me out of my mind!"

"Probably they are following us at this minute, taking note of your agitation, your terrible guilty reaction—"

"Stop it! What did you tell him? You must have told him no! You didn't lead him on, did you?"

"I didn't tell him anything. He decided to wait until the statute of limitations ran out—sometime this year, I think he said. I was willing to go along with that."

"You told my father no outright," she said bitterly.

"Your father was a different kettle of fish."

"Different how? All he wanted was his biography. He's had a fascinating life and you know it."

"I don't know how he was different." Both had made money, he mused. Why was one dull, the other interesting? It demanded thought. It was the word *made* that caused trouble, he decided.

She took a deep breath. "Listen to me, Drew, and please be serious just for this one time. We can't be involved in any way with this man. Not you, not me, not any of us. The law says you're guilty of harboring or something if you know where he is and don't tell. If you know he's committed crimes and you don't inform the authorities, you'll be found guilty, too. Do you know that?"

"Guilty of what?"

"Of aiding and abetting a criminal."

"I just listened."

"I don't care if you did anything or not, they'll find you guilty! Can't you get that through your head?"

He looked at her with new respect. "I'll be damned! That's another force. I thought it was just money, or habit, or duty that made people do things. You've hit another motive. Guilt. That's what makes people move when they'd rather sit still, makes them lie down when they'd rather stand up, makes them overeat when they'd rather—"

"Stop the car! I want out. I'm going home."

"I can't stop. I'm in the middle lane."

"Get out of the middle lane!" she said, her jaws clenched.

"Guilt. You've really hit on it, Pat. What an inspiration. That's why you work for the senator. And I never thought of it until now." He swerved into an opening in the right lane, then made a turn at the next intersection. "See, I'm taking you home."

"I don't care if they haul you in. I don't care if they lock you up forever. I'll deny I ever heard of that man or anything about him. I'll deny I know anything about anything."

"Will you visit me?"

"Shut up!"

He double-parked outsider her apartment building long enough for her to get out.

"I'm going to Richmond in the morning," she said furiously. "I don't want to hear from you or about you. Get lost, Drew. Just get out of my life for good!"

Behind him a horn was blaring, a voice screeching at him. "Bye, bye," he called after Pat, engaged the gears, waved to the driver behind him, and let himself be carried away by the surging traffic. He did not know if he was being followed, but if he was, he would lead the pursuer to the Princeton house. Let him get a glimpse of real class.

He was almost sorry that Pat was going to go into the bathroom and find his message; as upset as she was, she might break something.

It had not surprised Drew when Sorbies had confided in him. People did that. One time an old German grounds keeper in Richmond had told him how he had jumped ship and entered the country, how he had smuggled his wife in three years later. Forged papers, lies, they had managed ever since, forty-odd years. Another time one of the senator's youngest aides had confessed to a career of shoplifting. And

Pat's own Aunt Hazel had told him all about the lover she had maintained for fifteen years, in spite of a good marriage, three children, membership in every social club in Richmond. None of them had surprised him.

Sorbies must be seventy, he thought, driving sedately on the interstate, not wanting to alarm any follower. And he had said he was going straight, not passing the paper any more. He was at peace with the world, content with his rare books, secure. Maybe Lauder was getting desperate, knowing as well as Sorbies when the statute of limitations would run out. Maybe Sorbies had cranked up the press again.

"Why do you only write books about famous people?" Sorbies had asked in a complaining way.

"I don't know."

"Interesting, I guess, but hell, so's just about everyone else."

"That's true."

"World changers, is that it? You're interested in people who change things?"

"I guess so."

Then Sorbies had asked the question that stumped Drew, still stumped him.

"Think you can steal from a thief?" the old man had asked.

"You can receive stolen goods."

"Not the same as stealing."

"If you take something that isn't yours, it's stealing. By definition."

"What about taxation, then?"

Drew had thought about it. "By definition, that's stealing. Unless it's voluntary. They say we have the only voluntary system of taxation in the world."

"They say the moon's green cheese."

"But we know it's yellow."

"Right. If you were going to pass funny money, how'd you go about it?"

"I don't know."

"A smart man would buy diamonds in the Netherlands. Those merchants practically steal them, you know. Or buy gold in South Africa. You know how those people get that gold? But we don't want to get into morality, do we? Or go to

Hong Kong and buy Chinese antiques smuggled out from the mainland. Is that stealing? Can you steal from a thief?''

''That's what you've done?''

''Yep. And that would make an interesting book, don't you agree?''

''I do.''

''There are other ways, even more exotic. You'd want to choose your target after much consideration, not pick on the corner Mom and Pop store, that kind of thing. That would be immoral. But there are interesting ways.'' He had paused as if considering. ''Another time, not yet. Three years and I'll give you the whole thing. You interested in writing it?''

''I don't know.''

''No hurry in deciding. Once the statute of limitations has run out, then's time enough. If I ever decide to run for cover, I'll be in touch. I'll send you something or other, a catalog, something, just to let you know, and I'll be in touch later. Okay? Deal?''

Neither of them had mentioned it again. And now he had received the catalog. Well, well, he thought. Well, well.

THREE

In his office Leon Lauder was pushing a twenty-dollar bill in circles on his desk top. It looked perfect; even under a magnifying glass it looked good. Under ultraviolet it was more questionable but only because this particular paper had not been used for a few years. There was still a lot of it out there in circulation; it did not betray the bill as phony. Only if you really studied the serial number would you know it was play money. Not many people bothered to study the serial number.

"You think Lancaster knows anything about Sorbies?" Bob Samson asked. Bob was his assistant. Bob wanted Leon's job. They both knew that.

"Who knows? At any rate, he doesn't give a damn. No help there. I want that Indian."

"He's too big to hide long. We'll find him."

Leon Lauder grunted, pushing the bill. He admired that bill more than he was willing to tell anyone. Sorbies was a true artist, the best he had come across, the only one he had not nailed in a thirty-year career otherwise without a blotch. In his mind he called Sorbies the Artist because the bills were so good, the serial numbers painted in by hand, each one different—avoiding that trap—all else done on an offset press that was old but fine. Good old machinery, a quality product, not like the stuff the youngsters were turning out now—photocopying money, trying to pass what looked like Monopoly money. No, the Artist turned out a good product, too good a product. And if they didn't get him by the end of the year, he would get away with it, thumb his nose at them, laugh at them, even go public. Write a book? Leon's eyes narrowed and he was not seeing the bill now. Write a book. Was that the connection?

"Sometimes I think we should get out a couple of those bills and pass them ourselves," Bob Samson said. "Who could ever prove he hadn't done it when we nab him?"

"Beat it. Go on home. I'll put this stuff away," Leon said without looking at his assistant. They both treated the statement as a joke, but he knew that if he looked at the younger man, neither of them would be able to keep up that pretense. He had had the same thought too many times.

Eddie the Jumper had given him their first and only lead to the Artist. Eddie had sold Sorbies a pile of first editions stolen from the archives at the Vatican. Sorbies had called himself something else again, and Eddie had done time for that job. When he got out and went to his stash, he had found that he had been paid with funny money. Born again in prison, he had been filled with righteous indignation, and insane fury, and had come to Leon Lauder wanting justice.

For six months the investigation had gone forward. They had found Sorbies early on—that had been easy—but they needed paper, plates, ink, positive identification from someone who was not Eddie the Jumper. They had obtained photographs and sent them to agents in countries where the fake money had turned up. They had searched his apartment and his bookstore. They had followed him, located his three banks, knew where he ate and what, who he talked to . . . Once he had left town for the weekend and they had lost him, nearly giving Leon Lauder cardiac arrest. They had waited and he returned and now there were even more men on his case, keeping him on a tether supposedly. He had given them the slip again and this time he had not returned.

"But you can't hide, old man," Leon whispered. Not now, not when they had his picture, his prints, everything. The only real question was whether they would find him before the end of the year, and that question was making Leon restless at night, was wrecking his appetite, threatening to wreck his marriage. And Bob Samson was watching with a super-solicitous attitude, suggesting he take a day off, have a vacation, relax . . . One of his own men had been close enough to Sorbies to read Lancaster's name on the envelope he had mailed the last day any of them had seen him. Lancaster had been gone; the old man vanished; the crazy Indian lost . . . Well, Lancaster was back in reach, and Leon Lauder had told his agents in deadly terms exactly what terrible things he would do to them if they lost him. And, meanwhile, the search was on for Sorbies and for Jack Silver Fox—Tonto to his Lone Ranger.

Arnie Sorbies had been at lunch the day he realized that he was being watched. For several days he had had an itch that was not relieved no matter where he scratched, and now he knew why. It was the agent's right shoe, he reflected, not missing a bite of his spanakopittá. There was peculiar scrape on the outside of the right shoe, as if someone had pulled an eraser along the leather leaving a pale track. He had seen that scrape three times now. Of course, the man wearing the shoe could be a shopkeeper in the neighborhood, a new arrival who would appear from time to time at the same restaurants that Arnie frequented, buy newspapers at the same kiosk, walk along East Fourteenth during the same hours that Arnie kept. He did not believe any of his reasoning even as he went through it. He finished eating and had his usual two cups of bittersweet Greek coffee and left the restaurant to walk briskly back to his bookstore.

His first impulse was to bolt, of course, but he resisted and did nothing unusual the rest of the day. He thought through what it meant if they were this close without coming in the rest of the way. They had him, but not his house in the country, he decided. If they had followed him to it a few weeks back, they would have taken him in by now. They must be going after hard evidence, biding their time until they got a positive identification—which would not take them very long—or found the press and paper. There was no way for him to know if they had been on him when he left town the last time, but it mattered little one way or the other. He knew without a doubt that they had not followed him to the house in the mountains, or he would not still be a free man.

On Friday, certain that at least three men were with him throughout the day, he left. It was a last-minute decision to send a catalog to Drew Lancaster, and it amused him that one of his followers was close enough for him to elbow out of the way at the mailbox. He closed his shop a few minutes early that afternoon and hailed a cab on Fourteenth. He was carrying two books carefully wrapped and tied the way he usually did them. He thought the man browsing in his shop when he made up the parcel was probably a Secret Service agent.

He gave an address on Eighth Avenue and settled back. Traffic was terrible at that time of day; Friday evening in the summer was a nightmare on the streets. He did not look back; he knew they kept a car cruising for just such an event as this. They would be more careful than usual if they had lost him before. When the cabbie flipped the flag down and stopped, Arnie leaned forward and said, "It's going to take me just a minute to drop off this package. There's a twenty in it if you'll go around the corner and pick me up at the side door about halfway down the block." He paid the under five dollar fare with a ten and did not pick up his change.

"I won't wait," the driver said.

"You won't have to. I'll probably be out before you pull up."

The store he entered was Wasserman's secondhand shop, with merchandise that ranged from baby cribs to flutes to used books. He and Wasserman got together to play cards sometimes. No doubt the agents knew that. He went straight through the shop, waved to his old friend, put his package down, and walked out the side door. His taxi was slowing down and two women were waving frantically to the driver.

"It's my taxi," Arnie said pleasantly. "But I'll be happy to share it with you. Where are you going?"

The women were in their forties or fifties, suspicious. "Macy's," one of them snapped.

"Let's get in, then," he said. "I'll pay for it as far as Twenty-fifth." They all got in. He put a twenty-dollar bill in the pay box. "See, it really was my cab."

For the next two hours he wove his way in and out of the city, by bus, by cab, walking, and eventually he ended up in the Tube heading for Hoboken. He knew no one was following him.

After he left the railway station, he walked again. It was getting dark and he was hungry. Later, he told himself firmly. He would eat out on the road later. He stopped in front of a row of garages and took a key from his pocket, unlocked one of the doors, and entered.

A truck was parked there. An old panel truck with burlap bags and produce crates in the back. In the cab was a duffel bag. He opened it, drew out stained, faded jeans, a worn plaid shirt, work shoes and socks, threadbare shorts. There were holes in the toes of the socks. He changed clothes, folded his suit and shirt and underwear neatly and packed everything into the duffel bag. Now he went through his wallet and removed many cards: his driver's license, credit cards, all identification. He put them in a small canvas bag that already had in it five pounds of fishing weights. He added keys, all but his truck key and the key to his house. He put back in the wallet a few cards that had been in the duffel bag, looked it all over carefully, then put the wallet in his hip pocket. Arnie Sorbies was methodically being killed, he reflected. Too bad, he had grown used to him, liked being him, liked having a bookstore.

When the transition was complete, he left the garage, left Hoboken, and headed toward his country house. He knew where he could toss the canvas bag into a river, knew where he could stop to eat; he had been this way many times.

By one in the morning he was within twenty miles of his house on a state road that followed the Delaware River north. The river was deep here, the road empty of traffic now. There was a bridge over to Pennsylvania. He turned onto it, got rid of the canvas bag and returned to the New Jersey side. He was blindingly tired, no longer fueled by adrenaline. The road was winding, the night very dark. He rounded a curve, not traveling fast, and saw from the corner of his eye glaring lights, heard a screech of brakes, and tried to spin his steering wheel, tried to avoid the collision, and failed. He threw his arm up over his face, and felt an impact, felt himself flying, and then felt nothing.

When he opened his eyes again, the sun was shining, and he saw his room through a blur.

"Mr. Bramwell, how do you feel?" someone asked.

He blinked until the fuzz in his head began to clear. There was a doctor in a white jacket at the side of his bed. He was in a hospital, he realized, and he could not move.

"Mr. Bramwell," the doctor said. "I'm Dr. Dohemy. There was an accident. Do you remember?"

"I remember enough."

"Ah, I'm afraid that your leg is broken, Mr. Bramwell. Is there someone we should notify? Someone who can come get you?"

"Broken? My leg's broken?" Now he could feel it, a distant pain that reminded him of waves pressing upon a shore, one after another without letup. "I don't have anyone."

"Well then, a hospital. Or a convalescent home?"

"I don't have any money," Arnie growled. "Who hit me?"

"I wouldn't say anyone actually hit you," Dr. Dohemy said. "It was an accident. A collision."

"And I said I remember what happened. What's this place? It sure looks like a hospital."

"Yes, but not for the public. This is a private hospital for disturbed youngsters. This was an emergency, and I set your leg last night, but you can't stay here, obviously."

"Who hit me?" Arnie demanded. "Ask that guy who's going to take care of me."

"You must have hospitalization or something. Medicare? Medicaid?"

"It was you, Doc, wasn't it? Was it you?"

"Look, Mr. Bramwell, it was an accident. I came out of the drive and suddenly you were there, as much at fault as I was."

"I'll stay here," Arnie said, closing his eyes. "See if the insurance investigators think it was my fault. And I want a drink of water."

Dohemy looked at him murderously. "You can't stay here!"

"I'll sue the shit out of you."

Dohemy continued to regard him with murder on his mind. So simple. Pick up the pillow, hold it over his face a couple of minutes. Even simpler, overdose him. He should have hit him harder, he thought savagely, wishing he had been driving a semi or a tank. He turned away from temptation abruptly. Too many questions would come up, and this was the worst possible time for even one question. First thing they would ask, he thought, was where he was going at that time of night, and they would not like his answer that he had been on the way to Princeton to rob a house. The old man began to snore.

Okay, you bastard, he thought at him, you've got a place to stay for the next couple of months, and your own private physician. He would write out a release form and make the old fart sign it and as soon as he could drive that derelict truck again, out he would go. Meanwhile, he could keep him in isolation, away from the kids, away from guests, away from everything and everyone.

A few nights later Dohemy made another attempt to go to Princeton, and this time it was without incident.

FOUR

"Stanley," Irma Huysman said, "was very influenced by Nietzsche, his ideas about supermen. He saw no reason for evolution to take as long as it does to improve the human organism, as he called all of us." She sipped her tea and gazed reflectively at the Delft teapot. Sunlight shafted in through the window, highlighting the blue pattern, the glaze. Where the sunlight touched her hair, it looked blue also. "He was in Vienna studying psychiatry, you know. First under Dr. Freud and then under Dr. Jung. He left both of them in disgust after a time. Mystics, he called them. Looking for immaterial causes for what had to be material effects, behavior. In Berlin he studied under Hans Oberschmidt, a distant relative of my father's. And that was how we came to know him. My uncle often invited his students to our estate for a particular holiday meal. Most of them were very poor, of course. Stanley was very poor."

Drew nodded. Huysman had started his career as a medical student, then a psychiatry student, then as a racist? He waited.

"In Berlin," Irma continued, "Stanley was invited to contribute to the professional journal of physiology and that's what led to his being called a racist. You will read the articles in due time and see for yourself what they said. His point was that certain people are genetically superior to others, no more than that. But the Nazis used the articles just as they used words by Nietzsche and music by Wagner and so on. They used what they wanted in any way they wanted, and once tainted by their acceptance, the stain was difficult to remove. Stanley was not a racist, not a Nazi, not a fascist. He was truly apolitical all his life."

Drew had read the articles and they lent themselves to such

use. He did not say this. "Your family was very wealthy, isn't that right?"

"My father was a count who had vast land holdings that dated back to the sixteenth century," she said stiffly. She rose from the table and held on to her chair for a second or two, then started for the door. "My father sold me to Stanley in order to insure my safety in what he saw as very bad times ahead." She walked to the door leading to the hallway and paused. "That was not uncommon, you understand. The European nobility was for sale in those days. Now the European nobility has vanished. Which is better? Who can say? Stanley did not suffer from the bargain. I was a good wife to him, and the fortune is still intact. It was just a pity that there were no children of the marriage. I, of course, was not to blame for that. Stanley was too cerebral to care if there were progeny. His work was all that interested him. We all knew that from the beginning. It was acceptable."

"They were polite to each other," Florence Charmody said carefully. "I never saw either of them hit the other and never heard either swear at the other."

"Like that, huh?"

"Like that."

"She was sitting on the floor, her back to the file cabinet that she had been working with. "Did she mention their sex life at all?"

He shook his head.

"Nonexistent. And had been for half a century, I guess. He thought sex was for the lower animals, not enlightened human organisms."

"Is a Ph.D. automatically an enlightened organism?"

She laughed and turned back to the open file drawer, pulled out a manila folder. "Read your articles," she said as she opened the folder and began scanning the papers inside.

Which was he? he pondered, ignoring the stacks of articles before him on the broad, burnished desk. Probably a lower animal pretending to be enlightened. Or possibly an enlightened organism wanting to revert to lower animalism.

"I have an appointment with Dr. Lincoln Blackman," he said after a few minutes. "Is he a higher or lower organism? Or do you know him?"

"He's the head of the biology department and has been for

twenty years. Everyone who goes through Princeton must know him, and I'd guess he's a higher organism."

"Thank you. I won't bother to make a pass."

Dr. Blackman was a very small man of delicate appearance with diminutive bones and a doll-like face that seemed to be trying to make up for size with a bushy beard and mustache. His expression was benign and tolerant.

"What can I tell you?" he asked mildly. "Stanley was on the payroll for a long time and did not teach regularly for at least fifteen years. It was considered enough to use his name as a drawing card. That happens often, I'm afraid."

"What did he do? Did he come to his office at all?"

"What for? He had his own research, his own staff, his own resources. His position here was honorary. He was a graduate adviser now and then." He smiled at Drew. "He was not a popular man, I'm afraid. There might have been a little jealousy, naturally, but, more than that, he didn't care if anyone liked him."

"What was his research?"

"I don't know. That may be another reason for his unpopularity. He never shared anything with anyone if he could avoid it."

"But who financed his research, and where did he do it?"

Blackman shrugged. "I don't know for certain. The government? Probably. As for what he was doing, you might ask Claude Dohemy. I can't help you. It was classified, and for many years now I have suspected that it was, for the most part, imaginary. All in his head. He carried secrecy to such an extreme that it was quite difficult to take it very seriously, after all. I mean, what is there to be secret about with the study of genetics? Now, if you want to go back to fifteen years or more ago, why then you have the pure genius Huysman was for so much of his lifetime. A pity that such a man continues so far past the time when he should retire, don't you think? But who's to tell anyone something like that? Not I."

"Are you talking about his chimp experiments? His genius work?"

"Dear me, no. That was picked up by the media and exploited, but it was not serious work, no more than a sideline for Huysman, a throwaway thought or two. A mind like that has throwaway lines that would occupy a more ordinary mind for a lifetime. But believe me, that was not meant to be taken seriously at any time.''

''What work do you mean, then?''

''His paper on plant clones. Not even in his own field, you understand. But today they are referred to as a religious fanatic might refer to the Bible.''

''Plant clones,'' Drew said.

''Exactly. This is always the way it goes, Mr. Lancaster. The layman will seize on the sensational every time, but the professional . . . Ah, that's a different matter. Plant clones. That is what will make Huysman's name live forever.''

''And his twin studies? Are they meaningless? And the chimp experiments in which he seemed to increase the intelligence of the animals drastically, prove that they possessed some ESP powers? All that is without value scientifically?''

''Believe me, Mr. Lancaster. all that will fade away, has already faded away, but the plant clones will prove beneficial for a century or more.''

''You don't believe in ESP? Or in intelligent chimps? Or that identical twins who are separated at birth have amazing coincidences in their lives?''

Dr. Blackman laughed gently. ''I also don't believe in flying saucers and little green men from Mars. In science, Mr. Lancaster, unless your results can be replicated by others, I'm afraid they are pretty much discounted. For a long time it was flatworms that became smarter by eating trained flatworms, but we no longer look at planaria with awe, simply because only a few people achieved that effect. If you float to the ceiling before my eyes, I'm afraid, I would have to discount antigravity until someone other than you could also achieve it. That's how science works, Mr. Lancaster.''

''And his quantum field theory to account for the twin behavior? You discount that also?''

Dr. Blackman's laughter now was less gentle, almost boisterous in fact. ''Not even the physicists accept that.''

Drew stood up. ''Thanks for seeing me, Dr. Blackman. I'm gathering first impressions now, but perhaps later I can call again?''

''Please do. It's my privilege, I assure you.''

At the door Drew paused, then asked, ''What if I floated to the ceiling with you in my arms? Would you believe it then?''

Dr. Blackman's look was pitying. ''No, Mr. Lancaster.

I'm afraid I can't accept the impossible even if I experience it personally.''

Drew nodded and left. On the street outside Blackman's house he waited until he was sure his follower was alert and then started the walk back to the Huysman house. Huysman a crank? He had not considered that before, but the idea was intriguing, made the old man more interesting than anything he had been able to come up with previously. He liked the idea of his being a crank, believing in antigravity, little green men, psychic chimps. Asexual and mad? Mad because he was asexual? Not asexual at all but deprived?

Maybe if he explained to Florence that people who are sexually deprived often go mad and believe in little green men, she would agree to roll on the rug with him. Maybe he should suggest that they have dinner together first, and then tell her his theory. She was a scientist, she would see the logic of his train of thought. He began to whistle.

They ate in a dim restaurant that was vaguely French and overpriced. Florence was still wearing her sensible clothes—a suit, hose, comfortable shoes. She had taken off her jacket, a concession to the heat that persisted long after the sun went down. Over coffee she explained some of Huysman's work.

"Everyone knew about his chimps," she said. "It made *Time* and every newspaper in the country. He claimed that he had introduced genes that resulted in increased intelligence. He had them perform for observers; and all the nonscientists were convinced, but not a single scientist bought it. He was raked over the coals for going public in the first place and for doing it successfully, making headlines, having a best-seller. You know how that goes. They hated it and began tearing down the work instantly. It sank out of sight after a while."

"Was there anything to it?"

"Of course not. If he had done what he said, why didn't he keep up with it? Why let it go by the wayside?"

"I don't know. Why?"

"The usual reason is funding, but he never seemed to have a problem financing anything he wanted. That was all finished with by the time I came on the scene. By then he was back doing intelligence testing, personality testing, things like that. No more chimps."

"Was he a good teacher?"

"I don't know. He wasn't teaching when I was in graduate school. He was on my committee, and I worked for him two summers. I needed the money and he needed cheap labor trained to administer tests. I qualified. He was a devil to work for, demanding, nagging, double-checking everything, suspicious. It's a good thing he wasn't my teacher or I might not have made it."

"Can you explain what he meant by saying he established a quantum-mechanics field with his chimps?"

She shrugged. "I never read his books or the papers. They were all passé by the time I started graduate school. In the same category as the comet theory of Venus—you know, proving the Biblical flood and all that happened because the comet Venus came too close to Earth. Velikovsky was here at Princeton, too. I never read his books either. In graduate school you really don't have much time to pursue fairy tales." She considered him thoughtfully for a few seconds. "The one who might be able to tell you about all that period is Claude Dohemy. He's the only one I know of who stayed with Huysman a day longer than necessary for a degree or whatever."

"Was he crazy?"

"Huysman? Not on your life! Why?"

He explained his theory of sexual deprivation and madness to her; she was not impressed.

"Not very original."

"But the great theories are truisms that no one has articulated yet."

She laughed. "This particular one has been articulated to death, I'm afraid." Then, more kindly, she asked, "Is this your buildup to asking me to go to bed with you?"

He admitted that it was.

"Are you finished here? Ready to go? I have a furnished apartment. Not very fancy but comfortable and private."

He adored her, he realized. Her red hair was beautiful, her skin perfect, her frank appraisal the most provocative look he had ever seen. He paid the check and left an over-large tip, and they walked out to the street.

"Do you want to follow me in your car?" she asked.

They had met at the restaurant, and there were both cars at the curb. He looked past his to make sure his follower was behind his wheel. He wondered when the agent ate, if he had a hamburger in the car now and then.

"Who are you looking for?" Florence asked. "Isn't that your car there?"

"I'll follow you," he said. "I was just checking to make certain the agent knows we're leaving."

"Agent? Now what are you talking about?"

"Secret Service agent. He's tailing me. I think he realizes I'm about to go now."

Florence did not move. "Are you kidding? Secret Service agent? Why? How long has he been there?"

"He drove up right behind me, so I guess he's been there as long as we were in the restaurant. Two and a half hours? He thinks I'm harboring a criminal."

"You really are mad, aren't you? Are you haboring a criminal? And if you aren't, why do they think you are? How long have they been following you?"

"I don't know why they think what they think. I don't understand the mind of the police. They've been with me for days and days. And I am not harboring a criminal. Was that all of them?"

"All of what?"

"The questions."

"Yes. Let's say good night, Drew. Thanks for a lovely dinner. I'll see you tomorrow at the house."

"You changed your mind?"

"Yes. I don't think I want a parade to my apartment. Good night."

He watched her drive away and slowly went to his own car. Before he got in, he waved to the agent. After all, he thought, it really was not his fault, and probably he was hungry. A little friendliness might make all the difference to him after hours sitting out here, imagining the good food they were having inside the restaurant. He thought briefly of telling the agent that the food had not been all that good, but he decided not to. Even if it wasn't his fault, Drew didn't owe him that much.

FIVE

"Have you really read all the articles?" Florence asked. She was at one desk in the office, Drew at the other. For nearly an hour there had been no sound except for the rustling of a paper now and then.

"No one could read all those articles in less than six months," he said. "How did he manage to write so much?"

"A real stickler for work. A hyperactive kid all his life. I don't know. Most of it's very good work, too, or else absolute trash. That's what makes it so hard to take."

The air was heavy inside and out; a thunderstorm was building and it was as if its presence in the atmosphere had put an impossible burden on the air, squeezing it, weighing it down, trying to crush everything and everyone. Neither Drew nor Florence had mentioned the previous night.

On the desk in front of Drew was a complicated looking diagram. He put his pencil down on it, leaned forward, and whispered, "I have a plan."

"Wonderful." She turned another page and sighed. "Have you gone through the eugenics papers yet? Irma thinks every word he ever wrote should be in print, but no way would I touch any of them." She lifted another page by the corner and put it down as if it were covered with something she would rather not touch.

"My plan," Drew said, "is simple. You leave at the usual time, go hire a closed van and come back to the kitchen entrance and I get in and we head out. How's that sound?"

She shook her head. "Too complicated. I'd screw it up somehow. Are you finding anything beyond his work? Are you reading the diaries yet?"

"I thought you might not like the first plan. I have a

backup. The diaries are about as lively as the research papers. He must have had a friend out there in the world somewhere. He must have looked at a woman once in his life. I am not daunted. I shall persevere. You go home at the usual time and at a normal hour turn off your lights as if you've packed it in for the night. I'll call the fire department at twelve sharp, and in the ensuing confusion I'll duck out and climb your fire escape and knock four times. You open the window without turning on a light . . ."

She was laughing, shaking her head. "Why do they think you know where a criminal is hiding out?"

"Plan three," Drew said. "The criminal owns, or owned, a bookstore I visit from time to time. Plan three. We eat a quiet dinner right here with Irma, who is a very lonely lady, by the way, and we keep pouring more and more wine for her until she keels over, dead drunk. After we put her to bed, we retire to my room. I have a very nice and very private room of my own, you know, on the second floor of this mansion."

"I know you do. I picked it out for you. They can't be following everyone who ever entered his bookstore, surely. Unless you were his only customer, it seems it would require an army."

"You know," he said in wonder. "I never even stopped to ask." he took out his wallet and searched among cards, laid one on the desk. "I'll ask him now." He started to dial.

"You're not going to call them!"

He finished dialing and nodded at her. "They are public servants. I am part of the public. Who has a better right? Hello? Mr. Lauder, please: . . . It's Drew Lancaster calling." He smiled at Florence who was staring at him aghast. "Oh, Leon, how are you? It's Drew here. Look, it occurred to me that I don't really understand why you have agents following me about day after day. Is there anything new to report? Is there anything I can do for you?"

"I hope it's not an inconvenience," Lauder said. "Just in case Sorbies decides to get in touch with an old friend, we thought it would be a good idea to be on hand. You understand, I hope."

"Yes, indeed. Good thinking, but in that case why aren't you keeping tabs on his friends? I hardly qualify."

"Tell you what, Mr. Lancaster, you just might have a

point there. Let us think about it a couple of days. I'll get
back to you. Okay?''

They hung up and Drew said to Florence, ''He thinks I
have a good point, and he will get back to me. Meanwhile,
we have plan three to consider. We have dinner with Irma at
seven-thirty and we chat for an hour or so afterward. She's
filling me in on their early life. By ten she'll be nodding . . .''

''I haven't been invited to dinner,'' Florence protested.
''And I'm not in the habit of inviting myself.''

''Ah-ha!'' Drew exclaimed. ''I thought of that and suggested that you join us, and Irma was delighted with the
notion. She wants to ask you how many papers you're finding
that should be published.''

Florence laughed again, still shaking her head. ''We'll
see,'' she said.

Leon Lauder stared at the phone in irritation. What had that
been about? Why now? It was Friday afternoon and weekends
with an active case on his hands always made him nervous.
People did strange things on weekends, things out of routine.
He and his wife Mildred were due at their son's house for
dinner Saturday, for example, not at all part of their routine.
And tonight Mildred had a club meeting or something; he had
to fend for himself for dinner. Out of routine.

In the adjacent office Bob Samson was on the phone at the
moment to their Oklahoma office, but there was no news
about the Indian, he knew, or he would have been told.
Where was that damn Indian? Why had he dropped out of
sight now? And what was Lancaster up to? He knew about
the Huysman book that had lured Lancaster out of wherever
he had been hiding earlier in the summer, knew about his
temporary residence at the Huysman house, knew he had had
dinner with the Charmody woman, knew every move he had
made during the past two and a half weeks; but knowing all
that, he felt he knew nothing about Lancaster. And least of all
did he know what had generated that inane call.

Leon Lauder was good at his job and knew it and knew that
part of the reason he was good was that he listened to his
unconscious urgings, yielded to his intuitive itches. That
catalog had been a signal, he firmly believed, if for no other
reason than that Sorbies had mailed only the one, and it out of
date.

Lancaster was up to something, he decided, and pulled the phone to him to call his agent in Princeton, to tell him to be alert, something was up. Before he could even dial, Bob Samson stuck his head in the door.

"We've got him! Silver Fox has been spotted in Trenton."

Irma Huysman smiled gently at Drew as she spoke of her early days in Vienna. "My mother was a sponsor of opera, of course," she said. "Some of my earliest memories are of sitting watching rehearsals, transported. Stanley enjoyed music very much also, when he had time. We met in Vienna, you know. I was eighteen, a child, and he was so austere, so forbidding, I was quite frightened of him. I considered him my father's friend, of his generation."

It was nine-thirty; dinner over and Marion, the cook-housekeeper gone for the day. Irma, Florence, and Drew were in the living room, where, it was true, no food or drink was allowed. Their coffee had been served in a smaller sitting room.

"At first he visited only with others from the university, but after six months or so, he started coming home for dinner or to talk to my father. I don't recall that he ever looked directly at me during that time. It was not how things were done, you see. My father was very impressed by his intellect."

Drew glanced at Florence, who was listening to Irma with apparent fascination. Whenever Florence met his gaze, he detected a glint of amusement in her look. From the open door there came the sound of the telephone ringing in the study. No phone was in the living room. Irma started to get to her feet, but Drew was already up. "I'll get it," he said. "I'll plug the telephone in here if it's for you. Excuse me." He took the call in the office.

"The Huysman residence," he said.

"Daddy? Is that you?"

"Sherry! Is that you?"

She giggled. "You sounded like a butler."

"I'm working on it, but I don't have exactly the right inflection yet. When I get good enough I'll apply to your grandfather for a job. Tell me, am I nearly ready?"

"I don't think he'd hire you. Daddy, when are you coming down here?"

"Next Thursday, I think. Ask Pat."

Next Thursday will be too late. It'll be all over by then. If I don't see you again, I just want to say I love you and good-bye.''

"And I love you. What will be all over then? And where are you going?''

"I'll be a street child. And as soon as I'm old enough I'll join the Peace Corps or something. I might have to ask you for a little money now and then.''

"Will I have an address? Or will you come collect it in person?''

"I'd better send a trusted friend—if I can find one.''

"What if I turned up tomorrow? Would it be too late?''

"Probably, but maybe not. I suspect they'll announce their engagement even if you do show up. I mean, it's hard to stop something like that once it's gone this far, isn't it?''

"Is a party or something in the works?''

"Tomorrow night,'' she said gloomily. "A garden party. I have to wear stockings, and it's over a hundred degrees!''

"And the mosquitoes will be bad. Would you say this constitutes bad parenting? Enough to take to court?''

She giggled again. "Will you really come tomorrow?''

"Think I can crash the party?''

"I do have *some* rights,'' she said airily. "You can be my guest.''

When Drew returned to the living room, Irma was alone. "Florence said to tell you good night,'' she said. "She's had a tiring day. And so have I. I'll also say good night now. It was a nice evening. So thoughtful of you to ask Florence to join us. Poor child. I'm afraid her red hair alarms so many men that she leads a very solitary life.'' Slowly she rose and accepted his arm, and as they walked from the room together, she said, "It would be so nice if you and Florence . . . I'm sorry. Please forgive me. One must not make such suggestions, no matter how well-intentioned. Good night, Drew.''

She preferred to go upstairs alone, trusting the bannister more than anyone's arm. He watched until she made it to the top and turned to go down the hallway to her room. A roll of thunder sounded close by. He decided to take his follower for a walk in the rain.

The storm had hit early in the evening; now there was a light, intermittent rain falling, and somewhere in the north the

sporadic roll of thunder. No one else was on the streets as
Drew walked block after block, very gradually feeling the
rain penetrate his shirt, his trousers. It was not cold as rain
goes, but eventually it chilled him and he turned back toward
the house. Huysman had been dull, after all, he mused, and
thought that strange. A genius should not be dull, should be
incapable of being dull. Dull or so secretive that nothing of
the real man and his real goals had survived his death. He
realized that he had not yet committed himself to the book
and was vaguely surprised at that. So far, he told himself, all
he had looked at were the scientific papers and nothings
written in what Irma had called diaries. But as diaries they
were a miserable failure. Dates, speaking engagements, publication dates for forthcoming work, zilch. He had to have
had friends, someone he talked to about his soul, his needs,
his regrets. Everyone had to have that someone.

Pat had to have that someone, was on her way to finding
that someone, and she was due another disappointment, he
brooded. Senator Wiley was not a listener; he was not a
talker, he was a doer. Said so himself in speech after speech,
interview after interview. A doer, my friend, someone who
goes out there and gets the job done!

Thunder sounded again, louder this time, as if the storm
had its second wind and was coming back for a replay.
Lightning turned the sky bright violet. When he reached the
Huysman house again, the rain was coming down harder, and
was definitely cold. He checked his car doors to make sure
they were locked, the windows closed. One was not closed all
the way; the interior was gleaming with water. He shrugged,
fixed the window, and went inside the house, using the key
Irma had given him the first day. She had also called in the
neighborhood security people and introduced the several men
who regularly patrolled the area. Drew had not mentioned his
own followers. Let them sort it all out, he had decided. On
his walk he had not seen any of them.

The kitchen door was open; Irma called out to him. "Will
you join me for a hot toddy? Or something? You must be
soaked."

"Thanks. Be right down."

He was truly soaked. He changed and toweled his hair and
went down to the kitchen. Irma was seated at the worktable
there. She was drinking tea.

"I never could sleep when it's stormy," she said. "Please help yourself to whatever you want. The liquor's in the living room cabinet. If you'll bring the scotch, perhaps I'll have that. Tea's really a five in the afternoon drink, isn't it?"

He collected the scotch for her and bourbon for himself and made the drinks. Delicately she pushed her teacup aside and made rings on the laminated tabletop with the wet glass. "You do not seem very interested in Stanley. Is that correct?"

"I've hardly begun. I don't know yet."

"Yes, of course. Are you married?"

"Divorced."

"Was it a polite relationship? Please forgive me, but it matters."

"In a way, but not all the time. Not as polite as we are being now."

She smiled faintly. "That would be intolerable, wouldn't it? Stanley and I were always as polite as you and I are being this moment. Among our acquaintances there were the usual inharmonious couples, and I envied them sometimes. How refreshing it would have been to have been allowed the release of a scream, of throwing something now and then. Do you understand?"

"I think so." Thunder cracked overhead and the windows blazed with blue-white light momentarily. Irma sipped her drink. "Why don't you tell me why you waited for me," Drew said.

"I want you to do the book." She drank again, played with the circles of moisture, did not look at him.

"None of my books ever sold more than ten thousand copies in hardcover. You know that, don't you? There are too many good writers who would automatically have a best-seller with this material, but not me. You also know that. What is it you want?"

"Yes, I had you investigated. And I did read and admire your other books, but it was after the fact, I admit. I want you to find out what it was that Stanley was doing for the last twenty years of his life. You see, I don't know. I thought you would be able to find out, and if it was something shameful, you would not be interested in publishing it, but you would, out of honor, tell me."

"You thought you could pay me not to use anything you didn't want published?"

"Yes. In the beginning, but not now. Now I believe what I said: you would not be interested in it yourself. That is quite enough."

"Why not a private detective?"

"Anyone who goes through those papers has to be able to read them with understanding. I doubted I could find a detective with the qualifications."

Drew gazed at her without surprise. If she had confessed that it was she who had done all her husband's work over the years, that would not have been a surprise either. "What was he doing? What do you suspect?"

"Something hideous. Something horrible. Something he refused to discuss with me from the beginning, refused to discuss with anyone as far as I am aware, unless it was with that odious man Claude Dohemy."

"But what makes you suspect all that? Something must have made you suspicious."

"Of course. He asked me to finance a project many years ago and said he could not tell me what it was about—not yet. Naturally I refused. From that day until he died we were unnaturally polite to each other."

"Why did you stay together?"

She looked baffled by the question. "I was his wife. It was my duty. He was a great man, but to achieve his greatness he needed a good wife to see to things for him. I was a very good wife."

Another woman with an aptitude for managing money, Drew thought. Pat had asked permission to take care of his money when they were newly wed, and she had taken such good care of it that he had not had to think of money since. And that had been quite a modest sum. Apparently Irma had the same kind of talent.

Now Irma stood up, holding on to the chair back for a moment or two. "I realize that this may make a difference in your decision making," he said. "If you decide to go forward with the book, of course, I'll cooperate in every way, answer any questions I can, do whatever I can to make your work easier. One, I know, must be about our financial arrangements, in light of what I told you about my father. I shall turn over the files whenever you request them. Another, I suspect, is in regard to Stanley's work for such a long period. He turned to me for money because he refused to talk to anyone at the university about his project, and, of course, he would have had to divulge it in order to secure proper funding. The fact that he convinced someone in government to fund him makes me more suspicious than anything else about the legitimacy of his final project. I am not a subversive, Drew, but when a scientist must turn to secret funding from the government, I suspect the worst. Especially when someone like Thomas Wiley has anything to do with it.''

''Wiley? Thomas Wiley? He's dead, isn't he? Isn't his son the senator from Virginia? William Wiley?''

''There will always be a Wiley senator from Virginia, I'm afraid. It's a dynasty.'' She walked slowly to the doorway and paused. ''If you can make up your mind by Thursday, as we agreed on earlier, I would be appreciative.''

Drew nodded. ''I have to leave town for the weekend, but I'll be back by Monday. I have an appointment with Dohemy on Monday. It's looking more interesting right now than it was this afternoon, Mrs. Huysman. That's for certain.''

''Yes. If you decide you want to leave those agents behind, you are welcome to one of my cars in the garage. There is the back way out, through the alley to the street. We often left that way when Stanley and I did not want to be bothered by newsmen at the height of his notoriety over the twin nonsense. The keys are in the cars.'' Still she hesitated. ''If I had not refused, if we had discussed his proposed work . . . If I had not been recalcitrant . . . One wonders. After it is too late one must always wonder. Good night, Drew.''

The private security men and the agents must have got together for a beer, he thought. How long had she known about the agents? And why hadn't she fired him outright over that? What could Stanley have done worse than having the U.S. government assign an army of agents to keep tabs on him around the clock?

He made a check on the alarm system and turned off lights on the lower floor and then went to his room; he set his clock for four in the morning and lay down on his bed and fell asleep almost instantly. At four he got up, tossed a few things into his briefcase, and went downstairs where he turned off the security system, using a timer now so that in ten minutes it would be activated again. He left by the kitchen door, out through the covered walkway to the garage, picked the Peugeot over the Continental, and got in it. The keys were there. He used the garage opener and watched the door slide up silently, drove out and through the alley to the street, out of Princeton. Rain was still falling. No one followed him.

SIX

Glen Erin was twelve acres of paradise on the banks of the James River. There were majestic, moss-draped oaks, stately pines, spreading dogwoods; there was an untouched woods, formal gardens, a vegetable garden, winding paths, some covered with bark mulch, some with gravel; there were broad expanses of bluegrass like velvet; there was a river beach and there was a swimming pool cleverly designed to look like a natural lake in a white marble basin. There were grottoes under blue spruce limbs, and there were fairy rings spreading in slow motion ripples from year to year. There was a stable, no longer used for horses, and a four-car garage; overused. There were two guest cottages, formerly slave quarters it was said; but that was a lie because the estate had been built since World War II, complete down to facsimile slave quarters. When Drew pointed this out to Pat's father once in the foggy past when he and Pat had lived in one of the guest cottages, Randolf Stevens had asked him earnestly to please not mention that to anyone. It lent the estate a romance that would be sorely missed, Randolf had said.

The gate house at the driveway entrance was occupied by an elderly black man who waved Drew on silently after glancing with no apparent interest at his driver's license.

The drive curved twice before the main residence came into view. The architect had been overly influenced by Tara in *Gone With the Wind*. Mammoth, refrigerator-white with three-story pillars, wings shooting off at abrupt angles, and wide, shady porches, it looked like a movie set waiting for the film crew. Drew continued driving past the turnoff for the entrance to the house, around the garage, onto the gravel track that led to Willie Jo's bungalow. Her same old truck was parked there, and also there was a newer Toyota. It was three in the afternoon; the air still and as hot as he had known it would be—sticky, Virginia hot.

He parked and went to the door of the bungalow and knocked. When no one answered, he went around the small house and sprawled in the chaise under an oak tree and closed his eyes.

"Hey, Drew! How are you?"

The voice that roused him was hoarse and deep. Drew opened his eyes enough to squint up at Julianna Jones, Willie Jo's girl, as she would be called until she died of old age. Julianna was going on thirty, tall, square-shouldered, strong, and frighteningly intelligent. She was a physicist, or on her way to becoming one. The day she had been notified that she would be entering Radcliffe on a full scholarship, she had stopped calling him Mr. Drew, shocking her mother into obscenities Drew had been shocked at hearing. The day Pat kicked him out, Willie Jo had stopped calling him Mr. Drew.

"Tolerable, just tolerable. How are you, Julianna?"

"Tolerable."

He grinned at her. "Do you have the doctor in front of your name yet?"

"Next year or the year after that. I'm working on my dissertation. You here for the big shindig?"

"Yes indeed. Wouldn't miss it. Fortunately Sherry invited me, or I would have missed it."

"Lordy, Mistuh Drew! Shut yo' mouf, you hear me! Miss the gala event of the season, of the year!"

They both laughed and she sat down in the other chaise and stretched. "I'm on vacation. They're all going crazy up at the house about now."

"Julianna, think you could give me a capsule education in physics?"

"Probably not. You study it at all? High school, college, a popular book sometime or other?"

"I dozed through a course or two. You familiar with Stanley Huysman's work? His twin studies?"

"He was in biology. I'm in physics. Not a lot of crossover."

"Yeah, I keep getting that line. what does nonlocal causes mean?"

She sighed. "How long do you have? Never mind. Look, there's a famous experiment that goes like this. You set up a screen with two slits in it and a light source in front of it. And you put a photographic plate behind it where the light will hit. Okay. Now you shoot a beam of photons through one slit and you get a diffraction pattern on the plate, a blob of light. That's when one slit is covered. You uncover it and shoot the light through both slits, and this time you get dark and light bands, an interference pattern. Just to make sure, you cover a slit and try once more. A blob. Now the question comes up, how does the photon know the other slit is open or closed, as the case may be? How do those dark bands get there? Why doesn't the light hit them when both slits are open, since it hits there when only one slit is open?''

"That's it?''

"Try this one. This time you shoot two particles at once—one with a right-hand spin, one with a left spin. They're called a singlet, and they are always opposite in spin. You have a way to change the spin of one of them in flight before it hits the target. You don't do a thing to the other one, but you find that it has changed its spin also. That's what they call nonlocal cause. How did the particle know it had to change its spin? There's no possibility of communication between the two.'' She laughed raucously at his look of bafflement. "You want more? Probability waves, wave functions, the collapse of a wave function?''

"I always suspected that you were not a nice person,'' Drew said.

"There are other experiments, but they're more of the same. What they all say basically is that something is going on at the submicroscopic level that can't really be accounted for in our actual space-time world. Einstein believed that the quantum theory is incomplete, and he called the forces acting on the particles hidden variables. It's a wide-open playground right now. And I don't have to be nice. When God makes anyone as ugly as she made me, niceness gets waived.''

"Ugly? I think you're rather handsome.''

"I know you do, and that's why I'm sitting out here wasting my time trying to educate you when I should be inside pounding at the type—''

"Drew Lancaster! Is that you? What on earth are you doing back here? How are you? You look scrawny, if you ask me.'' Willie Jo stood over him, scowling welcome.

"And that's a perfect example of interference,'' Julianna

said and jumped up. "You crashing the party dressed like that?"

Drew had risen also to embrace Willie Jo, who was as thin as a pole herself and hard all over. Her hair was more gray-streaked than he remembered, but otherwise she appeared exactly the same as when he first met her nearly fifteen years ago. Her scowl was permanent.

"No, he ain't crashing the party! Dressed like that or any other way. Drew, if you came here to make trouble, you can just get yourself right back out, back where you came from. And you haven't eaten a thing all day, have you? Well, come on in. Come on. You'd better have a shower and shave, is all I can say, and a little food under your belt . . ."

He followed her inside the little house that was as messy as it had ever been with what looked like the same accumulation of newspapers, magazines, empty jars, bags of old clothes on the way to the Salvation Army, or from there . . . He took a deep breath, feeling very much at home.

Before Julianna vanished into the bedroom, he called after her, "Is there any way any of that could apply to people?"

Her look was pitying. "No way. Quantum mechanics deals with the statistics of probabilities, big numbers only, never with individual events. It never deals with real things in the real world."

Willie Jo was muttering about not a thing in the house to eat while she pulled a ham from her refrigerator and set it down on the table and went back for a bowl of stewed apples and a wedge of cheese. She noticed Drew still standing near the door and her scowl deepened. "Well, don't just stand like a bump, sit down. Cut yourself a piece of meat. Men! Have to shove their noses in food before they see it."

SEVEN

"Daddy, what do people mean when they say maturity?"

"As opposed to the dictionary meaning?"

"Yeah. The dictionary says something like at the peak of ripeness, or readiness. I forget—something like that."

"I guess most people mean grown-up physically, psychologically, and emotionally. Why?"

They were side by side in swings suspended from an ancient oak tree. The ropes were fifty feet long, the seats made of white ash. Pat had swung there as a child.

"What chance is there of telling if someone is emotionally or psychologically grown-up?"

"Damn little."

She was swinging higher than he was, and he spoke to her back and watched her hair fly. At birth it had been like platinum and for the first few weeks it had stayed like that, as fine as cobwebs. Then it had changed every year a little darker, until now it was more like wild honey than anything else he could think of. On the backswing the wind parted her hair in a neat line and it whipped about her face on both sides as she swept past him, going the other way.

"Mom says when I'm mature I'll understand Senator Wiley and appreciate his fine qualities. I don't think I have a chance in hell of growing up that much."

"Me neither."

"I guess not. A nerd's a nerd' that's all there is to that."

He remembered the first time he had seen her stretch the rope straight out horizontally, the wrench of fear that had seized his stomach. And the first time he had seen her go off the diving board, and the day he had taken her to school for the first time, how she had clung to his hand, her eyes enormous pools of blue terror, but she had not wept.

"Mom says I'm at a terrible age. Was twelve a terrible age for you?"

"Probably. And thirteen and fourteen. What have you been doing?"

"She found Peter and me spitting. I can spit farther than he can. Mom said it was disgusting."

"How far?"

"I'll show you." Her feet dragged in the dirt braking her flight. "I never swing anymore," she said. "Unless you're here. Did you always like to swing so much?"

"Always." He cleared his throat. "If we're going to spit, we need some water."

"Yeah. Willie Jo will give us a drink. Come on."

She took his hand and they ran together to Willie Jo's house. Julianna was in the kitchen. She shook her head at Sherry.

"Honey, your mother's going to have a fit when she sees you! What on earth have you been doing?"

Sherry looked down at herself in sudden guilt. Her shoes were covered with dust, her white-stockinged legs covered with the powdery red-brown dirt. She had been sweating and more than once had wiped her face or her forehead with a dirty hand. The streaks remained.

"A little dusting off is all she needs," Drew said uneasily. "What we really want right now is a glass of water each."

"We're having a spitting contest," Sherry added.

Julianna looked at them both, then threw her head back and laughed. Finally she said, "Lordy, lordy! Okay. Water coming up. Then maybe I can help you clean yourself up just a little before you go back to the house."

Sherry won, and Drew declared her a master spitter and promised to have a medal made to that effect. When it came to cleaning her up, it was hopeless. Julianna surveyed her and shook her head.

"Come along, honey. You've got to shower and change your clothes. Nothing short of that's going to do a bit of good. I'll help you."

"I'll see you at the party, Daddy," Sherry said and left with Julianna, talking to her earnestly about how maybe if they couldn't find another pair of white stockings, maybe she could wear her sandals because she was itching all over.

Drew wandered over to the small cottage that he and Pat had stayed in early in their marriage and then for weekends over the years. It had not been changed. There was a screened porch with an old-fashioned glider that still needed oil. He looked in the windows and saw that someone was using the building. There was a desk set up where once there had been a sideboard with funny dishes on display. On the desk was a minicomputer and beside it stacks of papers. He could see no more of the interior. He sat down on the glider and moved it gently a few times. They had sat here when Pat had told him she was pregnant.

At dusk he decided to join the party. Music had been playing for half an hour. As always, they started with Broadway show tunes, familiar to everyone, offensive to no one, danceable. Later, if it followed the pattern he remembered, the band would switch to the top twenty rock music, after the old folk had gone tottering off.

The many French doors to the ballroom had been opened; people were dancing on the terrace, others strolling in the gardens, some at tables on the lawn; and everywhere there were white-gloved waiters with trays, silent, watchful. Willie Jo had said this affair was being catered; she had little to do except guard her kitchen.

Drew snagged a martini from a passing waiter and wandered on into the house. His mother had said you always pay your respects first thing. He saw Randolf Stevens and drifted toward his onetime father-in-law. Randolf Stevens looked the Southern gentleman to a tee: dove-gray tuxedo, the glitter of diamonds in his cufflinks, silver hair, healthy tan, not an ounce over or under an ideal weight.

Randolf Stevens had made his fortune making tanks during World War II. He did not believe there was any such thing as too many tanks, but he had diversified, he liked to point out to people. Now he made tractors and minisubmarines and hang gliders, and other things that he was not free to discuss. No matter what he made, it was lucrative. The touch of Croesus was what he had. A decade ago he had become a corporation. He had penetrated megabuck country, he had boasted then. Now he was more discreet about his good fortune.

On two separate occasions he had tried to give Drew a job, and he had offered to subsidize his own biography, whatever it took, as he put it. He and Drew had become very polite to each other after that:

Randolf Stevens was talking to the family doctor and his wife—MacHenry, Drew remembered. Doctor Mac. He joined the small group.

"Good evening, sir," he said to Randolph. "Doctor Mac, you're looking very fit, and, Mrs. MacHenry, I swear you're getting younger and prettier every time I see you."

Randolf Stevens did the clever thing he could do with his eyes. It was as if he had nictitating membranes that he could pull over them at will, shutter them. It had always fascinated Drew to watch it happen. The hesitation before he extended his hand was probably unnoticeable to anyone except Drew.

"How good of you to come," he said perfunctorily. "In fact, no one mentioned that you were free this evening."

"Oh, I'm still free."

The doctor and his wife were smiling genially, and she talked about the terrible weather they had been having all summer—nothing but heat and more heat.

"And thunderstorms," Drew said sympathetically.

"If you'll excuse me," Randolf said then, "I should check the arrangements in the rose garden, make sure the TV people have everything they need."

"Yes sir," Drew said. "If there's anything I can do to help, you know . . ."

"No. No. Just enjoy yourself." He hurried off.

"Television and everything," Drew murmured. "How exciting."

"Isn't it, though," Mrs. MacHenry said. "Oh, listen!"

The band had started to play "Some Enchanted Evening." Her eyes grew misty and she took her husband's hand. "Let's dance to it. Remember when we went to New York and saw the show? How we danced . . ." They moved away together without a backward glance.

For the next fifteen minutes Drew wandered through the various rooms that had been turned over to the party. There must have been over a hundred people in them all and more than that out in the gardens and on the terrace. He smiled at those he knew and those he did not know without discrimination, still carrying his martini, which had grown warm and was more than a little disgusting to him now. Finally he saw Pat emerge from the library with William Wiley at her side. Pat was in a long, pale blue dress, cut a touch too low, he thought, although very handsome indeed. But she was outshone by the senator who was in a dazzling white tuxedo with a red rose in his lapel.

A waiter passed with a full tray of drinks and he reached for one without looking to see what he landed. It was a Bloody Mary. He sipped it and strolled toward Pat and Wiley.

They were engrossed in their conversation and did not see him until he called out. "Pat, you are incredibly beautiful! In fact, you're both beautiful! Good evening, Senator."

"Drew! What the devil are you doing here?"

Pat's eyes snapped with rage and two pink spots appeared on her cheeks. Senator Wiley looked startled but recovered almost instantly.

"Drew, how good of you to come. Always nice to see you, old man."

Drew was carrying the Bloody Mary in one hand, the unwanted martini in the other. He held out both and looked puzzled when the senator extended his own hand. Wiley laughed and shrugged. He glanced at his watch.

"Ten minutes to show time," he announced. "Then I'll have a drink or two. I'll feel I deserve it."

"What are you doing here?" Pat demanded again.

"Moral support?"

"We can use all the support we can get," Wiley said heartily. "Welcome aboard, Drew. Now, I think it's time to start moseying on out to the rose garden." He waved to someone behind Drew, beaming his famous full-of-teeth smile.

"Time, Senator!" someone called from inside the library.

A small clump of men moved in on them; one of them was carrying a notebook, another had a legal pad opened to a page covered with large words printed with a black felt marker. "We're all set," he said as he joined the senator and Pat, jostling Drew aside as he did so. Later Drew would claim that he was pushed and Pat would deny it and the senator would say with a fixed, glassy-eyed, shining-toothed smile that it had been an accident, pure and simple. An accident. Drew lurched forward and the martini in his left hand drenched Pat;

the Bloody Mary in his right hand arced out of the glass and hit the senator in the bow tie and ran down his white tuxedo. The lime twist got caught in a button for a moment or two. Pat screamed. Someone grabbed Drew as if he had drawn a gun. The senator did not move for an extended moment, then he reacted, tried to brush off the tomato juice, and he cursed.

"You goddamn sonabitch!" He caught himself quickly, and the smile appeared, glassy-eyed though it was. "Martin, tell the television people there's going to be a slight delay. Half an hour. Gary, get the car around front. And, Martin, call my house and tell Stan to have my other tux laid out by the time I get there." The two men rushed off.

"And you get out or I'll have you thrown out!" Pat cried, glaring at Drew.

"Now, Pat, we don't want to let anyone think this was anything but an accident," Wiley said. He did not look at Drew. "We'll be back within half an hour." He hurried away, out through the library. Pat did not run, but she walked so fast that people moved aside as she got near them. She was holding her head unnaturally high.

"I think you can let go now," Drew said mildly to the young man who was still holding his arms.

"Oh, sorry. Mr. Lancaster, why'd you do that?"

"You heard the senator. It was an accident. Someone pushed me."

The young man shook his head and wandered away. He stopped at the first cluster of people he reached, and they all turned and looked at Drew. He waved to them. Suddenly the house felt very warm. Presently Randolf would be roaming around, smiling his nice smile, looking for his one time son-in-law. The band began a spirited "Oklahoma" and someone screamed a hoarse "Yippee!" and Drew made his way through the house to the rose garden. This, he decided, was probably about the last place Randolph would search.

"What's happening in there?" a bearded young man asked at his elbow. He was smoking a joint.

"I don't know. You with the television crew?"

"Yeah. We just might still make the late news, but I doubt it. Politicians! Probably he didn't like the way his hair was combed."

There were Japanese lanterns strung throughout the garden.

They gave a soft yellow glow, enough to see the floodlights that had been arranged near a small pavilion and the half dozen or more men who were standing around, smoking, drinking, talking. Wires snaked everywhere in the area. Drew let his gaze follow them to where they converged in a power pack of some sort. Several party guests were still in the garden waiting for the next act, waiting for curtain time, waiting for something. A bar had been set up at the far end of the garden. Most of the guests were near it. A caterer's helper wheeled out a two-tiered serving table loaded with hors d'oeuvres and arranged them on the bar and they attracted most of the television crew as well as the party guests. The waiter left the table and returned to the house. Presently Drew wandered over to the bar also, helped himself to something pink on a cracker, and wandered off again, this time pushing the heavy table as if it were in his way. It rolled over the wires with difficulty. He gave it a shove that took it to the vicinity of the power pack, and then he ignored it.

He walked through the garden, and when he had left it completely he kept walking until he was no longer in any of the light from the house or from the lanterns. He circled the garden and approached it from the garage side, hidden from view by tall bushes. He kept off the paths this time and moved in among the rose bushes until he was close enough to the serving cart to pull it to him slowly. He lifted one end of it and pulled it over the heavy-duty utility cable that went into one side of the power pack box. He wrapped the cable around a wheel twice and eased the cart back in the center of the path and then withdrew.

Several minutes later he approached a chair at a table on the edge of the garden. "Do you mind?" he asked politely of two women who were already seated there.

"Not a bit. Did you hear that Pat Stevens' ex socked the senator in the nose?"

"No! You're kidding!"

"That's what they're all saying in there. I don't believe a word of it myself, but still . . . You never know."

"That's true. You don't."

"Psst," he heard then, and turned to see Sherry beckoning to him.

"Excuse me," he murmured and left the two women. "Hi.

I looked everywhere for you," he said to Sherry. They sat down at a small table.

"Did you sock him in the nose?"

"Do I look like the kind of person who hits another person?"

"I didn't use to think so. Did you hit him?"

"The last time I hit anyone in the nose or anywhere else was when I was twelve and he was fifteen. Come to think of it, twelve is a very difficult age."

"Anyway, if you did, you'll have to do it again because he came back. Hit him harder next time."

"Isn't it past your bedtime?"

She giggled. "They say blood was everywhere."

"It was tomato juice."

"They're coming out now. He only had one white suit, I guess."

"And a good thing. He looked like an evangelist in it."

The entourage appeared, led by the aide Gary, with Senator Wiley in the middle of a group of ten or more people. Pat was there. She was now wearing a long red dress. The senator was in a dark tuxedo. Pat saw Sherry and Drew and joined them. The television people had come alive and were bustling about. The lights came on blindingly and the cameraman had his camera mounted on a stand on wheels.

"We'll be ready in a second, Senator," one of the crew said. "If you'll just come on over here . . ."

"Drew, was it an accident? Have you heard the talk that's going around? After the announcement, you'll have to come inside and join us for a drink or something just to show that you didn't really attack him."

"Aren't you supposed to be over there?" Drew asked.

"No. Why should I?"

One of the caterer's helpers saw the cart on the path and rushed over to yank it out of the way. He tugged to get it moving and suddenly the lights went out; one of the floodlights crashed over and shattered.

"Good God!" Pat cried. "Now what?"

She jumped up and Drew caught her hand and pulled her down again. "You might as well stay back out of the way. Just in case this show never does get off the ground tonight, would you mind telling me what the senator would have announced if he had had the chance?"

"His candidacy," she said wearily. "Can you see what's going on over there?"

"I think they're wrapping things up. Maybe it's too late to make the news or they don't have backup equipment with them or something."

"This whole night's been a nightmare. I have a pounding headache."

"Maybe Saturn's in transit or something."

EIGHT

Pat left Drew and Sherry to join Senator Wiley. "You will come in and have a drink or something with us a little later, won't you?" she insisted before leaving. He assured her that he would.

He looked at Sherry, who averted her gaze and said, "I thought it was something important. He always runs for the senate."

"That's okay."

"I'm only twelve. No one tells me anything."

"Yeah, I know. If your mother is willing, you want to go with me tomorrow instead of Thursday?"

"Can I? Where? She won't let me."

"Maybe she will. I'll ask. And I don't know where."

"I don't care. No stockings? Just shorts and stuff like that?"

"Sure."

"Make her say yes, Daddy. Make her!"

He joined Pat, Wiley, and Pat's father for a drink, danced with Pat once, was turned down by Wiley, and left the party. Randolf's eyes had been shuttered, he thought, and William Wiley's eyes glazed over; he was a menace to the eyesight of America somehow. Pat had been very correct.

"May I talk with you in the morning?" he had asked.

"Of course. Good night, Drew."

On his way out he had met Willie Jo, who asked if he had punched the senator in the nose and was vaguely disappointed that he had not.

"Why don't you stay in the little cottage?" she had suggested. "Miss Pat uses it for an office sometimes, but she won't be working tonight, not with that party going on all hours.''

And now he sat on the glider, moving it occasionally, trying to harmonize the squeak with the noise of the frogs and the cicadas and the katydids and whatever else it was out there chirping or singing. Crickets, he thought, and a very distant mockingbird. June bugs? It surely was too late in the season for them, unless their name was a lie. A luna moth touched the screen, clung to it for a moment, fluttered away like the ghost of an idealized moth. A child's drawing of a moth with stylized wings.

The music from the party was filtered by the shrubbery and trees, acceptable at this distance. He dozed and came awake when someone entered the porch.

''Hello, Pat,'' he said softly, not surprised.

''What are you . . . ?''

''Is the party over?''

''No. I told Dad I had to leave. Headache. William left nearly an hour ago. It's two in the morning. Why are you up?''

''No reason. Come, sit down, relax a few minutes. Nice party.''

''It was a nightmare of a party. I hated it.''

She crossed the porch and sat on the other side of the glider. ''You said you wanted a talk. We might as well get it over with. I won't be able to sleep for hours, and you seem awake enough.''

''In a minute. Listen. Who ever said it was peaceful and quiet in the country?''

Neither spoke for several minutes. He had not turned on any lights; there was only intermittent moonlight that made it to the ground through the trees, leaving the porch in almost total darkness. He could smell her elusive scent, hear her breathing. The music had stopped. No doubt, people were now eating—those who had stuck it out to the end.

The wind started to blow in the tops of the trees, adding its voice to the night music. It was starting to cool off finally.

''Dad and William both say I have to tell you not to come here again,'' Pat said softly. ''You're trouble, they said. And I can't deny it or defend you. You're supposed to get in touch with me through my lawyer if there's any business for us to discuss. There isn't any, though, except Sherry, and that's already taken care of.''

"All right. Is that what you want, too?"

"Yes. We both have to start over, find a new way. Start living again. Both of us."

"All right. Want me to massage your neck?"

"No. Drew, please cooperate. I don't want to fight with you anymore."

"Let's not fight. Do you want to marry the senator?"

There was a long pause. "I'm not sure. And after tonight, we'll have to wait a long time. You know they're saying you hit him. It would look bad if we did anything right now."

"Yes it would. Are they saying I hit you, too?"

"Don't be ridiculous!"

"If I'd managed to soak you in tomato juice, do you suppose that's what they would say?"

"Probably."

He laughed. "Pat, why do you give a damn what the senator says? You're not engaged to him, married to him, related in any way to him. Why do you give a damn what your father says? You're not his little girl any longer. When do you start listening to what Pat wants?"

"You simply can't understand," she said fiercely and started to rise.

"Explain it in simple language and I'll try hard to understand," he said.

The glider shifted as she sat down again. "There is such a thing as appearance," she said. "It matters what people think. Our entire social structure is based on what people think is moral or immoral behavior. Civilization demands a certain code of behavior or there would be no chance of survival for any of us. We set certain standards of behavior and then try to live up to them, no matter how hard it is or how much we'd rather do something else. The alternative is anarchy and nihilism and destruction. If William is to succeed in politics, he has to be even more careful than most people about appearances. He is a role model, a guide for others, a standard-bearer, a moral guide. He can't advocate moral positions when he himself is open to accusations of living an immoral life. And it would appear immoral for him to associate with a woman who is still involved with her ex-husband. Do you understand any of that?''

"Is that how he explained it?"

"Yes. Both he and Dad have made it very clear that I have to stop seeing you altogether before William and I can even think of anything."

"But we're not involved."

"Tonight makes it look as if we are. That's what I'm trying to tell you. It looks as if we're involved, as if you're jealous or something. We can't have that." She laughed with a touch of bitterness. "If only they understood just how uninvolved we've been for years!"

"Is your headache in the back of your head?"

"Yes."

He moved to sit beside her. "Let me massage it out. It's tension." She became very stiff and still. Her skin was moist and warm under his fingers. "No wonder. You're tied in knots. Let your head droop forward a little. You never used to be political. Were you converted, born again to a political outlook?"

"I have to do something. We can't all drop out and pretend nothing matters."

"Right. Some things matter. Tobacco subsidies. Anti-ERA votes. More bombs. More weapons of all sorts. You're absolutely right."

"Stop it. Unless you're involved yourself, you have no right to criticize anyone who cares enough to try to handle those matters. Everyone has to make some compromises or nothing would ever get done. Everyone has to compromise sometime."

"I don't," he said softly. "Ah, I think this is the source of your headache." he kneaded her neck and she flinched, then relaxed slightly. "Good. How's it feeling now?"

"Better," she said. "I have to go. See you in the morning." She did not move away from his hands that now rested on her shoulders.

"I think for once appearances and reality coincide, Pat," he whispered, his face in her hair, his lips next to her ear.

"What do you mean?"

He bit her ear gently. "I think we're still involved. I feel involved as all hell."

"You're just horny!"

He laughed. "That too. Remember the night you and I sat out here and you told me what the doctor had said that afternoon? You were pregnant. I was thinking of that night a while ago."

She nodded. "I remember. You undressed me and carried me inside and kissed me all over. I've thought of it sitting out here. It's like someone else's life, not mine."

His fingers found the zipper of her gown and slowly he undid it. She shivered.

"Drew, after tonight, you can't come back here ever again. You really can't. And I won't see you in Washington or New York or anywhere else. I mean it."

He lowered the gown from her shoulders, down past her waist, leaned over, and kissed her just above the navel. "After tonight, who knows what'll happen," he murmured. "You're more beautiful now than you were that night. How can that be?"

"You can't even see me."

"Oh yes I can. Your eyes are glowing and there's a flush on your cheeks and your skin is like a dream of remembered satin clouds and your breasts . . . Ah, your breasts!" He kissed one, then the other as his hand moved down her body, between her legs. "Ah," he sighed then. "Did I ever tell you how much I loved it that you were always as horny as I was, just as ready, just as eager?" He picked her up and stumbled leaving the glider, hit the door frame with his shoulder, and nearly fell when he walked into something on the floor.

"You'll kill both of us," Pat said, laughing. "For heaven's sake, put me down. Give me your hand. This way."

Hand in hand they made their way through the dark cottage, bumped into the bed in the other room and fell onto it in a heap, laughing.

Their lovemaking was unhurried. His hands knew her, his mouth remembered, even his skin seemed to know her skin in a way that he could not fathom. In bed she was without inhibitions, she caressed him and loved him fully, responded to his touch, touched him in ways no one but she ever had done before or since. He murmured and she murmured and sometimes laughed softly or cried out, but when he finally entered her she always said, "Sh, don't talk," and he never did.

She would not stay the night. What would it look like? she asked pointedly.

"We never did get around to what you wanted to talk

about,'' she said. ''Have breakfast with me, okay? We can talk then.''

He walked to the house with her, watched her enter, and then returned to the little cottage and sat down on the glider once more. He was not sleepy.

Months ago, when she told him she was leaving he had asked why, but he had not really been surprised. It had been brewing, he had thought then, still thought. Her father had had something to do with it, he had thought then, and still thought.

Randolf had had what they at first thought was a heart attack, but turned out to be something more like indigestion. ''I have to go spend some time with him,'' Pat had said.

''Why? He's well now.''

''Yes, but what if he really had had a heart attack? And people think he had a heart attack. He needs me for a while.''

''And later, after spending time with him, she had said, ''He's doing things, and the senator is doing things. Important things.''

''But you don't even approve of the things they're both doing. You're not political in the way they are.''

''That's the problem. I should be. You should be. We have to get involved.''

''Why? In what?''

''In anything! You can't spend a whole lifetime in a cloud of lust! That's all we have going for us, lust! We have nothing in common in any other area. Nothing mental or spiritual or political. Nothing!''

''Spiritual?''

''Yes, spiritual! That hard bright core we all have that makes some people devote their lives to the welfare of others. We, you and I, have spent our lives denying it, ignoring it, and it's dying in us. I need it back. I'm going to work for the senator. Be a staff member on his team.''

''That's spiritual fulfillment? Working for William Wiley?''

''I knew you'd take that attitude. I knew you wouldn't understand. He's devoting his life to working for others, helping others who are less fortunate than he is.''

''What others? Who?''

''Everyone. The people. He has a cause: to help all the people.''

"Not me. He's not helping me a damn bit. He's taking my wife away from me."

"You say that only because to you I'm nothing more than an object of lust. But I need to grow, to develop, to become what my potential will let me become. I need to become a person in my own right!"

"I'll give up my money and take a vow of poverty. I'll donate it all to the charity of your choice."

"You don't have any money."

"I'll give up your money, then."

"Don't laugh at me, Drew. Whatever you do, don't laugh at me. I'm serious about this. You refuse to be serious about anything, and up till now I haven't objected. It's been fun with you, all fun and games, but that's not enough anymore."

"Why isn't it, Pat? Why is it wrong to be happy?"

She had stormed out without telling him and had not told him yet. Dawn was turning the tree leaves into black lace against a rose-streaked gray sky. He stood up and stretched. His shoulder ached from where he had bumped into the door frame, and his shin was sore from knocking against a stool or some damn thing, and there was an ache between his shoulder blades from too much driving without enough sleep. He felt marvelous, he decided, and went to bed for a few hours of sleep before his breakfast date with his ex-wife whose wonderful woman scent was still in his nostrils.

NINE

In May T.M. and Michelle Matthews had been audited. For weeks they had prepared the information that was demanded, gathered receipts, made photocopies of bills and canceled checks, reviewed their returns for the source of what had to be an error.

T.M. would handle the interview, they decided; otherwise Michelle would have to miss Friday, the busiest day in the doctor's office where she worked. It would not take both of them, they reassured each other nervously. They had been married just under a year and this was their first crisis, but they were handling it well, in an adult way, each being as cheerful as possible before the other, each wakeful and afraid to move at night for fear of disturbing the other. On that Friday morning T.M. was haggard looking and felt old, not his twenty-six years. Michelle had smudges under her eyes; she spilled coffee and dropped her toast.

"It's okay, honey," he said again. "Don't sweat it, okay?"

"Sure. I love you."

He felt the responsive catch in his throat, the tightening in his groin. They both looked at the clock, but there was no time. He did not touch her, did not dare touch her.

"Tonight we'll celebrate," he said huskily. "Dinner out, okay?"

She nodded. "Good luck."

It was time to leave the apartment, to catch the same subway train, he heading toward the Federal Building, she to her office. He was carrying his briefcase with the tax material, and a double roll of blueprints—three feet long, bulky. At the subway station they were like individual pieces of paper in a confetti storm, separated by the crowds even though they were within reach of each other.

T.M. had to wait no more than ten minutes in the scabrous room in the Federal Building that was already crowded that morning by nine. "See you in lockup, pal," the man on his left said cheerfully; the one on his right whispered, "Remember, don't say anything bad about the government, taxes, your auditor, anything!"

"Room number eight," the woman behind the reception desk said without looking up.

Outside the door of number eight, he swallowed, wiped his free hand on his leg, and entered. The man at the desk nodded at him but did not rise.

"George Reilly. Mr. Matthews?"

They shook hands and T.M. sat down opposite the auditor. George Reilly was a thin man with wispy hair going gray. He wore heavy-framed glasses that kept sliding down his nose, which was oily looking and narrow.

"Now, let's see what we have," he said, opening a file folder before him. On the end of the desk there were half a dozen thick books; there was a pencil, a pen, and the folder. Behind the desk, off to the side, was a metal table that held a telephone.

"Ah, yes. You're an architect, is that right?"

"Yes."

"And your wife is a bookkeeper?"

"Right."

"How big is your apartment, Mr. Matthews?"

"About nine hundred square feet, counting closets and the bathroom."

Mr. Reilly pulled a legal-sized pad from a desk drawer and wrote on it: Two bedrooms.

"You work for the firm Webbing, Trimble and Cooke? How many architects do they have, by the way?"

T.M. blinked. "In my section there are nine. Ten, counting Cooke."

"And they have rooms there for you to work in? Drafting tables, whatever architects need?"

He nodded warily. "I have here my records, the things your letter said I should—"

"So why do you have to do any of your work at home?

You are a full-time employee of the firm, aren't you?'' He was looking at T.M. over the top of his glasses, a thin smile curving his lips, as if they shared a secret joke.

''We have a big job, a skyscraper, and we have a deadline . . .''

''Did your supervisor order you to do part of your work at home?'' He glanced at the rolled-up blueprints T.M. had been studying at home. ''Or is that to impress me?'' His smile grew wider.

''No, of course not. I often take work home.''

''I see. What all is in your home office, Mr. Matthews?'' He shuffled papers in the folder and brought out a letter, a photocopy of the one they had sent to T.M. and Michelle. ''I see we asked you for a rough floor plan of your apartment. Did you bring one?''

T.M. dug through his briefcase and extracted the floor plan, not rough at all, but lovingly and accurately drawn.

''How very pretty,'' Reilly said, examining it, nodding, his smile spreading and spreading. ''Which bedroom do you use for your office?''

T.M. pointed.

''Of course. Why don't you just sketch in for me what you keep in that room. Would you mind?''

T.M. drew in his drafting table, shelves, then hesitated and leaned back.

''But where does your wife keep her computer? I noticed that you claimed a deduction for it.''

''It's in there, too.''

''I see. So she also uses the room for an office. Is that correct?''

T.M. nodded. ''She does computer programming for small companies—''

''But it says here that she works for a Dr. Saltzman.''

''She's programming his computer, for his records.''

''I'm afraid, Mr. Matthews, that the law governing the use of home offices is quite strict.''

''We looked it up! Look, I'll show you what it says.'' He held up his paperback tax guide.

''Please, Mr. Matthews. Perhaps we can save time if I just show you what the law actually says.'' Reilly slid the top book off the pile at the end of his desk and drew it to him, opened it where a slip of paper was sticking out. The book was several inches thick. T.M. looked from that one to the others in the stack, each with a slip of paper or more than one sticking out. Miserably he took a breath and slouched down in his chair.

That was the beginning. At the time, he thought that was the worst day of his life; two weeks later he knew he had been wrong. What really was the worst day of his life was the day that Jeremy Cooke announced that the firm was having to cut back, etc., etc., and when he walked out of the drafting room again, T.M. had been fired. he did not tell Michelle; it would be just a matter of a couple of weeks before he would find another job, he thought at first. He found his old resumé and updated it, filled out applications, had interviews, and applied for unemployment.

In the middle of June one afternoon he picked up Michelle at her office and they headed for the subway together. Two men approached, passed them, and then turned to come up behind them.

"Just let go of the purse, lady," one of them said.

T.M. felt his wallet sliding from his hip pocket. Neither he nor Michelle protested. She released her purse.

"Keep walking," the voice said.

They did for half a block without speaking. "We should go to the cops," he said finally.

"What's the use? How much did you have?"

"Maybe ten? You?"

"About that. I have money in my bra. Let's take a taxi home. I think I'm going to cry."

"In the cab she looked out her window and said in a low voice, "Today was my last day at the office. I quit a week ago."

His grip tightened on her hand. "What happened? Are you okay?"

"Oh sure. I just . . . I just couldn't take it any longer. He's such a crook and I was being crooked, knowing it was crooked . . ." Her voice broke, and she took a breath. "And now this . . ."

"It's okay honey. We'll manage."

"It just made me so mad, having to put his wife and his

daughter on the payroll, right after we were audited and have that big bill, knowing we're subsidizing someone like him . . . I'll get another job right away—''

The driver snorted. "You kids got money to pay for this trip?''

In their apartment they went straight to bed, scattering clothes on their way.

"God!" he said again and again, "you're so beautiful! You're so alive in there!''

She cried out and wept, and they clung to each other for a decent interval and started again. By the time they got up it was nearly ten. They showered together and played in the water, but neither could be aroused now, they were too hungry.

He scrambled eggs; she made salad and coffee and got out a package of frozen strawberries. He waited until they had eaten to tell her that he was also unemployed.

She stared at him. "You're not kidding, are you?''

"Michelle, what's wrong? You look . . . What's wrong?''

She could not have said what was wrong. For a moment she felt removed, that was how she would have described it if she had tried. Distant, somewhere else, someone else. She looked about the kitchen with its tiny table for two, past it to the living room, hardly furnished because they had decided to buy only pieces they both loved and only when they could afford to pay cash.

"We have to move, all the way out of the city," she said.

"Honey! It's not the end of the world. Not yet.''

"Out in the country.''

"Michelle, stop it! What's wrong with you?''

She blinked. "We'll move," she said quietly. "Do you want coffee now?''

"They've given me a great recommendation," T.M. said. "It won't take a month to find something.''

She got up and brought the coffee pot and two mugs back to the table, evidently paying no attention to his words. "We should go over our finances, I guess," she said, and the strange girl was gone, his own Michelle was back. A knot he had not recognized as such dissolved from his stomach. What the hell had all that been about? He pushed the thought away, unwilling to examine the question, unwilling to admit that anything had been screwy just seconds ago. Still, when he glanced at the kitchen, at the living room, it was with an uneasy feeling that nothing there was quite as solid as he had thought.

The next morning when T.M. brought in the mail there was a notice that their building was being turned into a cooperative. They were invited to buy into it; the price was eighty thousand dollars. Michelle looked at the letter indifferently. She was making sandwiches. Today, she had announced, they were driving out to the country to look at houses for rent.

She wanted to drive and he was happy to let her. Things felt out of control, unmanageable all at once; he knew nothing about this part of the country. He was a California native. They had been up the coast, out to Long Island, down to the Jersey shore, but never in this part of New Jersey that Michelle was taking him to today. Michelle had grown up in Trenton, he knew, had lived there until she went to school in Buffalo.

"Don't be a grump," she said, driving on a winding state road with forests on both sides. "You know as well as I do that we can't afford to live in New York now. And besides, you don't even want to work on super skyscrapers for multibillion-dollar corporations. All they'll let you do is plan where to put drain pipes for the next five years."

He glowered at her. When he had said that, looking for sympathy, she had teased him out of his foul mood. Not fair for her to bring it up now. What he really wanted to do, he had also said that night, was to build affordable houses for real people, energy-efficient houses using passive solar energy, pie-in-the-sky stuff, kid stuff . . .

"You can make your house plans and sell them to one of those companies doing that sort of thing. And I'll work on some program ideas I have. I can sell them. If we live frugally we can get by for more than a year on our savings and your unemployment even if neither of us gets a contract right away."

"You're out of your mind, you know that? Let's sell the car and the computer and find a cheaper apartment . . ."

"You can't sell the car. We'll need it in the country, and the new computers are cheaper than mine and have more functions. We're stuck with both."

He did not trust her cheerfulness. It was not natural. So they would waste gas and time and spend the day looking at trees and farms and hills and tomorrow settle down with the for-rent classified and get to work on finding a new apartment. He began to cheer up, knowing this was simply an outing, a day off; they could both use a day off, no fear of muggers, no announcements of doom and gloom in the mailbox, no bosses.

"All we have to do," she went on briskly, "is find a house to rent for under a hundred a month and we'll have it made."

He laughed and moved closer to her, patted her thigh.

It was eleven-thirty when Michelle pulled up in front of a small white building with a realtor's sign in the town of Harmony. T.M. was surprised at how pretty the countryside was; he had not known New Jersey was mountainous anywhere, had assumed it was all flat onion fields or industrial or beach.

"Hello. What can I do for you folks?" A man appeared from the side of the building, carrying a golf bag.

"We're looking for a house to rent," Michelle said. "Cheap."

The man laughed and set down his bag at the front door. "I'll be damned. How cheap, young lady? Sixty a month cheap enough for you?"

She nodded.

"Well, come in. I'll tell you what I have." He opened the door, ushered them inside where there was a desk and several chairs. Pictures of houses covered one wall, most of them farm houses, some of them quite beautiful.

"Name's Fensternacht. Sarge Fensternacht," the man said, rummaging through a pile of papers on his desk. "Just got a letter yesterday . . . Ah, here it is."

T.M. muttered their names, eyeing Michelle warily, uneasy again with an unfamiliar sense of things not right.

"Let's see now. Just came yesterday, like I said." Fensternacht read part of the letter: " '. . . out of touch for the next year maybe and hate to think of it empty all that time. So just try to rent it for enough to cover the taxes and pay them for me when they come in. Add enough for your commission, of course. Thanks. Your pal, Joe Bramwell.' " He looked over the letter, beaming first at Michelle, then at T.M. "Sixty a month will do it."

"We'll take it," Michelle said.

"Hey, hold on! We have to see it first," T.M. protested.

Michelle looked at him and nodded. "Sure." She turned back to the realtor. "Can we move in right away?"

TEN

Joe Bramwell had bought the house as a fixer-upper, Sarge Fensternacht had told them. Dirt cheap, abandoned for fifteen years but basically sound. Then he had made changes. T.M. thought it had to be the ugliest house in seven states, maybe in the world. Where the front door had once been, there was now a forsythia bush, gone wild. Bramwell had taken out the stoop, the steps, had boarded up the door, and the house had no entrance that was easily detected. He had built on a garage with no square corner, no perpendicular wall, but a shelter for a car, and through the misshapen structure there was now a door that opened to a four-foot square entrance inside, with the kitchen to the left, the living room to the right. The living room was the width of the house, twenty-six feet and thirteen feet wide. It had a fireplace that was sufficient to heat the house, Sarge had insisted, but if they wanted to use it, there was also a furnace in the basement. Upstairs there was a room that was exactly the same size as the living room below, and two smaller rooms, one of which Michelle claimed as her office, with the other automatically becoming T.M.'s studio. The large room was their bedroom. There was furniture of sorts in the house, but nothing they wanted to use. They put it all in the basement where there were heaps of broken chairs and tables, junk furniture of all sorts, cans of paint, varnish, tools, sanders of various kinds, and dirt. Mostly dirt, T.M. thought, standing at the bottom of the stairs surveying the hodgepodge.

He was whistling. All in all, the move had proved workable, to his surprise. He and Michelle had climbed the hills across the road from the house, had explored the swamp behind it, and had swum in the river which was less than half a mile away. Their road was dirt and unused except for the four or five families that lived on it, and none of the other people lived within sight or sound. In the beginning he had thought the place too isolated for either of them to bear; gradually over the last few weeks he had come to accept it, the quiet, the funny house, the mosquitoes that attacked as soon as the sun went down, and most of all the chance for him and Michelle to relax, to play when they wanted to play, work when they wanted to work, take walks, talk, experiment with cooking—all the things there had been no time for.

If only money were not an ever-pressing problem, this would be ideal. He was actually making drawings that he was proud of—good plans, good houses—and Michelle was at work with her computer for hours day after day. If only they had a rich uncle who would finance all this for the next year or two, let them try their wings as freelancers. But, although they did not talk about it, he knew this was a time-out, dream time, play time, and before the end of the year they would have to face reality again. And there were no jobs in Harmony, New Jersey, for an architect and a computer whiz. Meanwhile, he would try to get the furnace in working condition because in a month they might be needing it and better find out how if it worked at all. The problem was in getting to it.

Bramwell, apparently, was retired, lived in Jersey City with a bossy daughter, and used this house in the country for his safety valve. He had bought it for cash and started "improving" it instantly. He only spent six weeks to a couple of months in it each year, but he built onto it when he was around. The back deck was a nightmare of construction, wobbly, crooked, dangerous. The garage was laughable. And in the basement was all this junk furniture that Bramwell had said he intended to fix up, refinish, and sell to make a little spending money. T.M. shook his head at the mess he had to force his way through. Cobwebs were thick, dust was thick, shelves built into the wall were so loaded with junk that it was impossible to see if anything useful was there or not. A workbench sagged from the weight of its miscellaneous burden. And the light was terrible.

He had cleared a path nearly to the furnace when he decided that he would not be able to see anything anyway without more light. He returned to the stairs and went up

them three at a time. At the top he flicked every switch up
that was down and pulled down those that were up. Bramwell
had fancied himself something of an electrician, also; the
wiring in the entire house was incredible.

T.M. had bought light bulbs the week they moved in. Now
he took several of them with him and returned to the basement. He filled every socket he found and tripped switches,
pulled strings, pushed buttons, but the lighting was not im-
proved. When one light came on, another went off. It was as
if Bramwell had done it deliberately, he thought in exaspera-
tion. Anyone who knew how to string up the wires he had
strung knew enough to make them work better than this.

The basement was not that big, he thought, surveying it;
why so many lights to begin with? Presumably because
Bramwell wanted to work on his junk furniture down here.
There were three lights over the workbench area alone. None
of them came on if the light by the furnace was on. He was
ready to admit defeat when Michelle came partway down the
stairs.

"Mail's here," she called. "Your sister sent you a letter."

"Be right up."

"Are you going out again today? If you're not, I'll close
the garage door. It looks like another storm is coming."

"Go on and close it." He looked around for a rag to wipe
his hands on. He was grimy from basement dirt that apparently had not been disturbed for over a decade. He was at the
work bench when all the basement lights went out. The black
was unrelieved for several seconds until his eyes adjusted and
then he could faintly make out the windows, covered with dirt
and almost hidden by junk; the door to the kitchen was a pale
rectangle floating high over his head. He dropped the rag he
had found and groped for the workbench, knowing there was
a gauntlet of junk between him and the stairs. His fingers slid
along the edge of the bench as he gingerly felt his way toward
where the clear path had to be, and suddenly the entire wall
beside him shifted.

He stopped moving, feeling as if a hole had opened in the
floor. Carefully he pushed against the bench, and it shifted
again and continued to shift as long as he kept pushing. He
could now see a black space opening as high as the basement
ceiling, at least two feet wide. He took his hand away from
the bench and the wall moved back, the space disappeared.

Cautiously he felt along the bench for the spring, the release, whatever it was that he had found before; nothing happened.

"T.M., what's wrong? Did we blow a fuse again?"

Michelle was outlined against the pale rectangle of the kitchen door. She flicked a switch and the main basement light came on. "This house has the craziest wiring I ever saw," she muttered and retreated.

T.M. hunted until he found an overlap in the molding that had been used to finish the bench top. That had to be it, he decided, and pressed it, tried to push it forward, then back, tried to move it in any direction, any amount. Nothing. Finally he went upstairs in frustration.

"I broke the garage door," Michelle said glumly. She was seated at the kitchen table with mail in two messy piles before her. One pile was bills, which they had agreed not to open until each Friday; the other was mostly advertising, but there were also one or two first-class letters.

"What do you mean, you broke it? How?"

"You know how we never can get it to close all the way down? I was determined to make it close, or the rain would have come in again the way it did last time, and I grabbed it and swung on it to pull it all the way. I think it broke. It made a terrible noise and slammed down the last foot. Then I couldn't get it to open."

They went out to the garage together; here again the lighting was terrible. There was one dim light over the door to the house; it left most of the garage in the darkness. Michelle opened the car trunk and brought out a flashlight, which she held while T.M. felt around the edge of the metal door, searching for a lock mechanism. He found it finally and released the door; it rose about a foot from the ground, the position it usually maintained. He tugged on it, and with each pull it sank down a few inches but went back up when he let go.

"That's what it kept doing and I grabbed hold and swung," Michelle said. "What are you looking for?"

"I don't know. Something's screwy around here. Why install a door that won't close unless you force it? Why panel one wall of a garage like this?" The wall next to the house was finished with knotty-pine paneling. It turned the corner and ended at the overhead door. He pulled the door closed with some effort and then used the flashlight to examine the track. Slowly he took a step backward from it after a moment. "That's it," he whispered. "I found the release."

"What are you talking about? What's wrong with you? What did you find?"

"Come on. Let's go back to the basement."

"I thought I was acting nutty," she said, "playing Tarzan with a garage door, but you win. What are we doing?"

They were at the top of the basement stairs. She reached for the light switch and he caught her hand. "No lights. The lights all went off and it opened, but when you turned on the light I couldn't find it again. Come on."

"T.M., you're going strange on me."

"Here, let me hold the light." He took her hand and led her down the stairs, shining the light on the steps in front of them, then on the floor, picking out a path among the clutter. "Over here," he said, lighting up the bench, then playing the light along the edge of it. "I held it right about here, I think. Yeah, here's the rag I dropped." He went down on one knee, examining the underside of the bench until he found the place where the molding was thickened, doubled. Carefully he touched it, slid his finger forward, then back, and the wall shifted.

The bench moved with the wall, opening a passage into a pitch-black interior. Michelle gasped and held her breath for a long time. When she exhaled, the opening was complete. Her exhalation sounded like a sigh.

"What's in there," she whispered.

"Let's find out." His words came out in a whisper also.

They moved forward, not quite daring to enter the black space. T.M.'s light swept the room and they gasped.

"Good lord! A press! And, look!" His light stopped moving, fixed on a table where there were stacks of money.

All the hokey wiring, T.M. thought later, sitting opposite Michelle at the kitchen table. All that hokey Sunday carpentry. All a fake. The room in the basement had been built by a master craftsman with enough alarms and traps to make it almost impregnable. It had been a fluke that he had stumbled onto it. If Michelle had not slammed the garage door shut, if she had changed any one of the switches that he had raised or lowered, it would not have opened. If he had not put light bulbs in every socket there, it would not have opened.

"I'm really scared," Michelle said. "We have to call the police, don't we? We have to, but I keep feeling I don't want to."

"Yeah, me too."

"What are we going to do? We can't just forget the whole thing."

"Honey, have you ever done anything really illegal?"

She shook her head, wide-eyed.

"Do we have a magnifying glass anywhere?"

"In the *O.E.D.* I'll get it."

They examined the twenty-dollar bill they had brought up from the basement, and it took the magnifying glass to find the small imperfections, the hazy cross-hatching, the sharp peaks that were clotted slightly. Even with the glass, it did not look all that different from a twenty-dollar bill that Michelle had dug out of her purse, except for the missing serial number.

"I could draw in the number," T.M. said in a faint voice. "There's ink down there."

"I know you could."

They stared at each other. He moistened his lips and shook his head. "They'd catch us and we'd serve twenty years for something like that. In separate prisons."

She took his hand and held it against her cheek. "I'd die if we were separated," she said softly.

One thing led to another and they decided to go to bed and think it all over. Much later that night T.M. opened his sister's letter. As he read it, he felt the world go soft again, the way it had done back in their New York apartment when Michelle had announced that they were going to move to the country. All at once there were no hard edges to anything, nothing seemed solid, nothing seemed fixed in place and real.

"What is it?" Michelle asked, watching him.

"Susan and Jerry are coming east in two weeks and want to meet us at Atlantic City for dinner."

"Atlantic City?"

Both of them turned to stare at the bogus twenty-dollar bill on the table between them.

ELEVEN

"This little piggie went to market and this little piggie stayed home . . ." Mildred Lauder squeezed toes and her grand-daughter of eleven months squealed in delight, and on the opposite side of the sun-baked patio Leon Lauder brooded. The infant let out a piercing shriek of joy, and Mildred's responsive laughter was hardly less piercing. Leon lifted his beer and drank.

"Think about it, Dad," his son Anthony said at his left elbow, and at his right elbow his grandson Tony asked if he could have two hotdogs on one bun.

"The price is right," Anthony went on, "and there's plenty of space for just two people. Who needs such a big house at your age? Always grass to cut, roses to spray, something to do. Relax a little, Dad. Let Mom relax a little."

"I don't like buns," Tony whined. "And I don't like pickles and onions and relish. I just like hotdogs and catsup. And Coke. That's all I'll eat."

". . . piggie went Wee, Wee, Wee! all the way home." Two earsplitting shrieks punctuated the rhyme.

The third child, Jennifer, aged seven, came out to the patio and stood before Leon staring at him. He smiled at her; she continued to regard him soberly.

"No tomatoes," Tony said after a moment. "Can I have my cake now?"

"Now that Becky's back at work, it's a little hard on the kids, not having one or the other of us here all the time. And Mom gets such a kick out of them, doesn't she?"

"Peekaboo!" Mildred cried; the baby shrieked.

"Little Bo Peep has lost her sheep and can't tell where to find them leave them alone and they'll come home wagging their tail behind them,'' Jennifer said in one rapid breath. She curtsied and ran back into the house.

"Isn't she something else! How about that!" Anthony cried.

"From inside the house they heard the phone ring, and in a moment Becky called from the door, "Father, it's for you."

". . . hate mushrooms!" Tony was saying when Leon escaped.

Leon listened with growing disbelief, staring at a print of a matador killing a bull. Blood spurted like a fountain from the wound in the beast's side.

"You let him go," he finally said with long spaces between the words. "And you're not sure just when he took off. Is that right?"

He listened, staring at the bull that did not know yet that it was dead. Lancaster's car had been parked in the driveway. He had taken a walk in the rain. He had checked his car windows and then had gone inside, presumably to bed. He had not been seen since. One of Mrs. Huysman's cars was gone. And after the one glimpse of the Indian in Trenton, he had dropped out of sight. No one had been expecting him; the only available car had been heading the wrong way, and by the time the driver had been able to turn, the Indian, his truck, and the black kid he claimed was his grandson were all gone.

Leon gave orders in a deceptively quiet voice. He scowled at the stupid bull and turned to see Jennifer standing just inside the doorway.

"For the whitest white for the brightest bright for sunshine light it's Dandy!" she said and curtsied. She turned and ran off.

From the patio he could hear Mildred's voice: ". . . the clock struck one and down it run!"

Yesterday, minutes before he was due to leave his office, the director had called him in.

"Look, Leon, I know what this guy means to you, your only failure, but what the hell, he's an old man. He'll be dead soon. So what if he does get off? And anyway, he's inactive. And meanwhile down in Alabama there's someone passing dollar bills drawn on brown paper who's getting away with it. You've got an army on this one case, and with our budget these days . . ."

The director was in his forties. Anthony was forty. "At your age . . ." Anthony had said. An old man. At your age. And his army of men were all twits. His only son was a twit, married to a twit, with three twit children. At your age!

"We're ready to eat," Becky called to him as she passed the door carrying a platter of hamburgers to go on the grill. "When we're finished, we thought you and Mother might like to take a ride over to see those new condos that are going up. They're so nice!" She passed on out of range.

They were condemning his house that had been paid for for twelve years. Under the law of eminent domain they could do that. A new road was needed, a new bypass for airport traffic. His house was in the way. His house, his roses, his two apple trees that were as old as Anthony. At your age . . . A peal of Mildred's manic laughter made him wince. She would love being minutes away from the kids, he knew; she had told him so many times, by now taking it for granted that that was how it would all work out. It was true that anything you said often enough became somehow true, he thought, not moving from the phone yet. She had said it often enough to convince herself that it was what they both had agreed on. For a long time it had been. "When you retire . . ." but now it was, "When they make us move . . ." That was going to be sooner than his retirement.

He walked slowly to the patio but did not actually go out. Tony was crying because there were no hotdogs, only hamburgers. Jennifer was reciting something to Mildred who appeared absorbed in the child's words. The baby, who had been put down in her bassinet, was howling furiously. Anthony was singing as he burned the meat, and Becky was making up plates for the children, talking to Mildred apparently or maybe to herself. It was hard to tell.

"I have to go," Leon yelled over the noise. "Something's come up that I have to attend to. Anthony, can you give Mildred a ride home later?"

There were protests. Mildred looked martyred and Becky looked like a junior martyr; she had not had time to practice that look yet, but it was coming along. When he got in his car and turned on the key, the radio came on. Promptly he turned it off and took a deep breath. He would find a restaurant, he decided, have something to eat, and then he intended to go to Princeton and raise some hell.

* * *

T.M. and Michelle had had their dinner with his sister and her husband on Friday night and had casino hopped for a few hours with them. They had picked out the casino they intended to hit, the biggest and most garish of all, one where whole busloads of people entered at a time, got in line to buy chips, and then lost themselves in the crowds.

T.M. had a fatalistic feeling about the whole thing. He had found some money, had drawn in the numbers skillfully, had accepted that they were meant to use it. He could not have defended any of this, but on the other hand, neither could he resist doing what they planned to do. They each had one bogus bill only. At first he had insisted that only he pass one, but Michelle had objected, and in the end, they both tucked a bill inside their wallets.

"We're just going to try it out," he had said. "If anyone gives us any trouble, we say we got it in change. Right?"

"Right."

She looked like a scared kid, pale, shaky, big eyed. He thought she never had looked so beautiful in her life. For a moment he wavered. What in god's name were they up to? This was a federal offense, he knew, not kid stuff, nothing they could beat if they got caught. But the bills were too good for anyone to suspect! He knew they were. And Bramwell must have lived off them for years without getting caught. And, he thought, it did not even feel like stealing. He had lifted a pen in a drugstore once and he knew what that felt like, and this was not it. This felt okay, right in some way he could not define. It was that auditor, he told himself. Every single item he had questioned, they had lost, and they had tried to be honest. Stupid they had been, but not dishonest, and it had cost them two thousand dollars! They should have been allowed that office and her computer, if nothing else. He knew he was rationalizing and stopped.

"Ready, honey"

She nodded. They walked out of the coffee shop where they had waited for a bus to start unloading outside the casino across the street, and they crossed over and joined in the hordes heading for the entrance.

Brilliant sunshine, heat, afternoon all faded instantly in the dim mammoth building. Red carpeting, paneling, an oversized reception desk, bustling bellboys, women in tights carrying trays of drinks, a strikingly tall black woman carrying a tray of silver dollar chips, women in shorts, in evening dresses, in jeans, men in tuxedos and others in denims, and everywhere the sound of slot machines, the rattle of coins in trays, the staccato sound of the metal arms being released, the hum of voices and the punctuation of laughter . . .

Michelle got in one line, T.M. in another. He was slightly behind her. When she got to the window and passed a bill under the grill, the man behind it glanced at her, then looked more sharply.

"May I see some ID?"

"Why?" She groped in her purse and pulled out her wallet, opened it. She looked around almost desperately, so pale that she looked as if she might faint. "I'm . . . I'm here with my husband!"

"Sure, sure." He glanced at the driver's license. "Just checking for underage, ma'am." He pushed a roll of chips toward her and already was looking past her at the next customer. She picked up the roll and fled.

T.M. changed two twenties into silver dollar chips and even he could not tell which bill was which.

He grasped her arm. "Let's get a drink," he said urgently. "I've never been so scared in my life as when he stopped you! Why did you say you were with your husband?"

"I knew I had to say something. He must have seen how scared I was. I thought he'd think I was guilty of that."

They had walked away from the cashier's window and were standing before endless arrays of slot machines. Most of them were being used. There was a white-haired woman in orange shorts who moved like a zombie, feeding coins and pulling the lever mechanically over and over. When coins fell into the tray she did not even glance at them. Another machine had a young man who put in a quarter, made a note, then pulled the arm, again and again. An elderly man divided his coins in the tray into stacks and then fed them all back into the machine.

"Would you like a drink?" a woman asked. She was in red tights, carrying a tray. T.M. said two Bloody Marys and she made a note, moved away.

Another woman, this one with a tiny black skirt over her red tights, approached them. She had a change maker around her waist. T.M. held up his rolls of chips and she kept going.

"Sit down and let's wait here for our drinks. Just in case anyone's paying any attention to us, we'd better make it look good. Here, that's a dollar shot. Be my guest." He held out the silver dollar chips for her to take. She took three and put them in the machine and pulled the lever down.

Michelle was not watching the machine, but was gazing at the people at the other slot machines—old, young, well dressed, in little more than rags . . . T.M. touched her arm and nodded toward a heavily made-up woman in a black sheath. She stood before her slot machine swaying from side to side. "Cobra," T.M. whispered and they both giggled. But suddenly the machine Michelle had played began to ring and coins fell out in a cascade, flights flashed, an alarm sounded. Michelle screamed and jumped away from it. Around her people were laughing and applauding. The change-making woman hurried to them.

"Well, pets, you've hit the jackpot! The machine pays off the first hundred and one of our cashiers will come around and pay off the rest. Congratulations!" She beamed at them with what seemed to be genuine happiness.

"The rest?" Michelle said weakly.

"You have ten thousand coming." The woman handed T.M. a plastic pail. "I don't think you can carry all that, can you?"

"While T.M. was scooping up the coins a man in a tuxedo appeared, consulted with the woman, and began counting out hundred dollar bills. He was not as happy as she was, but he was friendly.

"If you don't want it in cash, we can arrange something." He handed the money to T.M. and also a card. "Please be our house guest for drinks, dinner, whatever you like." He grinned then and looked from T.M. to Michelle and back. "Do you want an escort to your hotel room?"

They ended up checking into the casino hotel, saw their money put in the hotel safe, were escorted to their room, and so deep was their state of shock that it was nearly half an hour before they tumbled into bed.

TWELVE

Sunlight streaked the porch where Pat was reading the Sunday comics when Drew joined her. The porch was screened, and there were enough plants there to deceive anyone into thinking that this was a jungle—monstrous philodendrons climbing trellises, dieffenbachias in all variations, some in bloom, miniature citrus trees with flowers and fruits . . .

"Good morning," Drew said, taking a chair at the table opposite Pat. She made a muffled noise. When he said good morning to Willie Jo she had grunted. With her it was expected. She was in a dilemma, he knew. She could not call him by his first name where others could hear her, but neither could she bring herself to call him Mr. Drew. A grunt was sufficient from her, but from Pat? He poured himself coffee and tried to see her around the edge of the paper.

"Our party made the society page," she said bitterly. "Not a word on the editorial page or in the news, just in the gossip column. Whose former husband tried to engage which senator in a fistfight at the brawl given by Randolf Stevens? I knew it! I just knew it would be like that!"

"I give up," he said after a moment. "Whose? And which?"

"You said you had something to talk about," she said coldly. "I have to leave in half an hour. What was it?"

"Two things," he said, then waited until Willie Jo put down a plate of ham and eggs and a basket of hot biscuits and left again. "First, will you look in the senator's files for something for me?"

"Absolutely no. What's the second thing?"

"I want to find out why William's father agreed to finance a very expensive project that Stanley Huysman proposed.

That's all. It has nothing to do with Billie Boy at all, just his father.''

''I don't betray trust in me,'' she said pointedly. ''I said no. What else?''

''Okay. But what if the senior Wiley betrayed his trust? Would you feel you could let me know? Never mind. If you come across anything, then decide.''

She looked at her watch. ''That one's already decided. What else?''

''Do you mind if I take Sherry back with me today? Instead of waiting until Thursday?''

''We have our agreement about that. I see no reason to change a word of it. I have to go now. Good-bye, Drew. Remember, if there's anything to discuss, we'll let our attorneys handle it.''

''No, Pat. We'll handle it right now, right here. I'm taking her today.''

''You wouldn't care! You could lose all your visitation rights and you know it. Why are you acting like this? Why this sudden show of concern? You didn't fight anything before.''

''My mistake,'' he said quietly.

''And you think you know better than I do what's right for her? Is that it?''

''No. You know better, but you're not acting like it. She's feeling like an orphan, Pat—unwanted, in the way, invisible. You're so busy mooning over the senator, flitting back and forth between here and Washington, you've lost track of her.''

Pat's face flushed and she jumped up, threw down her napkin. ''No! And that's final! Now just leave. She'll be ready to go with you on Thursday, just as we planned.''

''Remember how it was when you were twelve? Your mother gone, your father so busy making money that he didn't see you for weeks on end. Remember, Pat?''

''I never said anything like that!''

''You didn't have to spell it out. It was there to see. It's there to see with Sherry. I'll bring her back on Labor Day, just as we planned, in time for her to start school.''

''If you take her, I'll call the police! That's kidnapping!''

''Do it yourself, Pat. Don't let your father do it or the senator. You do it, sign the charge yourself. Here's the address and phone number of the Huysman place in Princeton.

I'll be there with her until Wednesday, maybe Thursday, and I'll let you know when we'll be leaving there and where we'll go.''

He had risen and stood on one side of the table, she on the other. Her face was very white.

"Why didn't you show some fight before? Why didn't you even pretend that you cared?"

"God knows," he said. "Maybe I didn't believe one adult could save another adult. You had to do it for yourself. But she's not an adult."

"You think you can make love to me and then turn around and do this? Was that your plan last night? That's despicable!"

"Pat, I don't believe for a minute that Willie Jo would tell me to use the cottage without permission. And I don't believe for a second that Randolf would give it."

It had been a peaceful divorce in most ways. She had said it's over and I get Sherry, and his lawyer had shaken his head and said that's how it goes. There wasn't a court in the South that would give him any rights she hadn't approved of from the beginning. That's just how it was with a mother and child, especially a daughter. At no time had she been furious, and now after all this time, she was furious.

"Go to hell!" she cried. "Just get the fuck out of here!"

He began to laugh. "What a way to talk! What a choice of words!"

She wheeled about and ran from the porch.

The day was sunny and hot, traffic heavy. Drew and Sherry stopped for lunch and lingered over the scant display of books near the cash register. She hardly glanced at the comics, and not at all at the coloring books, but went to the paperbacks, looking at one romance after another.

"Mom says I can't read any of these yet."

"Do you want to read them?"

"My friend Susan reads them all the time. She reads her mother's."

"Do you read Pat's books?"

She looked at him with surprise. "They're on economics and junk like that! Do you know what I am, according to her books? I'm a dependent economic unit!"

Drew burst out laughing and said after a moment, "Now, that's what I call dirty!"

"I've got enough books. Let's go. How much farther is it now?"

"A couple of hours, three maybe if the traffic doesn't thin out a little. Tired?"

"Yeah."

They returned to the Peugeot and started driving again. Traffic was even heavier than it had been. Drew dawdled in the slow lane, content to let everything pass him.

"Grandpa says you let Mom support you, that you were dependent on her. Were you?"

"I don't know. We never talked about money."

"He said you don't know a dollar bill from a piece of kraft paper." She gave him a sidelong look. "I was cutting out Christmas trees with the paper. That's what it reminded him of."

"I'm sure he loves you very much, anyway," Drew said.

"Sometimes. Sometimes he says I'm my father's daughter. What's wrong with that? Whose daughter would I be if I'm not yours?"

"Beats me."

"Remember that game we used to play in the car? I'd tell you three things and you made up stories about them. Want to play that?"

"Sure, but make it easy on me. I'm an old man."

She laughed her little-girl wicked laugh and thought for several minutes; then she asked, "Do you know what a coelacanth is? We studied fossils in school last year."

"I know what it is. Is that one of the three things?"

"Yeah, and a unicorn. And a peanut butter sandwich." She finished with a giggle.

"You're sure about the peanut butter sandwich? Are you still hungry?"

She laughed again and settled back to wait.

Finally he started. "Once upon a time there was a prince who had wealth beyond dreams, a father and a mother who loved him dearly, and a heart of gold."

"Boring," Sherry said.

"Wait. In spite of all his good fortune, the young prince had one thing that made all else insignificant. He had a polka dot tongue." He glanced at her; she was grinning broadly. "Now, anyone who has a polka dot tongue will tell you that life can be hell, people can be cruel, and the future can certainly look bleak.''

''What colors?''

''I thought you'd never ask. Green and purple.''

''Yech! Blech!''

''Exactly what everyone said. That's the beginning. Want me to skip the middle part?''

''I know the middle. They took him everywhere trying to find someone who could fix his tongue. Then what?''

''That's the middle. Okay, it happened that the neighboring king was coming to visit with his daughter, who was the most beautiful princess on earth and the richest and all that stuff. You know this part?''

''Yeah. The prince and princess were supposed to fall in love and be married, but.''

''What could the poor boy do? There was this monstrosity of a tongue. He tried eating a peanut butter sandwich and coating his whole tongue with peanut butter to hide the polka dots. The princess got close to him and curtsied low and excused herself; she complained to her father that the prince was just a child and of no interest to her at all. There was a great sadness in the kingdom. Now one day an old woman gathering huckleberries came across the prince who was moping in the woods. What you have to do, the old woman said—she was a witch in disguise, of course—is ride a unicorn to the bottom of the sea and consult with the coelacanth who lived forever and knows everything.''

Drew glanced at his daughter. ''You know about unicorns? Who can ride them? Just very good people?''

''I thought it was virgins.''

''Okay. Whatever it was, he could do it. That very night he drew a magic circle and waited and sure enough a snow-white unicorn got nosy, and he caught it and flung himself upon its back. Take me to the bottom of the sea, he demanded, and off they went. Never mind how he breathed on the way down, there is a certain element of magic in a story like this. Anyway, eventually they found the ancient coelacanth dozing away, encrusted with barnacles and grandsons of barnacles too numerous to count or even think about.''

Sherry laughed aloud. ''Then what happened?''

''Well, the old fish was annoyed at being awakened by a mere human being and he blew bubbles furiously for a time.

When he had finally settled down again, he listened to the prince's sad story, ate a passing crab, and then gave the prince some very good advice. The prince returned to the dry lands and released the unicorn that had served him so well, and went home. From that day on he was known as a wise and tolerant prince, and later as an even wiser king who held his own counsel and said little, but acted with firm justice in all matters. When his own son was born with a polka dot tongue, he did not bemoan the fate of the child. When the time came, he took him aside and gave him the same advice the wise old coelacanth had given him many years before. What he said to his son was: Keep your mouth shut.''

"And they all lived happily ever after," Sherry said. "That's a silly story."

"Oh dear. You're too young for romances and too old for my stories."

"It's silly, but I like it anyway," she said firmly. She pointed. "Look, that girl's got a flat tire. Let's stop and help her fix it."

"You mean, let's stop so I can fix it." He braked and pulled over to the shoulder some distance in front of the disabled car. "Come on, and stay on the edge of the shoulder away from traffic."

Actually there was not a heavy flow of traffic now. Most of it had turned east toward New York or west toward Trenton. The young woman who was watching them was hardly old enough to be out driving, Drew thought. She looked like a teenager at the oldest. And probably she didn't know a spare tire from a doughnut.

"Hi! Need some help? My rotten kid wants me to play Galahad." They were even with the car now. He looked at the tire, making a tsk, tsk sound. Flat and bald. "Have a spare?"

"That is the spare," she said. "It's the second flat today. I changed it less than an hour ago."

"I'm Sherry. And this is my father. He's Drew Lancaster. What's your name?"

"Lisa Robbins. Are you the writer?"

He nodded, still studying the tire. There was no way it was going to roll again, but there had to be something to do in this situation.

"I've read your books," Lisa said and held out her hand. It was dirty. "They're very good."

He looked at her again. "Thanks." Old enough to read his books? They shook hands and he wiped his off on his handkerchief.

"Sorry," she said. "Can you give me a lift to a garage? If we take my tire I guess they can fix it and bring me back to put it on."

"If you were my daughter, I'd say: Don't on any account get in that man's car with the midget bank robber disguised as a kid. You never know who you'll run into on a highway. But what the hell, come on. Open up the trunk and let's get at it."

The trunk had suitcases on top of the tire. Drew frowned at them when he had unloaded them all and hauled the tire out also. "You can't leave all this behind," he said finally. "Someone's bound to break in before anyone gets it rolling again."

In the end he backed up to her car and they loaded all her things into the trunk and then left the car with the flat tire. Sherry hung over the seat and questioned their guest.

"Where are you going? Do you live around here? Is that your car? It has a California license."

Lisa Robbins was very pretty, Drew decided, and very nice. She answered every question gravely and fully. "I lived in Sacramento with my mother until a few months ago," she said. "Then Mother got married and moved to Hawaii and I was on my own. I'm a commercial artist, and I decided to leave the west coast and work in Philadelphia. There was a job, I thought, but I didn't get it after all. The magazine publisher hired his wife's niece instead. So I'm not sure right now what I'll do. I wanted to see Princeton since I was this close. You know, look at the house Albert Einstein lived in."

Could he just come right out and ask how old she was? He glanced at her in the rearview mirror and thought not. She might consider it an insult. Sherry had no such compunction.

"I'm twelve," she said. "How old are you?"

"Twenty-four."

A child, Drew thought. Out on her own in a cold, uncaring world, stranded with bald tires likely to go flat at a moment's notice.

"I really need a job," she said. "I was so sure of the Philadelphia position I was pretty careless with what little money I had."

Stranded, broke, hungry, she was a child waiting for a terrible accident to happen to her, a terrible fate to overwhelm her.

"Where is your father?" Sherry pressed on with the ruthlessness of the very young.

Lisa shrugged. "I have no idea. I never even knew my father. He left before I was born."

Sherry turned to Drew. "Can you hire her to stay with me? Maybe then Mom won't have you arrested for kidnapping me."

Lisa gasped. Drew looked at his daughter coldly. "You were listening?"

"Sure. That's the only way I ever find out what's happening. No one tells a twelve-year-old anything." She turned to look at Lisa again. "Mom probably has the cops looking for us right now, but they don't know about this car. It isn't his and they don't know what it looks like or anything. They won't find us."

"Whose car is it?" Lisa asked carefully.

"Don't worry, it isn't stolen, no matter what the little blabbermouth seems to be suggesting. The car belongs to Mrs. Stanley Huysman. I borrowed it."

He glanced back at her in the mirror in time to see her fall over on the seat in a faint.

THIRTEEN

Michelle had a stack of computer magazines on the table and a notepad and calculator. She said, "I think we should pay off the IRS altogether and be done with it. It just makes us both mad when we have to make the payments. And I guess I've decided to go ahead and get the modem. We'll still have five thousand for emergencies or whatever."

"Okay," he muttered. They were in the kitchen, the money on the table between them, and Michelle was acting as if they had always lived with ten thousand dollars spread out on the table, ready for whatever came to mind.

"T.M., do you feel at all guilty?"

"No. Well, not much."

"Neither do I and that worries me. Is that degenerate, do you suppose?"

Degenerate? Criminal maybe, but degenerate? Or were they the same thing actually? "I keep thinking I should feel guilt or something, but it's just not there. I was scared to death at the time, especially when he stopped you and asked for identification, but that was different. Definitely not guilt."

She nodded. "Same as with me." Then more briskly, she said, "Tomorrow let's go to Trenton for the modem, and we can visit my mother. Okay?"

"Sure." In a way he could not fully understand he thought of it as her money. She was responsible for it; she had created this moment step by step. And now if she wanted to use her money for another piece of computer equipment, that was fine with him. He went to the refrigerator for a can of beer, and she gasped.

"I still have my funny money!" she cried. "Look, it's still in my purse. I must have used a real bill!"

She pulled the bill from her purse and held it up and they stared at each other. T.M. thought, of course. It just took one.

All the cashiers had been questioned and all had gone through the pictures with no results. One of them remembered fleetingly the frightened girl who was out cheating on her husband, but he did not mention her. No point in giving the kid any more grief than she was giving herself. Anyway, he had paid attention to the bill she had given him. You always do when the customers look that guilty. Nothing wrong with that twenty, he knew. He was not certain he would have spotted the paper; it was pretty good, but he knew that kid's money had been okay. And that was all he had to know. He never gave it another thought.

Leon Lauder glared at Bob Samson, who was on the phone. Samson hung up and shook his head.

"One bill, one piece of paper, and he stops for the night. It doesn't make sense," Leon said. He turned his glare to the piece of paper on the desk. It was good, but not up to par for the Artist. But what it was good for, he thought savagely, was to justify his working on this case. It was not, by god, inactive. It was wide open again, and he would have his army out there by daylight and nab that goddamn Indian, and if Sorbies was in the States in a cellar or an attic or hiding out in a doghouse, he would nab him too. If it took a hundred agents, two hundred . . .

"I'm going home," he said abruptly. "Call me if anything breaks. And you might tell that flea-brained crew in Princeton to keep an eye on the back entrance of that house as well as out front." And just where the hell had Lancaster spent his weekend? Tomorrow, he thought. It would keep until tomorrow. He intended to go to Princeton and talk to the famous writer in person and then set up office in Trenton or maybe even Princeton and see this through. Sorbies should not have mailed that catalog, his only real mistake in all these years. A signal to Lancaster, that's what it had been, clear and simple. A signal, duly sent and received. And Mr. Lancaster so cool butter wouldn't melt and all that crap. Well, Lancaster did not know it yet but tomorrow they would have a long, confidential talk, and Mr. Lancaster would learn something about the

penalties for aiding and abetting a counterfeiter in any goddamn way whatsofuckingever!

Pat clamped her hands over ears and cried, "Will you both
just stop badgerinig me! You've been at me for hours and I
can't take much more!"

"Now, Pat, we're not badgering," her father said in his
reasonable tone, the tone he used when he was taking over a
competitor. "It's just that you can't let that man walk in and
disrupt all our lives whenever he takes a notion to make
trouble."

"It isn't fair to me, Patricia," William Wiley said, also
reasonable suddenly. "I don't know where I stand. I had to
call off making my announcement, as you know, because of
him. And now this. I really can't understand why you are so
reluctant to exercise your rights under the law."

"You've got to get rid of him once and for all," her father
said. "Can you imagine what it's going to be like when you
and Bill are married and he comes waltzing in at will, creat-
ing havoc?"

"No, he won't," William said darkly. "Haven't you seen
my bumper sticker? I SHOOT INTRUDERS. That's how I feel
about uninvited guests."

"He wasn't uninvited. Sherry asked him to come. She
admitted it to me."

"Not on her own," her father said. "You can make book
on that. He put her up to it. But this is how it's going to be
unless you nip it in the bud right here and right now. If you
don't make that call, I will. You just take yourself up to bed
and let me handle it."

"That's the best way, Patricia. Let us take care of it."

"Why are you both so determined to put him in jail? He's
not evil or even wicked. He's Sherry's father and he loves
her, and she wanted to go with him. Bill, are you so desperate for revenge that you'd put him in jail for an accident? And
you, Dad, are you still mad because he wouldn't write your
book? I just don't understand why you're both so determined."

"I gave him every opportunity to join the family, to become a real part of the business, to become one of us, and he
just looked at me as if he saw dandruff on my shoulders. That
man doesn't appreciate any consideration. He used you, used
your money, your position. He doesn't make enough money

to buy his own erasers. And he's got about as much pride as a rattlesnake. A real man isn't content to spend his wife's money. You have the opportunity now to get him out of your life for good, out of Sherry's life, out of our hair for all time. Once that's done, you and Bill can start making real plans. There's a future for you with Bill, a future for Sherry."

She did not look at the senator then, but said, "I won't make that call, and you can't. You have no complaint, after all. I'm going back to Washington and get some sleep and think. Maybe tomorrow I'll decide to complain; I just don't know. Do you mind if I drive the office car back? I flew here. My car's in the city."

"Pat," Wiley said then, "none of this has a thing to do with how I think of you. I hope you know that. You're my most valued staff member, my most valued friend, and some-day, I hope, much more than that. You're right. You need to rest and think. But try to see it from our perspective while you're thinking. We both agree that he's taking serious advantage of you and that there can only be more trouble in the future if he isn't stopped completely right now. That's all. You run along. Drive carefully. The car's outside. I'll have someone come pick me up later."

Drew firmly believed that when slender young women fainted, it was because they were pregnant or because they had not been eating properly. Accordingly, when Lisa had opened her eyes in confusion, he had asked point-blank if she was pregnant. She shook her head, her confusion deepening.

"Are you sick? Recovering from an illness?"

She was pushing against the seat, trying to sit up. Again she shook her head.

"Then we'll go find a restaurant and have dinner," he said, glad it was settled so easily. "Sherry, maybe you'd better sit back here with Lisa, hold her hand or something."

Sherry's eyes were enormous. The way she jumped to the opportunity to help, he was afraid for a moment that Lisa would think it was an attack.

"I fainted?" Lisa asked then. "But I've never fainted in my life."

Drew shrugged and got behind the wheel again and took them all to a restaurant. When Lisa excused herself to wash her filthy hands, Sherry asked in a whisper, "Can we keep her? Please!"

He was gratified to see both girls eat ravenously, his theory confirmed.

Now they were both sound asleep in Irma Huysman's house. Irma had blinked a time or two, then rallied and said that indeed no, they were not to go to a hotel or motel or any other such nonsense, they were to go upstairs and pick out bedrooms and put themselves to bed. To Drew she had added before following them up slowly, "Florence asked if you will please give her a call. Good night. They are charming children, both of them."

Florence sat behind the desk and Drew sat in a leather chair. Florence had brought over three or four of Huysman's books, which she had spread out before her.

"I skimmed through them," she said. "I thought if you're going to talk to Claude Dohemy tomorrow, you should have a little preparation. Are you too tired for a lecture?"

He really was, since he had not slept for two nights, but he did not like to say this after she had gone to so much trouble on his behalf. "I'm in good shape," he said, lying bravely.

"I'll keep it brief and simple," she said with a grin. "It's not in the books, by the way. Anyhow, years ago Huysman got interested in the study of monozygotic twins. Identical twins. He did some important work, good research. There are anomalies in twin behavior that have yet to be understood completely. If they are separated at birth and raised separately, there are often similarities in their lives that are hard to understand. For instance, say Carol and Karen are born in New York and Karen is taken a few months later to grow up in California. They both marry a man named George on a June day in the same year at the same time. They both have two sons both at the same time. They have the same illnesses and the same accidents. And so on. This is repeated over and over. They don't know about each other, don't know they are twins. In fact, when twins are raised together this pattern is less likely to occur."

Drew felt at a loss. "There must be some reason. I mean, it isn't just Carol and Karen. It's also the Georges and the people driving the other cars involved with their accidents. Or not clearing snow off their sidewalks, whatever the accidents are. In fact, it's like an infinite regression of what ifs. You know, the what if I hadn't been on that corner at the time you came out, we'd never have met. And so on, back through their entire lives.''

"Very good," Florence said approvingly. "Exactly what Huysman asked: what's behind all this? Anyway, moving on. He then got involved in a series of experiments on chimps. He did genetic manipulations on them, and linked them in what he called singlet fashion. We're back to the quantum mechanics area, by the way. He was convinced that he could pair them in such a fashion, and he accumulated tons of material that seem to bear out his claim. Of course, these animals were all controlled in such a way that they couldn't make choices the way the twins can and do. He had to introduce other factors. He stressed one of the paired chimps and watched the other for the proper reactions. And he got them, over and over."

"Stressed?"

"Electric shock is the usual method. No permanent damage, but a definite reaction, which is what he was after, of course."

"Of course. Go on."

She looked exasperated at his tone, then continued in an even drier voice. "At the height of his excitement over this work, he made extravagant claims about establishing a field with his chimps that defied space, and this is when the physicists dumped on him. He set up experimental animals in two separate laboratories, using Dohemy as his chief assistant at that time. When Dohemy stressed his chimp, witnesses observed the effects on the other one. Increased blood pressure, increased heart rate, things like that. But no one would buy it. No one else could replicate it, for one thing, and that's the first criterion of a good experiment: that anyone else can do it with similar equipment."

"Why couldn't anyone else do it if it really worked?"

She shrugged. "That was the rub, of course. Finally he made a statement that tore it all. He said that as the observer he was part of the field, which is what the physicists claim, apparently. But he went further. He stated publicly that as observer he believed in his results and chose for them, caused them to happen. No one else wanted those results and they chose for the opposite. After that, his name was mud with that particular work. He dropped it soon afterward and went back to personality testing and psychological testing, both his fields of real expertise, incidentally.''

After a time Drew asked, ''What happened to the chimps?''

She pulled a folded paper from one of the books and pushed it across the desk toward him. ''It's in there. He never published it. He claimed that whenever he sacrificed one of the paired chimps, the other invariably went into a decline and died soon after from no discernible cause.'' She stood up and stretched. ''I'm going to find something to drink. You want anything?''

''Anything. I'd better read some of this stuff tonight.''

She nodded and left. Drew opened the folded paper and rested his chin on his hand, started to read. Almost instantly his vision began to blur and again he remembered how nice it was to sleep, how good it felt to close his eyes and let his muscles relax. He put his head down on his arms, just for a second, he thought, and fell asleep. When he opened his eyes again, it was to see Florence standing at the door holding her purse.

She was shaking her head. ''I think it must be fate or something,'' she said lightly. ''Good night, Drew. Pleasant dreams.''

And he realized that this was their night to roll on the rug, and he was in no shape to roll anywhere or anything, except himself into bed. He did that.

FOURTEEN

"You!" Lisa Robbins gasped when Florence entered the dining room the next morning. She had finished eating, and she and Sherry were waiting for Drew to tell them what they were going to do this day. She seemed to take it for granted that whatever plans were being made included her.

Florence looked back over her shoulder and then said, "Me. Who are you?"

"This is Lisa, and I'm Sherry, Daddy will be right back. He's on the phone with a government agent. Would you like some coffee?"

Florence looked them both over suspiciously. "Does Mrs. Huysman know you're in here?"

"We're her guests," Sherry said. "Who are you?"

Drew entered the room then and said cheerfully, "Good morning, Florence. I see you've all met. Coffee?"

"Are they going to arrest you now?" Sherry asked.

"I will see Mr. Lauder at four, and that means I have a reprieve until at least this afternoon. So, who wants to drive out in the country with me? I'm going to talk to a man for about an hour, and after that we'll have the rest of the day until my appointment at four."

"Can we take a picnic lunch?" Sherry asked.

He nodded. He had become aware of the unnatural intensity of Lisa's state, still fixed on Florence. "Do you feel faint again?"

Lisa shook her head. "For a minute I was sure I knew you," she said to Florence. "From a long time ago."

"I'm sure not," Florence said with a touch of unease in her voice. She said her name; Lisa shook her head again. "Did you go to Princeton or to Sarah Lawrence?"

"No. I've lived in California most of my life, since I was twelve anyway."

"Well, I've been to San Francisco once. And I would remember if I'd met you there." Florence looked relieved and now sat at the table and said to Drew, "When's your appointment with Claude Dohemy?"

Lisa made a strangled sound and jumped up. "What's happening to me?" she demanded. "Everyone I see, every name I hear makes me think I've been here before, that I know these people. What's happening?"

"I don't know," Drew said. "Maybe you and Sherry should wait for me here. I'll make it as fast as I can and then we'll have a picnic."

"Let's all go," Florence said quickly. "I'll stay with the girls while you talk with Claude. Come on, Sherry, let's see if there's anything in the kitchen for a picnic. If not, we'll have to make a shopping list. When are we due out there, Drew?"

"Ten-thirty," he said helplessly. It seemed out of his hands. But if Florence went to look after Lisa, it would be all right, he thought, and tried to banish the feeling of uneasiness that had overcome him.

They had taken Lisa's tire and her car key to a garage the night before and someone had changed the flat and had driven the car into town, but obviously she was in no shape to take possession, continue on her way alone. Looking at her moments ago, her large expressive eyes, the new firmness in her face as she nodded vigorously at Florence, he knew he was in no hurry to send her on her way. Whatever was happening, she was a part of it; she belonged here for now. And by tonight, or tomorrow at the latest, he would tell Mrs. Huysman that he really thought there was not a book here that was compelling; and then he and Sherry would leave, perhaps for Disney World or the Keys. And Lisa would have to be on her own again. But meanwhile he had this appointment with Claude Dohemy to get through. And why not take all three females along? Make Leon Lauder eat his heart out. Leon was not taking it at all well that Drew had ducked out on him over the weekend. He had made it sound like a betrayal, in fact, as if Drew had more or less promised not to leave without permission. He sighed and poured more coffee and thought about the coming day, the interview, a picnic with three women, an interrogation by a Secret Service agent, the possible arrival any minute of F.B.I. agents, or at least local police looking for a kidnapper. Life had become so exciting, he thought glumly, that his best course of action now would be to buy an airplane ticket for anywhere.

"We will play Tsohg," Drew announced at the outset of their trip. Florence and Lisa were in the back seat of his car, Sherry in the passenger seat by him.

"Do you have rules, or do we have to guess them?" Florence asked.

He did not like the way Florence was hovering over Lisa, as if she knew something that she would rather die than tell. And Lisa seemed afraid of her. He liked that even less.

Before he could describe the rules, Sherry said, "You spell words backwards and Daddy is the judge of whether or not they're spelled right. Mom cheats when she plays."

"She does not cheat," Drew said indignantly. "She simply can't spell worth a damn. You start."

Sherry thought first, then said, "Y. That's the last letter. Your turn, Lisa."

"There are just a few more rules than that," Drew said emphatically. "One, you don't want to finish a word. A word has to have a least five letters. If you finish a word you're a T, then an S, and so on until you're a Tsohg and you lose. If you're challenged, you have to say the word and if it's all right, the challenger gets a T or S or whatever. Now, let's resume the play."

He wanted no conversation. He wanted them all deep in thought and silent while he mulled over the various things he had learned about Claude Dohemy and his hospital for disturbed children. It was an old hotel, he knew, built at the turn of the century, used during World War II for an officers' retreat and later used by Huysman for his chimps. After that project was abandoned, it had become a hospital with Dohemy in charge. That was the puzzler. How had that come about and why? And why did Lisa blanch and turn faint every time a new player came into the ball park? And what did Florence suspect, or worse, know? He noticed with satisfaction that a dark green sedan was keeping a steady three car lengths behind him. There were two men in it. He had not been able to restrain Sherry from waving to them. Neither had waved back. Unfriendly, he thought. They were definitely unfriendly.

He followed the Delaware River north on a road badly in need of repairs. Already a heat haze was rising in line-distorting eddies, forming mirage pools of water in the distance. By the time he reached the turnoff for the old hotel, now hospital, he was an O and losing the game.

"To be continued," he said, braking at a high gate. There was a wide spot here for turnarounds; a narrow road beyond the gate twisted out of sight among trees just a short distance away.

A heavyset man appeared on the other side of the gate. "Do you have an appointment?"

"Drew Lancaster to see Claude Dohemy," Drew called from the window.

"Wait a minute," the man said and vanished inside a small gate house. He stuck his head out the door a moment later. "Who're all the people with you? The doctor says you're supposed to be alone."

Drew glanced in the back seat of the car and was appalled to see Lisa looking like a ghost herself. Florence was holding her hand, a vaguely smug expression on her face. He turned and yelled at the guard, "They're going to wait for me. Can I walk up to the building?"

The man disappeared again and when he reappeared this time, he came to the gate and started to unlock it. "Your friends can wait here. I'll run you up to the hospital in the jeep."

"We passed a turnoff for a park back at the bridge," Florence said. "I'll take the girls down there for an hour or so. We'll come back up here then. Okay?" She patted Lisa's hand as she spoke.

Drew shrugged. "Not much more than an hour. Don't fall in."

The green sedan had pulled to the side of the road; one of the men was consulting a road map. Drew got out of the car, Florence took his place behind the wheel; he waved them good-bye, went through the gate, and waited until the guard relocked it. The men in the sedan were undecided, he thought with a grin. Wait for him by the side of the road or keep an eye on his car.

"This way, Mr. Lancaster," the guard said, and he did not

get to see which decision the agents were forced to make. He
followed the guard to a jeep, got in, and they were off on a
winding road that took them to an imposing, five-story building that had once been an elegant hideaway for wealthy city
people looking for the serenity of the countryside and was
now rather tawdry and overdecorated with gingerbread everywhere. The grounds were impeccably kept, the lawn luxuri-
ant, sheared, shrubbery trimmed by experts, nothing to indicate
that this was a hospital. There was a deep, shaded porch,
double doors with stained glass halfway down them. Under
some trees in the distance a few young people were watching
him. There was the sound of a lawn-mowing tractor.

The guard opened the door and ushered Drew inside, and
the first person he saw was Arnie Sorbies sitting in a wheelchair, his leg in a cast, wheeling himself through the front
lobby of the building.

Arnie came to a dead stop, then nodded and continued on
his way. Drew turned to see a white-coated man approaching
from the other direction.

FIFTEEN

Claude Dohemy was a tall, smooth-faced man in his forties. He had pale hair, not quite blond, and pale blue eyes that gleamed under contact lenses. "Ah, Mr. Lancaster," he said genially. "Please come this way. My office is through here. I'm Claude Dohemy. Whatever I can do for you, I'll be delighted. So good of you to take on Stanley's biography. Irma is so very pleased."

They shook hands at the door to a wide corridor. Now Drew could see that the original lobby had been partitioned. There was a second door into the rear portion of it; that door was closed.

"You were surprised at seeing Joe, weren't you? A faithful old grounds keeper here for thirty years at least. A nasty fall from a tractor. Poor fellow, couldn't just turn him out, now could we? He'll be up and around again in no time. Oh, just a moment." He looked into an office with an open door. "Vera, I'll be in conference with Mr. Lancaster for the next hour or so. Please see that we're not disturbed."

Vera, Drew saw, was young and very pretty with long smooth black hair, dark eyes. She was wearing a lab coat. She looked at him directly, dimpling, and nodded. "Do you want me to bring coffee or anything?"

"Nothing, nothing. This way, Mr. Lancaster." He opened the next door they reached and ushered Drew into a spacious room with windows on two walls. There was an extralong leather-covered couch and matching chairs, and three or four other chairs grouped with end tables in easy-conversation arrangements. At the far end of the room was a round table with leather-covered chairs on casters.

"Nice," Drew said.

"Isn't it, though? We like to keep it comfortable and informal. This is where we talk to the young people, meet guests, whatever. I like it. Please, that chair is very comfortable."

Drew nodded and walked to the windows instead of taking the chair. From one set of windows he could see the rear of the property, acres of rolling lawn, and in the distance a tennis court where people were at play. The other windows overlooked a large swimming pool with yet more young people either in the water or lounging in deck chairs. Some of them were reading, others dozing or chatting. It looked like a fashionable country club.

"Pretty, isn't it?" Dohemy said, joining him. "And so very effective. What you see out there, Mr. Lancaster, is not merely a group of children enjoying themselves, although, of course, they are doing that. What you see is a break-through in the treatment of adolescent schizophrenia. Did you know that schizophrenia is primarily a disease of the young? Or that until now the prognosis was very dim for any child so diagnosed before the age of twelve? We are making history with our treatment here. And that is why I had to deny your companions entrance today. I am sorry about that, but it is one of our ironclad rules that no outsiders may be in contact with our patients during the course of their treatment. Now, then, Mrs. Huysman, dear Irma, asked me to cooperate with you in any way I can, and I shall be happy to do just that. What can I tell you?"

"I don't know," Drew said and followed him across the room where they both sat down in the brocade chairs. "Just about when you worked with him, when you were a student under him, whatever comes to mind."

Dohemy nodded thoughtfully and began to talk about his student days, about being a graduate student, how he had done much of the work that Huysman was publishing in those days. "I don't blame him, you understand," he said. "That's how academia works. The master lays out the guidelines and the students do the real work. It has to be that way. We were beseeching the ramparts of ignorance in those days, Mr. Lancaster. Germinal work, the importance of which has not yet been recognized. He was a hard taskmaster, but a genius doesn't have to be easygoing or maybe can't be easygoing."

"And you gave it all up to run a hospital?"

"We were still working on the new tests. I was his colleague right up to the end, although I had less time for it during the last ten years. He was failing rapidly, even though we all pretended it was not happening. He used to come out here and talk about his plans. Sad, Mr. Lancaster, it was very sad."

"What did he hope to prove with his chimps?"

"That was a sideline. Of no consequence. Oh, very briefly he believed he was onto something of great importance, but when it proved not to work, he gave it up without a backward glance. That is the way of true science, you see."

"He kept them out here, didn't he? Who funded all this work of no importance?"

"I really don't know much about his finances, I'm afraid. He was closemouthed about all that. But, yes, he kept the chimps out here. There are extensive laboratory facilities in the basement still. I inherited them when the church opened the hospital. Another one of those happy coincidences that make life always surprising."

"You're still doing research, aside from the children and their treatment?"

"Indeed. Just to demonstrate how science works, let me tell you what I was trying to do for a time. Think about what makes you unhappy, Mr. Lancaster. Anything that makes you unhappy. When you have something in mind, let me tell you what you have actually done. Ready? Good. You are comparing a situation that exists now with one that either existed in the past or existed in a fantasy where it was better. Am I right?"

Drew nodded. Actually he was thinking that he wanted to get out of here, back to the girls and Florence, find out what was the matter with Lisa.

"Now, this is my hypothesis. Life is a series of comparisons, measuring now with the past, what we anticipate with what we have already had. Fear is a memory of something unpleasant. Right? You remember the pain of the dentist's drill and fear it. What if we could erase bad memories? Selectively, of course. Then there would be only pleasant, even very good memories, in our heads, and when you thought of something pleasant it would not be the feeling of dread that it would evaporate momentarily. I had to give up the whole line of work, however. And I did give it up without a moment's hesitation, without a backward look. On to a new hypothesis, new ground to be broken.''

"Why did you give it up?"

"I came to realize that only bad memories save us from continually repeating the same mistakes. So fundamental, isn't it, and I overlooked it.''

"Are you telling me that Huysman discovered a fundamental error of that sort in his work?"

"Of course he did. He was trying to carry over to the macrocosm events that work only in the microcosm. Who cares if physicists call the things they work with waves or particles? They admit they don't even exist except as probabilities and then only when you go looking for them. So they can tunnel through impenetrable barriers. What does that mean if they don't exist anyway? Stanley had to come to the same realization I reached. There was a fundamental flaw in his concept. Experiments that worked with submicroscopic events simply won't work with material objects like people.''

"Chimps, Dr. Dohemy."

"That's what I said. They won't work with chimps." He stood up. "I know this is merely a preliminary conversation today. Irma said you might want to come again, and you're more than welcome any time. But now, I'm afraid I must excuse myself. Work, you know. Always more work.''

Drew got to his feet. "I wonder if I could see the labs before I leave. I'm trying to get a feel for the various places Huysman worked, his environments at home, school, here.''

Dohemy looked at his watch and frowned. "Perhaps the next time? I have a consultation very soon.''

"Maybe Vera could conduct a tour?"

"It will only take a few minutes," Dohemy said. "I'll give you the thirty-second tour this time and a longer one when you return. We can reach the basement through here. We keep the various parts of the building isolated, you see. There's no access to the hospital facilities or the laboratories from the areas used by the youngsters.''

He led Drew down the corridor again and at the end of it unlocked a door that opened to wide stairs.

"I didn't know the building had been used as a government hospital," Drew commented.

"They called it an officers' retreat, but they treated them for various afflictions while they were here.''

"And then the church took it over for a young people's hospital. What church is that?"

"The Church of Inner and Outer Harmony. My brother is its pastor."

"A visionary and missionary," Drew commented. Dohemy smiled. They were in a basement corridor now, concrete floor, concrete walls painted off-white. There were fluorescent lights the length of the corridor. And there were metal doors.

"As you can see, it was extensively remodeled for the army. The church has kept it up very well."

"That must be some rich church."

"It is. In here is where the chimps were housed, caged, I should say."

The cages had been removed, leaving a room nearly empty except for workbenches along one wall and several rows of heavy plank tables.

"Not much to look at, I'm afraid," Dohemy said.

"How about the labs?"

"I'm afraid I really do have to put that off for this visit. Time, you see. When you return I'll be certain to schedule nothing else that will interfere with what time you have."

"Okay," Drew said cheerfully. "I'll be back. What are you working on now, Dr. Dohemy?"

They returned to the stairs; on the way up Dohemy said, "Do you know the most pressing issue of our time, Mr. Lancaster? Hunger. Too many people. Too few resources. And yet everywhere on earth, or nearly everywhere, there is grassland. I am working on an enzyme that will permit the human gut to digest grass. That's not for publication. I wouldn't even tell you if it weren't for Irma and my promise to give you what help I can. I trust you, Mr. Lancaster, to keep a confidence."

"It's safe with me," Drew said solemnly.

Dohemy walked to the door with him and saw him inside the jeep again, waved once and reentered the building. The driver took Drew back to the gate house. Neither spoke during the short trip.

As the driver was unlocking the gate, he said, "Oh, you forgot your book. One of the kids picked it up." He pulled a paperback book from his pocket and handed it to Drew.

"Oh, of course. Thanks."

He walked through the gate and saw that the green sedan was still on the roadside. His own car appeared around the curve and he waved good-bye to the guard and walked forward to meet Florence. Only after getting into the passenger seat did he glance at the book. It was a dog-eared copy of *Les Misérables* in French.

"What the hell?" he muttered, but now Sherry was clamoring for his attention.

". . . back to the river for our picnic and you can see their house. The Indian's name is Jack, and Lisa's brother's name is Franklin. They won't be there because Jack said the agents are after him too, and you'll bring them back with you."

Drew turned halfway around and faced her. "Someone, not you, start at the beginning and fill me in. This is like entering the theater in the middle of the third act."

Lisa was smiling happily, Sherry was pink with excitement, and Florence looked more self-satisfied then ever.

"Well?"

"Well," Florence started, and at the same time Lisa said, "He isn't really my brother." They both stopped and Sherry said, "You might as well let me talk."

Florence looked at Lisa in the mirror. "I'll start. All right?" Lisa nodded. "We went to the park I told you about and the girls were skipping rocks in the water when this boat, a rowboat, came along. There was a large, old Indian in it, and a young black man. I thought Lisa was going to jump right into the river or fall in. And the young man looked as if he were seeing the Virgin at Guadalupe. They came ashore and I talked to the Indian while Lisa and the young man, Franklin, stared at each other." She looked at Lisa again. "Your turn."

They had reached the turnoff, and she pulled into a small parking lot and stopped the engine.

"It was the same way I felt when I fainted in the car," Lisa said. "As if I was here and somewhere else all at the same time. Me and someone else at the same time. It's too hard to describe. Nothing felt solid and real all at once. That's not right either," she said helplessly. "Anyway, I knew him, but I never had seen him in my life. And he knew me the same way. And there are others, a lot of them in that place back there where you were just now."

The green sedan parked in the small lot and the agents stared at the river.

"Let's take the stuff out and go down there and eat," Drew said. "This looks too much life a conference or something."

They carried the picnic basket and cooler down a slope to a table on the riverbank, only feet away from the water. The river was smooth here and clean; it reflected the trees on the other side and the blue sky and fluffs of clouds serenely.

"One of them is standing up watching," Sherry reported. "Can I wave to him?"

"Why not? Okay, Lisa, go on."

"We talked about when we were kids," she said. "His mother always called him a devil spawn, and he ran away when he was twelve. He ran away when people came to his school and he knew they were after him." She took a deep breath. "When I was twelve one day people came to my school looking for me and my mother ran away with me. To California. That's why we went there—because they were looking for me. She was looking for me," she said, nodding toward Florence. "She was looking for him, Franklin, too."

Florence handed him a tuna fish sandwich. "Nineteen seventy," she said. "The year I was working for Huysman, doing testing. On three occasions there were students missing, the results skewed. He was furious. Called us—Claude Dohemy and me—dolts, nincompoops, and much worse things. That was the last time I worked for him." She took a bite from her sandwich and chewed deliberately. Then she asked Lisa, "How did you know we were looking for you? I didn't know it, although Claude probably did."

Lisa shrugged. "I just knew. Franklin said it was like that with him, too. He just knew. My mother said if it happened again, if they came looking for me, she would take me to England, change our name, really hide. She said it was my father trying to get me back and she wouldn't let him have me. She said he was cruel and vindictive, a lot of things that made it seem a good idea to run away. For a long time in California we were afraid, but nothing else happened and we forgot about all that. I forgot about it. And then . . ." Her voice faltered, stopped completely. She took a bite of her sandwich and gazed at the river. "Something happened, but I don't know what it was," she said with her mouth full.

"Eat," Drew said. "What's to drink."

"Beer, Cokes, orange juice," Sherry said. "Can I have some beer?"

"Don't be ridiculous. Are they still watching?"

"Oh sure. They never wave back. They have to pretend they don't see me wave to them, I guess."

"You said you can see where Franklin and the Indian are staying from here. In a minute let's walk to the water and you can point to it. Point to a lot of things, that first. Okay?"

He thought he never had seen Sherry so happy, so excited. He signed. If she told Pat they were out playing cops and robbers and spies and god knew what else, that would really tear it. In a minute he and Sherry left the table and stood at the edge of the water, and he saw the small house she pointed to and then a tree and a log floating downstream and probably a fish, and finally he said that was enough of that and they sat down again. Lisa had picked up the book on the table and was holding it with her eyes closed. She opened the book near the middle and then looked at it.

" 'Come back before Friday,' " she read softly. " 'Bring *him*.' "

"Good god," Drew muttered. "Now what? Let me see." The message was written in the margin. "That could have been in there for years."

Lisa shook her head. "They mean Franklin. They know he's been trying to find a way to get in. There isn't any way except over the fence, and it has an electric wire, or through the gate, and it has a guard. You can take him in with you."

"Oh sure. I'll say he's my Seeing Eye dog."

"You'll think of something," she said with confidence.

"Why before Friday?"

"Something awful is going to happen on Friday," she whispered. "That's why Franklin and I had to come here now. There's someone else around, but we don't know who it is. Someone like us."

Drew took a deep breath and let it out explosively. "You said something happened. You mean today? Meeting Franklin?"

She shook her head. "In California I had a good job, friends, no problems at all, but back in May, all at once, I began to feel as if I couldn't stand it, I had to chuck everything, job, home, mother, everything and come back here. I had to, and I couldn't. It was too crazy, too irrational. Then the company I worked for went out of business. The partners quarreled and split up and it was over, my job was done. From Friday until Monday was all it took to end it. And my mother met a man and fell in love with him, married him, and moved to Hawaii. A whirlwind romance, as they say. A couple of my closest friends were transferred to Texas unexpectedly with good promotions, raises . . . It was as if . . . as if something or someone had been calling me, but there were too many things, too many people in the way and I couldn't leave. Things, people began getting out of the way and all I could think of was that I had to come back east. I came.'' Very softly she added, ''I don't think I could have done anything else. I didn't really have a choice.''

''Christ!'' He looked at her helplessly. ''Sherry, take Lisa for a walk, will you? I want to talk to Florence. In private.''

''What's the use of that?'' Sherry asked. ''Lisa's the one who knows everything.''

''Just humor me. Get lost for five minutes.''

They went upstream slowly. Drew waited until they were too far to overhear, although he felt as Sherry did, there was little point to it.

''Huysman went into human experiments, didn't he? That girl, the black kid, all the kids in the hospital up there, could they all be the result of his experiments.''

''When Claude and I were sent out testing, he was searching for her, for Franklin, and for another girl. Their mothers had not cooperated, had run away. And he wanted those kids back. They already had the hospital, but by then it was for unmarried mothers. All the others were born up there, kept up there in prison ever since. What do you think?''

''You told me the twin studies indicated that twins who were kept together didn't show the same parallels that the separated ones did. Maybe all the kids in the hospital are perfectly normal and Lisa is just a little . . . strange.''

Florence shook her head impatiently; her eyes were wide and almost frightened. ''Franklin and Lisa are paired, a singlet. And the kids in the hospital know about them.'' She tapped the paperback *Les Misérables*.

For a moment Drew felt the world shift, go soft and uncertain with no hard edges, no boundaries, no firm ground. He clutched the table until the feeling passed, and when it did, he knew nothing was what he had thought it only moments earlier.

SIXTEEN

Arnie Sorbies had learned much more than Dohemy would have believed possible in so short a time. He had learned that there were over a hundred young people in the home, that the youngest was about thirteen and the oldest no more than twenty-two or twenty-three. They were in a prison, not a hospital, no matter that there was a surgery in the basement and laboratories and even intensive-care rooms. Dohemy and a few assistants used the laboratories, but no one else went into that section of the basement, at least not in the daytime. And he had learned that whatever was the matter with the kids, it was not insanity or criminality or anything he could put a finger on. Hell, he thought, they'd flunk right out of juvenile deliquent school first hour. Not a one of them that he had talked to knew a damn thing about street life, about the real world, about anything that wasn't spoon-fed to them, in fact. They were taken out now and then in small groups—no more than three or four at a time, as far as he could tell—to concerts, museums, even a ball game, and they had every-thing kids could want right here: movies, computers, teach-ers, swim coach, tennis . . . They were like royalty, pampered and isolated and imprisoned.

The setup was weird, and the kids were strange. There was something not quite right about them. At first he had gathered his nuggets of information gleefully, ready to throw them in Dohemy's face the first chance he got, but he had dropped that idea. Now he pretended he saw nothing, heard nothing, guessed nothing. He exercised and practiced walking on crutches and kept his eyes open and mouth shut. Right now Dohemy was like a frog on a griddle, ready to jump at a sound, at a look. So spooked that Arnie was making it his business to stay out of his sight altogether. He remembered with a feeling of great disquiet the looked on Dohemy's face that first day, and now he wondered just how close he had been that day to not waking up at all.

And there was Albert Dohemy, who they said was Claude's brother, but he guessed was something else. On his third day here Albert had come to visit and threatened him openly.

"This is a religious establishment," Albert had said, "and the people funding it are not terribly tolerant. Claude was stupid allowing you to stay even one night, but that's done and you're here. You could still have a relapse, if you understand my meaning."

"Well, it's good that I got a letter off when I did, now isn't it?" Arnie said. "Otherwise my pals wouldn't know where to come and claim the body."

"You mailed a letter? Who mailed it for you?"

"Now don't you go getting yourself in an uproar," Arnie said mildly. "I dropped a line to my lawyer and told him about the accident and the good care the doctor was taking. I told him I'd be in touch in a couple of months."

Albert had stalked out, and Claude had come to visit that night. "We're doing experiment work on schizophrenic young people," he said without preamble. "It's vital that no one upset our schedules or our treatments by introducing concepts the patients are not yet able to cope with. They are coming along very well, and even one wrong word could nullify years of treatment. If this project is as successful as it seems it will be, it will revolutionize the treatment of children all over the world. Do you understand the importance of such work?"

Arnie allowed that he did.

"Very well. Of course, we cannot keep you out of sight. They already know someone is here with a broken leg. It would be more upsetting to them to try to hide you than it will be to let you mingle with them, but you must agree to our conditions."

The conditions had been that Arnie not talk to them about the world, as simple as that basically. Oh, Claude made it sound like more, but after he left Arnie that night, that was what he had been able to translate all the conversation down to. Keep your mouth shut around the kids. Period.

That night Arnie had breathed a short prayer of gratitude for the inspiration that had struck him to rent out his house.

Joe Bramwell would not be needing it for a good long time, he had decided that night, and an empty house might attract attention, just in case Leon Lauder and his snoops had traced him to this area. He felt even more gratitude to the cook who had brought his dinner that night and agreed to mail his letter for him, not giving the matter another thought, apparently. At least Claude and brother Albert had been able to confirm that a letter had been mailed, and he suspected that the letter had saved his life.

And so, here he was, Joe Bramwell, a local farmer who had had an accident, sitting at an upper window watching the one man who knew who he was leaving the grounds where he was being held captive. He had no doubts now that he was as much a prisoner here as the kids were. Dohemy had made that clear to him.

He started at a noise and looked behind him; three of the older boys were in the room, also watching Lancaster leave.

"Is he a friend of yours?" one of them asked.

"I know him."

And he wondered how they had got into this section of the building but not for long. They went where they chose.

"Do you trust him?" the boy asked.

"As much as anyone," he said cautiously.

The boys exchanged swift glances; one of them slipped from the room and closed the door softly after him. He was standing on the other side of it, Arnie thought and waited.

"Mr. . . . Bramwell," the spokesman for the trio started, and the pause was long enough to raise goose bumps on Arnie's spine, clear up his scalp. "Will you help us?"

He looked from one to the other and then nodded.

Jack Silver Fox had not felt this uneasy since the last time he rode into Mexico with over a million dollars of paper in his saddlebags, and that had been . . . He couldn't even remember how long ago. Too long for the memory to flood him now, that was certain. He glanced at Franklin from time to time, but the boy was concentrating on the spread across the river, paying him no mind at all.

"Have they all left yet?" he asked eventually.

"Yeah. Ten minutes ago. The agents took off after them. You can relax now. What'd you do, Jack? How come they're after you?"

"Too long ago to remember," Jack said, but he did relax a bit. He was six feet five and weighed over two sixty, how much over no one knew because he had not been back to a doctor for twenty-three years, not since they had weighed him in and then out of prison. He knew he had gained a little weight since then, forty pounds maybe, but it did not matter to him or anyone else. His parents had raised him on antelope and rabbit and corn tortillas and beans—good food, the kind of food that encouraged a boy to reach his full growth. Franklin, on the other hand, was slender to the point of frailty in appearance. Jack knew the boy was wiry and tough, able to keep up with anyone on the spread back home in Oklahoma, but people tended to add another helping to his plate, urge him to have more dessert, another scoop of ice cream. He stayed skinny, hipless, and healthy.

"Boy, I think it's time you and me had a little talk," Jack said finally.

Franklin lowered his binoculars and grinned at him. "I reckon. Sure is pretty around here, isn't it?"

"You've got the wrong role," Jack said, heaving himself to his feet. They were in front of the cabin they were renting by the week, supposedly fishing. The shade was deep here and it was cool, fresh smelling with leaf mold and river water and the less definable smells of later summer, of growing things at maturity. Jack stood surveying the river and slowly let his gaze climb up the bluff on the other side. On top of it, set back fifteen or twenty feet, was a high fence. What they called a cyclone fence back home, open wire to let the wind through and nothing else. This fence was interlaced with electric wire, not like the fences back home. The fence surrounded the property; the only entrance was by the road that was barred with an iron gate, guarded day and night. The first week they had been in the area Franklin had announced that he was going up in a small plane, sightseeing, and reluctantly Jack had gone too, feeling certain the light craft had not been built for someone his size. The pilot had thought that was funny. Franklin had taken pictures up and down the river, real estate speculators, he had told the pilot blandly, snapping away. They both knew there was no way to get inside the fortress called hospital. And that was all right with Jack. It looked too military to suit him, government at the very least, and he had tangled once with the government and had no intention of doing it again.

"What are we doing here, boy? And how long you aim to stay here doing it? When I took off in that truck with you I didn't plan on staying the rest of my life. You're supposed to be the talkative one, me the enigmatic one. So talk."

Franklin laughed in the good-natured way he had, showing every tooth in his head. It was this as much as anything that had made Jack take him home that night twelve years ago. He had stopped his truck at the sight of a skinny kid hitching on a road that might not have anything else moving on it for a day or more. "Where you going, boy?" he had yelled out the window.

"You going to scalp me?"

"Maybe. You hungry?"

"Maybe. You a real Indian?"

"Hell yes! Now get in here and stop your sassing!"

The boy had laughed in delight and got in.

Now Franklin put the binoculars inside the case and snapped it. "Problem is, Jack, I don't know what to say. You remember what you said when I asked you how you know where you're going to find water? You said, the closer you got the less you itched. Sort of like that with me. The closer we got to this place, the less I itched."

Jack nodded. "All I wanted, an explanation, I'm hungry." He started to go inside the cabin.

"What explanation? Man, I ain't explained nothing, because I can't explain nothing!"

Jack shrugged and went inside. It was a logical explanation, he knew, as logical as when his mother had cooked extra beans because someone was coming, only no one knew who or why or exactly when except her. Or the times she had sent him and his two sisters to watch for their father when no one else knew he was even on his way yet.

Jack knew all about the itches that came over people and made them decide to get up and go, get up and do something they hadn't thought of doing before. Just such an itch had taken him to Dallas over thirty years ago; there he had met the man without a name. He still thought of him that way, and he knew the name he had finally called him was not his real name, not the name he had now or the name he had used most of his life until that day. The paperhanger had appeared in his life because he had itched and had gone to where the itch stopped pestering him, and a friendship had been formed. And eventually he had had enough money to buy his spread in Oklahoma and they had shaken hands, parted.

"Listen, my friend," the paperhanger had said that last day. "Start a fire with any paper you still have. Don't keep it. Don't carry it around with you."

Jack had listened but had not really heard. It pleased him to have one bill, a souvenir, memento, a tangible something to look at and hold now and then. Sometimes out on his own rangeland, sitting at his camp fire, smoking his pipe, he had taken out the bill and examined it, pleased at his good fortune, and the bill had come to be his lucky piece. They had stolen this land from his forefathers, he thought then, and he had stolen it back. Justice had been served in a roundabout way. That pleased him.

Then, in Tulsa, he had been picked up for public drunkenness although he had not been drinking, merely fighting. He had been locked up and three days later Leon Lauder had paid him a visit. The little piece of paper had betrayed him finally.

"Don't be a dumb lummox. He used you. You were no more than a packhorse for him, a mule. A smooth talker, was he? Convinced you that it was all right, no harm done?"

Jack had said only that he knew nothing about anything. He did not know who gave him the bill, how long he had had it, if there were others like it anywhere. Then nothing more. The questions went on for days. They went out to his ranch and searched, even dug here and there. Where had he got the money to pay for it? Savings. Where had he earned the money he saved?

Lauder was a man who followed his itches, Jack knew. They were both aware that he was lying, each aware of the other's awareness, and that was that. They had got him for drunkenness that time. When he came out, he had hired a lawyer and they left him alone after that until recently. He wondered if the paperhanger was plying his trade again, but it was an idle thought. He had not wanted more questions and had agreed to go on this trip with Franklin just to avoid them, but he knew he had nothing to fear. They couldn't prove anything last time around, and there was nothing to prove now. He was a man with a clear conscience who wanted simply to be left alone in his old age. He was humming in a monotone as he started to heat the grill to cook steaks. That boy needed more food, he thought, get some flesh on his bones.

SEVENTEEN

Michelle and T.M. had driven to Trenton, had shopped the computer stores and bought the modem she wanted, and were on their way to visit her mother.

"I hope her tongue is well," T.M. said, grinning.

"What's wrong with her tongue?"

"She nearly bit it off when she came and saw our house. Remember?"

Michelle laughed at the memory of her mother's expression when she visited them a few weeks ago. "Turn at the next corner," she said. "That's the way I used to walk to school."

He turned and they cruised the quiet residential street of small houses and neat yards. This was one of the subdivisions north of the city and it had not changed much over the years. The trees had grown larger and the shrubbery had reached maturity, but the houses were not old enough yet to start having the dilapidated look of so many subdivisions built in the past few decades.

"This must have been a neat place to grow up," T.M. said approvingly. "At least they let the streets wind a little and avoided that grid pattern."

Michelle nodded, but she was staring ahead with a distant look. "I never really graduated from grade school," she said suddenly. "I had forgotten all about that. I went home to school that last day, pretended I was sick and went home, and I never went back."

"Pretended? I didn't try that for years after sixth grade."

"They came to school and I really felt sick for a few minutes. I wonder why I forgot that. Mother must have gone back for my certificate or whatever they give kids in sixth grade."

"Honey? What's wrong? You sound . . ." Like that night in their apartment, he realized: distant, gone, wavery somehow. "Michelle, snap out of it!"

"Halfway down the next block," she said in her strange voice. "That's our house." It looked much like the others on the street—frame with stone facing in front, neat lawn, rose bushes at the front entrance.

Michelle's mother, Laura, was very young looking, in her forties. They could have posed for mother-daughter commercials for hand cream or hair conditioner. She was slender with blond hair like Michelle's and the same large expressive blue eyes. She was a legal secretary with a very demanding job, and enough clout that she could leave the office early, give them drinks at home and treat them to dinner.

"Darlings!" she greeted them, taking their hands and pulling them inside her house. It was cool and dim after the glare of the August afternoon.

Michelle stopped just inside the door. "Mother, I have to talk to you. Tell me about my father."

Her mother paled a little and walked into the living room, sat down. "Come on in," she said resignedly. "I guess I knew this would happen eventually. Do you want something to drink first? Coffee? Iced tea? Beer?"

Michelle took a chair across the coffee table from her mother. "Nothing," she said. "Who was he?"

Laura held up her hand and shook her head. "Let me do it my way," she said. "The way I've done it in my mind a hundred times or more. You have to understand what it was like in the fifties for a girl like me. As soon as I got out of high school there was pressure to get married. From my parents, from my boyfriend, my girl friends. That's what they expected all of us to do, get married right away, have four kids, scrub the kitchen floor and wax it every week, the whole thing. I was eighteen and not ready for all that, but there wasn't much I could do. I knew a little Latin, a little math, a little science, and so on. And nothing useful. I got a job in a department store and made twenty-one dollars a week. And had to pay ten for room and board to my parents. We lived in Philadelphia, you know, but I had a girl friend who had moved to Trenton. She sent me an ad from the newspaper. Someone was advertising for people to take some tests, psychological tests, and they were willing to pay twenty-five dollars for about three hours. She was going to do it if she qualified, and I came up to do it too. The tests were being given at Princeton. We both went over by bus. We couldn't figure out just what they wanted, but they turned her down and used me. I got my twenty-five dollars and decided not to go back to my parents' house, but to move in with my friend and share expenses and got a job in Trenton. She was working already in a chemical plant and making a lot of money for those days."

Abruptly she jumped up. "I guess I need a drink after all," she said and rushed away to the kitchen.

T.M. started to follow her, but Michelle caught his hand and shook her head. "She needs a minute alone," she said softly.

When Laura came back she brought in a tray with three tall drinks in frosted glasses. "Gin and tonic," she said. "The perfect August drink." She picked up one and drank deeply, then set it down and continued.

"My friend insisted that I apply at her plant for a job and I did and was called to work in just a couple of weeks. And I had more money than I'd ever had in my life. She got engaged soon after that and we separated; I got my own apartment and everything was wonderful. Then the doctor called me from Princeton. There had been a question on the test I took about willingness to cooperate in future testing procedures. There were a lot of questions I didn't understand or see the significance of, but that didn't matter. Twenty-five dollars for a Saturday morning, that's what interested me. I went back alone."

Michelle was staring at her mother as if hypnotized; Laura was oblivious.

"There was a private interview with two men, both scientists. One was Dr. Huysman and everyone knew about him even then. He had won the Nobel Prize, been in all the magazines. You know. The other was his assistant, Dr. Dohemy." She picked up her glass but did not drink now, simply traced water drops as they ran down and fell off. "They were doing pioneer work in artificial insemination and needed volunteers who would be very well paid. The answers I had given on the tests indicated that I was the kind of person they were looking for." She drank all of her gin and tonic.

T.M. put his glass in front of her. She seemed unaware of him.

"I was stunned. And outraged. And frightened. I ran out. The young doctor came after me. He took me to a coffee shop and talked to me." She shook her head helplessly. "The next thing I knew I was back in the office and they were both talking to me, explaining everything, making it sound as if I would be as important as Madam Curie, as Dr. Huysman himself was. I would have to move to Princeton, where they would get me an apartment. They would place me in a hospital out of town for the insemination process and keep me there for a week or two, and then I would go there to have the child when the time came. They would pay me a salary and all expenses for a year during the pregnancy and three months following the birth, and after that they would pay me every time they examined the child and tested it. And there would be a trust fund set up for the child's education. They made it sound so . . . businesslike, so normal! My salary would be twenty-five thousand dollars!"

Mother and daughter were both so pale that T.M. would not have been surprised to see either or both fall over in a faint. Laura was drinking his drink that he had placed before her. Michelle was gulping down her own.

"Well," Laura said, "they had the test results; they knew me better than I knew myself at that moment. I went to school that year and took business courses and eventually you were born."

"Who was my father?"

"I don't know. They wouldn't tell me. I suspect it was one of the doctors, but I don't know. When you were eight I told them I was through. We moved to this house and I changed my name and that was the end of it all."

Michelle shook her head. "They came back to test me again in the sixth grade. They were looking for me. I came home sick that day."

"They never came again after that?" T.M. asked and realized with the question that he was not doubting a word of any of this.

Michelle shook her head.

"But why not? It would have been easy enough to find the two of you if they'd wanted to."

"They didn't need me anymore. They had a lot of others locked up safe somewhere."

She said it as matter-of-factly as if she had just read it in a newspaper, and T.M. felt a chill race through him.

All the questions T.M. and Michelle asked elicited little more than the original story Laura had to tell. She did not know how many other women were involved with the project or who financed it. She had received her payments regularly as long as she presented Michelle for testing at the intervals they had specified. She had not been allowed in the testing room and did not know what they had tested for or how.

"I asked you again and again, and you just said it was a game they played with you," she said to Michelle finally. "Don't you know?"

"Not really. I have vague memories, but there were tests all through school; those didn't seem any different from the others. Achievement tests, psychological tests, the usual junk they put kids through."

"But if they just seemed like the usual thing, why did you leave that last time?" T.M. asked.

"That one was different," she said slowly. "I was really afraid that time. I felt that someone was hunting for me and if I took the tests, they'd find me. Cornered."

They went to an Italian restaurant a few blocks away and talked about the weather and the funny house T.M. and Michelle were living in and anything they could think of except what was on all their minds. It was only eight when T.M. and Michelle took her mother home again. This time they did not go in.

"The hospital you went to," Michelle asked, "is on the highway up the river? Is that what you said?" She consulted a map and showed her mother the road. "There's nothing indicated here, but I guess there wouldn't be on a state map, would there? About an hour's drive from town?"

Laura looked from her daughter to T.M. and back, then sighed. "I didn't want to talk about any of this. I hoped it never would come up. It's over and done with. I did something terrible and I know it, but it has nothing to do with you. You were a beautiful baby and a completely normal child in every way. Forget it, darling. Don't let it change you now. Please.''

''Normal? Who's to say? What's normal? I have to know more about this. Who was my father and what was he after? What did he do to me?''

Her mother pointed to the map. ''It was about a quarter mile past the bridge. It's not there anymore. It's a home for mentally disturbed youngsters now or something like that. I used to drive by there now and then, trying to make sense of it all for myself. There aren't any answers. You just have to live with it. Huysman's dead and it was his work, no one else's. Just his. And I guess it was pioneer work. They're doing it more and more all the time and no one thinks anything of it. We were just the first.''

T.M. drove. They were both silent until they were in the neighborhood of the children's hospital. Then Michelle said, ''When we get to it, pull off the road or something, will you? I want to see if there's a telephone number or anything.''

T.M. did not question her. He felt as if he were in a state of shock or near shock. All he could do now was accept whatever happened next. He drove into the turnoff and stopped. There was no number on the neat, bronze sign on the gate of the property. It said simply: THE CHURCH OF INNER AND OUTER HARMONY and beneath that: NO ADMITTANCE.

''Are you satisfied?'' he asked after a moment.

Michelle did not reply. She was gazing ahead with a fixed stare, concentrating, a slight frown creasing her forehead.

''Honey? Can we go now?''

''Let's go home,'' she said calmly. ''I want to try out my new modem.''

In the back seat was the modem they had bought in Trenton. T.M. drove glumly, not even pretending to understand anything at all, waiting for a sign or something from the place that was hidden from sight by a forest, and now all she wanted to do was go home and play with her new toy. Okay, he thought, whatever came next, he was ready to go along with it. He picked up speed and in little over half an hour they were home and she went into her office.

''Won't that be awfully expensive?'' he asked when she had the interface connected, everything working. ''Won't it be on our telephone bill?''

She looked surprised. "No. I'm going to find the code and charge everything to the Church of Inner and Outer Harmony.

He nodded and walked downstairs carefully. Of course. A little counterfeiting, a little stealing now and then, charge it to someone else, why not? He remembered her outrage, enough to make her quit her job, over the doctor's corruption when he put his wife and daughter on the payroll. But that was different, he said in a falsetto in his head. Of course. He put on water to make coffee.

They didn't want law and order, he thought bleakly, they wanted justice. The Romans had had law and order aplenty when they tossed the Christians to the lions. The slave traders had operated under law and order. the movement west, ousting Indians right and left, had taken place under the law of the land. But people who wanted justice instead of law and order, he thought then, often ended up in prison, and he was afraid that Michelle had started down that road and would not be able to turn back. Criminal beginnings, a criminal act of conception—or had that been done under the law of the time?—had put engrams in her head that were only now finding an outlet, making her a cheerful criminal, seeing nothing wrong with criminal activity, even liking it, choosing it.

And it was his fault, he added to himself. If he had not lost his job, if he had been able to decipher that stupid tax book better, if he had not claimed the office and her computer, if he had found a new job right away, anything that brought in an income, if they hadn't been mugged, if they had had another apartment lined up in New York or had had enough money to buy into the one they had been living in . . . He made the coffee and decided he had to start back even further. With her mother. If she had not felt compelled to leave her parents' home, get a job in Trenton . . . And that beginning demanded backing up again to Laura's parents. If they had been less rigid, less demanding of Laura, more understanding . . . And their parents, and theirs . . .

There was no place to begin. He poured coffee and sat down to sip it. No place to begin unless he went back to Adam and Eve or maybe Cain and Abel, he corrected himself unhappily, thinking of his wife upstairs trying to find a way to cheat a church.

EIGHTEEN

"Daddy," Sherry asked just before he left for his visit with Leon Lauder, "how can you carry on surreptitious activities if they follow you everywhere you go?"

"I'll bring that up with him. And meanwhile, little big mouth, keep mum, okay? No blabbing to anyone about anything."

"You mean Mrs. Huysman and Marion?"

When Irma had introduced her housekeeper, Marion Skolnick, Sherry had giggled and said, "Maid Marion." For a second or two Drew had thought that was it, they would all be tossed out, but Marion and Irma both broke into laughter along with Sherry.

"Dear," Irma had lectured then, "we don't have maids now. We have housekeepers or cooks or companions. Come along, both of you," she motioned to Lisa to join her and Sherry, "and I'll show you the doll furniture I had when I was a child. I've kept it all these years. Can you believe such a thing?"

When she got up, it was with a smooth motion. All three went upstairs, and Drew left for his appointment. And where had he and Sherry ended up with his admonishment to keep her lip buttoned? he was not sure.

"What do I tell Mom?" she had demanded. "I'm not supposed to keep anything from her."

"In spite of all my efforts," Drew had said to Florence, "she was born a Jesuit. She argued with the doctor even before he swatted her, and not hard enough by half, if you ask me. Sherry, there's no reason to tell Pat anything about any of this. At least not right now. She'll ask are you eating properly and getting enough sleep and stuff like that and you know it. Unless you introduce another subject it will end there. Right?''

"Maybe," she had said darkly.

He met Leon Lauder in a motel coffee shop. "This could be habit-forming," he said cheerfully as he sat down in the booth opposite Leon.

"God, I'm glad you didn't say we have to stop meeting like this," Leon said. "Would have put money on it. Coffee?" He waved to a waitress. He was having iced coffee and ice cream.

Drew said coffee and pointed to Leon's drink. "At least you don't use strawberry."

"Mocha or vanilla. But chocolate's pretty good too."

The waitress brought Drew's coffee and departed. He tasted it and added sugar and cream.

"That's why I have mine this way," Leon said. "Only place I can get good coffee's at home. I'd rather have a beer, but that looks bad."

"My daughter wants to know how you think I can carry on surreptitious activities with your men on my heels all the time."

"Makes it hard, I guess. But they aren't there all the time."

"Sorry about that. Just wasn't thinking. I drove to Richmond and picked up my daughter and came back."

"Did you really punch the senator in the nose?"

"Not yet."

"Come back by way of Atlantic City?"

"Nope. I don't believe exposing children to vice."

"Yeah. Know what you mean. Who's the other girl?"

"Sherry's nanny. Lisa Robbins."

Leon looked mildly shocked. "We don't have nannies any more."

"Actually I'm putting together a harem. Today I took my women and my daughter and drove out into the country where I parked them while I had a chat with Dr. Claude Dohemy at the Church of Inner and Outer Harmony Home for Disturbed Youngsters."

"Crazy kids up there?"

"Disturbed. I waved to Arnie Sorbies but we didn't chat. I watched the kids play tennis and swim and talked to Dohemy about Stanley Huysman who was a genius. I'm considering writing his biography. Dohemy was his associate for many years and I'll be going up there again from time to time, with or without my harem. I don't think your men will be allowed inside the grounds."

Leon watched him broodingly. "That's where Huysman did the monkey operations? I read about him."

"Chimps. I saw the room they were kept in, but the cages have been taken away. It was uninspiring."

"You know an Indian by the name Jack Silver Fox?"

"No."

"Big man, over six feet tall, broad as a door. If you'd seen him, you'd remember. Never saw him with Sorbies in his bookstore?"

"No."

"Funny. He's in the area. Used to work with Sorbies, and now he turns up in the same area where you turn up. Sorbies sends you a message, and his Indian friend appears after cooling it for more than twenty-five years. I don't like that kind of coincidence, Mr. Lancaster. It doesn't set right."

Drew nodded with sympathy. "I don't blame you," he said truthfully.

"There are two government agencies you don't want after you," Leon said reflectively. "The IRS is one. From the president on down no one wants those dudes after them. Including me." Drew nodded. "The other one's my agency, Mr. Lancaster. There's a saying about us. We never close a case until the guy's in the pen and his press and plates in our little museum or destroyed. We have a neat museum. You might want to come have a look at it sometime."

"I'd like to see it."

"When you're in town give me a call. But the point is, we always get our man. Always. And his accomplices. Every one of them. Equally guilty under the law. The Law's hard on counterfeiters because if you don't protect the sanctity of your money, the whole thing might come falling down. One of the first things an enemy thinks of during wartime is putting out bogus money to mess up the economy of the other side. Works, too."

"I didn't know that," Drew said. "Maybe I can find some books on the subject."

"I'll send you a reading list."

Drew pushed his cup back and stood up. "Well, you've given me things to think about."

"Mr. Lancaster, it would be a real feather in my cap if I nabbed someone with a name like yours. You know? Might even up my grade rating, let me retire at a higher pension. We bureaucrats have to think of things like that."

Drew nodded. "See you around, Leon."

"Oh, yes, Mr. Lancaster. That you will."

Drew walked back to the house thoughtfully. Why was he so reluctant to turn in Sorbies? None of his business, but was that enough of a reason? He kept coming back to the question: Can you steal from a thief? He still had no answer. He was not happy with Leon's threats, he decided, and did not doubt that Leon had been telling him the truth. But he had been truthful, also, and what the hell.

Florence had drawn up a chart for him to look at by the time he reached the house.

"Here's where the files are missing," she said, pointing. "I have his papers from day one until the mid-fifties, then nothing. He started the chimp research in nineteen fifty-three and published in nineteen sixty, but I have only the finished papers, not his notes or the date, nothing else. Then in nineteen sixty-six he was doing the psychological test in public schools. And some of those notes are missing. Then more blanks until his work on plant clones began appearing. Too many blanks, Drew. I don't like it. You don't just sit down and write a scientific paper. There are stacks of notes, the experimental data to back them up, tons of stuff."

"Could he have kept it all at the hospital? Or in his office at the university?"

"The hospital I don't know about, but he kept hardly anything at school. He was a secrecy nut and didn't trust anyone at school worth a damn."

"How long would it have taken to clean out the files that thoroughly? Maybe he did it himself before his stroke."

She shrugged. "It would have taken some time, but remember that Claude was in and out of the house a lot that last year, especially the last months. It wouldn't be too apparent to anyone not looking for the blank spots, anyone just taking it all in as a whole. God knows there's enough material in those files to keep a researcher busy for a couple of years."

"Why were you looking in those years?"

She looked at him with a twisted, almost bitter smile. "You never met him or saw him?" He shook his head and she went on, "He had lovely eyes, very big, expressive, his only really good feature. Lisa's eyes."

He stared at her in disbelief. "You can't be sure. Sherry has blue eyes as big as saucers and she, by God, is my child."

She waved that away. "You think he operated on her? Altered her brain surgically? The way he did the chimps in the beginning? No, he couldn't have. And he didn't have to. By the end of the chimp research he was doing genetic manipulations and in vitro fertilizations. We have to talk to Lisa tonight after Sherry's in bed. She told us she lived in Kansas City with her mother until she was twelve, but, Drew how much do you want to bet that her birth certificate says she was born in New Jersey, somewhere around here."

"Why did you say he couldn't have operated on her?"

"Because he didn't get any results until he started the genetic manipulations before conception. He lost all the chimps he operated on without proving a thing. He gave up that approach very early and never returned to it because it was working the other way."

"How do you know that?"

She waved at the books on the desk. "He says so in there. That's one of the reasons no one else could replicate his work, it was truly revolutionary and very difficult. Especially for anyone who didn't believe in it to start with. At that time the world was focussed on the double helix, the DNA research that was coming out. He talked about genes and chromosomes and never even mentioned DNA; crank stuff, old-fashioned. And it didn't work for anyone else."

She folded her chart as Lisa, Sherry, and Irma Huysman entered the room. "Later," she said.

Sherry babbled about the neat dollhouse and its furnishings, and Irma beamed at her and Lisa. They all had dinner, and Irma talked about growing up in Europe—in Berlin, Vienna, Paris. It sounded like another world, another era. It was another world and era, Drew thought, half listening. A simpler world? Maybe not, but not such a dangerous world as it had become since. Science and technology had been flexing their muscles, but since then they had demonstrated their joint

power and the world would never be simple or not dangerous
again. Sherry would never know the world Irma had taken for
granted. The thought saddened him.

Sherry was asleep; Irma had gone upstairs; and now Drew,
Florence, and Lisa were in the office with the files. Somehow
it seemed a better place to talk about Huysman than the
luxurious living room.

Lisa was shaking her head in bewilderment. "How did you
know I was born in New Jersey?" she asked Florence. "I
only lived here a few months. My mother came from Kansas
City originally. She was a student at Princeton when she met
my father, I was born, and he ran out. I didn't even know it
for years and years, not until I happened to notice it on the
birth certificate."

Florence looked at Drew. She appeared more troubled than
smug, he thought with satisfaction. It was because Lisa was
such an appealing child, so trusting and vulnerable, he decided. He felt troubled about her too.

"How in hell can we prepare anything, offensive, defen-
sive, or even passive without knowing what Dohemy is up
to?" Drew gazed at Florence thoughtfully, but not with much
hope. She had made it clear already that she did not have a
clue about what Dohemy was up to, not specifically anyway.
They both suspected that whatever he was planning for Friday
had to do with finances.

"Huysman had the funding," Florence said. "With his
reputation back in the late sixties, the seventies, he could
have had whatever he asked for. Not so with Claude. He's
never been more than an assistant. He has the soul of an
assistant."

"Okay, funding. Government funding is what he's after.
And that isn't much to go on. Huysman got the funding by
calling it a church establishment, and there's no such church,
just a name. Why doesn't Dohemy use that ploy?"

They were in the office; Lisa had gone to bed without
adding a thing to what they already knew or suspected.

"Maybe that's exactly what he's trying to do," Florence
said. "Use the church as a front." She was silent a few
minutes, then said, "I hate this but let me tell you what I'm
thinking."

He nodded glumly. "He needs something as dramatic as the chimp experiments to demonstrate his results?"

"Just so. What do you think?"

"Exactly how were they set up?"

"Okay. Claude was at one end, Huysman at the other, with assorted assistants, no doubt. The paired chimps were separated, one with Claude, one with Huysman. There were government observers at both ends. If I were setting it up, I'd have one of them actually administer the shock, let him pick the time, note it, everything, just so he would know that no collusion was taking place. I'd have closed circuit television to let the two groups of observers communicate, inspect what's happening at each end."

"How severe were the shocks?"

She shrugged. "That would be in the notes that are missing. For demonstration purposes it wouldn't take much. For dramatic effect . . . ? I just don't know."

"Those were animals. We're talking about people, children . . ."

"Did you read about the Tuskegee syphilis study?" Reluctantly Drew nodded. She continued, "Those were people, men with syphilis carriers. There was a cure but the observers did not administer it, they simply observed right up until the men died off. Government funded, Drew. Government employees, doing their job, observing."

"Christ!" He got up and paced the office. "So what do we do? We can't even get inside that place. It's a fortress, a castle, complete with moat. And if those kids have the ability to communicate in any way with each other, if they know something terrible is going to happen, why are they staying? There are over a hundred of them. They could get out with any kind of concerted effort."

"I don't know," she admitted. "It doesn't make sense. I can't even guess why they haven't taken over the place by now."

"I'll think of something," he muttered. "I have to find a way to get Franklin in with me. I have to talk to someone on the inside . . ." Sorbies, he thought grimly. He wanted to talk to his old buddy Arnie Sorbies

Florence stood up and stretched. "I'll be going. See you in the morning. I'll come over pretty early. Good night, Drew."

He continued to pace the office, then expanded his area to

include all the downstairs. Sorbies, the Indian, the kids who
were drawn to each other, the experiments . . . It was just too
much, he decided. Too fucking much! What was he doing
here? Tomorrow, he told himself. Tomorrow he would tell
Irma so long, tell Florence so long, kiss Lisa so long, and get
the hell out of here. Head for Florida, Disney World, on to
the Keys. Tomorrow. Meanwhile, he continued to pace angrily.

He had not wanted to become involved with any of this,
had not asked for it, and could still back out of it all. He
already had one government agency nosing around. He certainly did not need a second one annoyed with him. Which
one would it be? Health? Interior? Defense?

He grimaced and came to a stop in his pacing. If you had
people in tune with each other and one of them was in Cuba,
for instance, and the other in Washington, then what? Then
nothing, he decided after a moment. They did not talk to each
other, they were simply aware of each other, drawn to each
other. He started to pace again, more bothered than he liked
at the idea of the Defense Department interested in those
strange kids. But no matter how many different ways he tried
to see them being used, he could not find a single way that
seemed worth the effort. The Post Office on its worst days
seemed a better bet for anyone who wanted to send or receive
a message.

NINETEEN

Late Sunday night in Washington, Pat Stevens had found herself before the files in William Wiley's office. The watchman in the Senate Office Building had checked her in and periodically trudged down the hallway trying doors, testing locks, shining his light into dark interiors. She almost envied him the job, simply because it was so clear-cut. He knew exactly what he was supposed to do, had no trouble in doing it, and slept with an easy conscience when it was done.

"Damn you, Drew," she muttered, not for the first time. The files she was looking for had belonged to William's father during his tenure as senator. When he died after a brief illness four years ago, the governor had appointed his son, William Wiley, to fill out his term, and William would continue to fill the post for as long as he wanted it. No Wiley had ever been defeated in Virginia. William was heir to the office, heir to the files.

After midnight she went to the cafeteria in the basement for coffee and a doughnut, anything to help her keep awake. There were a few others down there, working late that weekend for their various bosses, taking a break. She decided she was not fit company for anyone, and took her coffee and pastry back to the office, and sat at her desk ignoring the doughnut after all. There wasn't anything to find, she knew, had known all along. This was another one of Drew's fantasies, and again she had let him involve her. She wanted to throw something. All day she had refused to answer her phone, letting her answering machine handle calls, listening to her father, to William plead with her to call back. The only call she had returned was Sherry's.

"Damn you, Drew!" she whispered vehemently. Sherry

was having a wonderful time, was eating okay, sleeping okay, and lying through her teeth about something.

It was twelve-thirty. Another half hour, she thought, and she would be done; she would finish all the files so that when she told him there was nothing, she would make him believe it.

At one she was sitting back on her heels staring at the folder she had open on the floor. She carried it to her desk and sat down with it and started to read the documents; an hour later she started to photocopy them.

It was nearly three when she left the office numbly, not even seeing the watchman who waved in friendly greeting. She drove back to her apartment. Inside her living room, she lifted the telephone, then put it down again. It was three-thirty! All at once she felt totally exhausted, incapable of thinking, of doing anything except sleep.

In bed she found that she could not sleep. Did William know? Was this what Drew had expected her to find? Huysman had been Senator Wiley's star witness back in the fifties, during the witch-hunts. He had named names! There was correspondence with McCarthy, with others also involved in witch-hunts, blacklists. And Huysman had been promised funding for an indefinite period, of an indefinite sum of money. It was not stated that simply, that directly, but she had learned to read ambiguous documents by now. She knew what this one meant. She stared at the ceiling, barely illuminated with light leaking in around her drapes, and thought of the phrase that had crept into the correspondence again and again: Huysman's Pets. First the chimps had been called that, and then children had been called that. Huysman's Pets! And he, Huysman, had labeled them constructs! They were all crazy! Huysman, the senator, all of them. Crazy! What in god's name had he thought he was doing? And for what? For what possible purpose?

William could not know about any of this, she decided much later, when the light in the bedroom was diffuse, morning light. He had not been part of his father's schemes, had not participated in any of his father's affairs. He had been off to college, then in a law firm in Richmond and Washington. He had been a boy when his father and Huysman had made their deals. It had nothing to do with him, nothing to do with her. Terrible things had happened during those years, everyone knew that, but no one now was to blame, no one now responsible. Now that Huysman was dead, the senator dead, the project would come to a natural end and be just as dead. But she knew she had to talk to someone about this, someone who could tell her what it was that Huysman had done to those children. The papers had not gone into any detail. He had created them, created constructs, Huysman's Pets. But exactly what did that mean?

She wished, as she was falling asleep at last, that the senior Senator Wiley had been the prime mover in this business, but he had not been. Senator Cummings had that honor, and Senator Cumminings had the primary reports, the detailed reports, all the hard information somewhere in his files. And Senator Cummings was a toad, she heard herself saying, drifting off, drifting . . .

"I have to talk to you," Pat said over the phone to William Wiley. "Are you coming to Washington?"

"No. You know I've been planning to go to London and Paris, on to the Middle East. What's wrong?"

"Nothing. Nothing. I'll come out there. I'll be there in a couple of hours. Will you be around this evening?"

"Pat, my darling, you sound so mysterious. I'll be here. And, yes, we do have to talk. I've been thinking, as I know you have been doing. As soon as you get here, just give me a call, all right?"

She nodded and said good, and they hung up. She had forgotten his coming trips. He would be gone until the beginning of October, six weeks. Fact-finding. The image of Drew's face rose in her mind; he was grinning sardonically.

She drove the staff car out for William, since she had taken it from him. She would fly back, she decided. In her suitcase were the papers she had photocopied. She thought this must be how a spy felt on his way to an assignation to deliver classified material. Her trouble was that she had no one to deliver the papers to, no one who would know what they meant. Drew? Never, she told herself firmly. He had made her do this, had made her become a traitor to the senator, but that was as far as she intended to go with Drew. She was not sorry she had pried; if she was going to be an effective aide to William, she had to know what had gone on before, where they stood, what they intended now. That was where her loyalty was now: with him—not with his father or the project or anything else—just with William who had hired her, who trusted her thoroughly. Who intended to marry her at the first opportunity.

William was waiting for her at Randolf's house. Her father was in his penthouse offices downtown.

"Look, Pat, as my aide, you have a right to travel with me. Right? Right! You're not tied down with Sherry now, so do it, come with me!"

William held both her hands and spoke earnestly, even intensely.

She pulled free and shook her head. "That's not what I want to talk about." she said. "You're not leaving for a week, are you? Let's get back to that. William, do you know anything about Stanley Huysman and his project that your father sponsored?"

He looked blank.

"It was a project that your father and Senator Cummings were jointly involved with. It's concerned with experiments with children."

"Les Cummings? Really?"

Pat saw the change come over his face: his gaze went inward as he calculated, his eyes changed, looked almost glazed. "William? What is it?"

"Where did you come across this, darling?"

"In the files at the office. Why?"

"Les Cummings, now isn't that interesting. It's his project now? Is that how you read it?"

She nodded slowly.

"Pat, you're a marvel! An absolute marvel! For more than a year I've been looking for a way to get a little leverage with Les Cummings and here you hand it to me on a platter! Come to London with me! To Paris! Let him keep Sherry, see if we care!"

She shook her head. "It would get out. The press would have a field day with it."

"Then let's set a date and to hell with them."

Her father came rushing in then and seized her in a tight hug. "Why didn't you answer your phone? Can't you imagine how upset I was, knowing you were at your wit's end and not taking calls! Honey, don't do that to an old man with a bad heart."

"Jesus!" she cried and yanked free. "You aren't an old man and you don't have a bad heart! Stop it! Don't you play that game with me anymore!"

"We were talking about setting a date," William said gravely.

"Are you now? Well, this calls for a little something extra, doesn't it? I'm sure we have a special bott—"

"We are not setting a date! There's no call for a celebration, not yet! I . . . I'm going to go shower and take a nap. This house is crazy!"

Under the stinging shower Pat tried to remember exactly when she had decided that her life was a wasteland. After her father's illness that turned out not to be a heart attack, she knew but could not remember the minute, the day. She had a vivid memory of her argument with Drew about it later.

"What do you mean, wasted?" he had asked, massaging her stiff shoulders. She had driven from Richmond to New York.

"I don't have anything real to do. I don't do anything of any importance to anyone. I'm intelligent, educated, some say talented, and I don't do anything."

"What do you want to do?"

"I don't know. Something with meaning. Something memorable."

"Like building a cultural center?"

She twisted out from under his hands. "I don't know why you think it's funny for my father to be doing just that. He, at least, recognizes that he should do something for others."

"I know. The Randolf Stevens Concert Hall." He started to laugh again.

"Goddamn it, Drew, stop! What should they call it? The Smith Building? The Music Hall? What?"

"Exactly what they are calling it. Can we go to bed now?"

"Forget it! I'm going to read the paper."

That was how the end started: with Drew laughing at her father, with her going off to the living room to glower at the newspaper without reading a word. It had steadily become worse over the next six months, at least when she was home. She had spent more and more time in Richmond with her father, who was pathetically grateful, whose need was touching, who labeled Drew a slacker, a shirker, immoral, half

alive, and other things that had shocked her at first. She had
not realized how bitterly opposed to Drew he had been. Had
it really been because of the stupid biography? She could no
longer deny it or admit it. She simply did not know. When
things start to go sour, she thought, the smallest pinprick
becomes a mortal wound.

"He wants his biography," she had said lightly, almost
dismissive about the topic. She might have said: he wants
heavy cream in his coffee instead of half and half. It meant
little more to her at first than that.

"Why?"

"What do you mean, why? Why does anyone? To put his
life on record, to make a statement. I don't know why. Why
did Eisenhower?"

"He was dead when I did his. He expressed no preference
one way or the other."

"You know what I mean. Why does anyone else?"

"Damned if I know. I don't. Do you? Want all your warts
out there showing, your secret wishes, petty little dislikes,
ancient crimes—"

"Which warts? Which petty little dislikes?"

"Not you specifically. You, generic you. Anyone."

"I know you don't mean me. You mean my father, don't
you? His warts? I hope you wouldn't try to paint him lily-
white, but neither should it be a smear job. After all, he is my
father."

Drew stared at her in bewilderment. "I'm not going to do
it at all, Pat. I never said I would."

"Why not?" she practically screamed at him. "What am I
supposed to tell him?"

"I already told him no, more than once, in fact. Don't tell
him anything."

"Why are you being so stubborn? He will self-publish,
promote it, do everything you're always complaining your
publisher won't do for your books."

"He wants to be forgiven in public for being a warmonger,
I suspect. For manufacturing weapons. I'm not the one to
forgive him."

"He doesn't! That's . . . that's a terrible thing to say about
him! That isn't what he wants!"

"If not, it's even worse," he had said slowly, thoughtfully. She had run from the apartment, from the city, back to Richmond.

All her married life, she realized, she had been in the position of trying to explain Drew to her father, trying to explain her father to Drew. And it had been hopeless from the start. Early she had said to her father, "He isn't a slacker. He's a writer, an observer of life. He appears to be just sitting there, but he's thinking, watching, taking note of everything. Not everyone has to go out and make a million dollars in order to be a success."

He had looked at her with pity.

Over the years the argument had lost all meaning to her, also. Why, for heaven's sake, hadn't he at least become a best-selling author? But even if she could forgive him for not being successful, for not doing important things, she could not forgive herself for doing nothing. She had come to see her own life as insubstantial, meaningless, barren. William Wiley, trying to make order out of the chaos his father's death had created, had asked her to help, had made her help seem vital, indispensable, and she had found a direction of her own. The end of her marriage had come very fast after that decision. And with the divorce, her father had started talking about the marriage made in heaven she would have with William Wiley.

Why? she asked herself, dressing in shorts, a sleeveless T-shirt. Why was it so necessary to her father for their family to be joined to the Wiley family? Not just prestige, she felt certain. There were other, more prestigious families in Virginia, some of them even worse off financially than William. Did her father see this marriage as royalty saw marriage all through history? Power plays. Buttressing of authority. Empire building.

She shook her head in disgust at the idea, but she could not rid herself of the memory of Williams's eyes changing when he thought she had given him a wedge to use against Senator Cummings. He would send Gary back to Washington to dig out those files, she thought then, and they would find someone who understood what they meant and then use them accordingly. She had watched him enough times to know the process. She had to find someone to explain those papers to her, she decided. Not for Drew—he would never know—but for herself. She had had enough science in college to be uneasy, to doubt her own preliminary conclusions drawn from what she had read, but she knew she needed help.

From her bedroom windows she looked out over the river and cursed her father, cursed William, cursed Drew. Then she saw the tall powerful figure of Julianna move out of sight, going toward Willie Jo's bungalow. Julianna would know, she realized. She was a science whiz; she would understand what those papers meant. She ran downstairs, avoiding the areas of the sprawling house where she might run into her father or William, if he was still hanging around. She jogged to Willie Jo's house and knocked and when Julianna answered, she realized that she never had talked to her as anything but a housemaid, a personal maid, the daughter of a lifelong servant.

She did not know now what to say. Julianna gazed at her, waiting, curious. Finally Pat spoke and what she said was, "I'm sorry."

Julianna nodded, as if she understood exactly what that meant, and she opened the door wider to admit Pat.

TWENTY

"Are you sure?" Pat asked for what had to be the tenth time. She examined Julianna's face, as if searching for a telltale sign that what Julianna had told her was not really true, that it was a hoax, a game. Julianna was frowning intently at the photocopies Pat had brought home with her.

"The proper question," Julianna murmured, not looking up, "is what are we going to do about it?"

"Do you really believe all this?" Pat asked, waving at the papers generally. They were in her bedroom, the door locked. The papers were spread out on the bed and the desk.

Julianna was sitting cross-legged on the floor, taking one paper at a time from the bed, rearranging them, regrouping them according to some scheme that made sense to her. Pat had not been so bewildered for many years.

"Believe, not believe. Who knows? This says what they were trying to get, not what they ended up with," Julianna said.

"What should we do? What can we do? Now that Huysman's dead, does it even matter any longer, except as a cautionary tale—See what happens when you give money to research without limits, without someone to oversee what's being done? But what's the use of that? Who cares?"

Julianna glanced at her curiously. "You work for the senator. Isn't that the line he'll take if all this is made public?"

"Maybe," Pat said. She started to pace the length of her bedroom as Julianna continued arranging the documents. She had to do something, Pat knew. She could not simply pretend none of this had happened. And William was the logical place to start. Her reluctance was deep-seated, out of reach of logical examination. She knew only that she did not want to talk about this with William, or her father either, for that matter. None of the papers was classified, and that must mean that nothing had come of the research. Cummings, Wiley Senior, others had owed Huysman and this was how they had paid their debt. Filed away, forgotten. Now it would be discontinued, paid in full. Wiley was dead, the scientist was dead; why even consider going public with it? It could only damage William's career, even though he had had nothing to do with it. There would be a little bit more of the public erosion of confidence in government, and no one needed that.

Julianna finished with the documents and sat with her back against the bed, looking out the window across the room. Her hair was in an Afro, a foot across, high; she was large, tall, big-boned, and muscular but not fat. She could have been a priestess, Pat thought suddenly, or a princess, a warrior princess. She realized that not only had she never really talked with Julianna, she never before had actually looked at her. And she knew, with something akin to relief, that even if she wanted to do nothing about what they had found, Julianna would not be willing to bury it, forget it. Julianna was committed to action in this cause; she had said so as soon as she had grasped the meaning of the papers, and she said so now in her attitude, her watchfulness, her narrow-eyed concentration.

"Let's put them all somewhere safe," Julianna said at last. "This needs a little thought. I wish Drew was here."

"This has nothing to do with him."

"I think it has," Julianna said, standing, stretching. "He asked me about the physics involved in Huysman's work. A quick lesson in physics, that's what I gave him. He didn't have all this, I'm sure, but he's onto something."

Pat had not told Julianna that Drew had suggested she search the files. She turned away now and started to pick up the documents on the desk. She could hear Julianna gathering up those still on the bed.

"Let's both think about it and get together later tonight, after dinner. Maybe one of us will think of something."

Julianna nodded and silently watched as Pat stuffed the papers into a large manila envelope and put it in a desk drawer that she locked.

"Here's my girl now," Randolf Stevens said when Pat went downstairs again with Julianna at her side. "Will you tell Willie Jo to bring some munchies out to the porch," he said to Julianna. "Come along, Pat. William and I want to talk to you."

"Julianna doesn't work here, Dad," Pat said sharply.

"It's all right. I'll tell Mam on the way out," Julianna said and left, walking like a warrior princess.

"Isn't that Willie Jo's girl?" Pat's father asked. He looked bewildered.

"Yes. Oh, forget it. I want to talk to William too."

William was already on the porch, sipping a frosted gin and tonic. "Pat, darling, here's a drink with your name on it," he said rising, handing her a tall glass.

"Thanks. Listen, William, about that research that your father got funding for, did you know that it continued for over twenty years? That it was human research, illegal research on people?"

"Now, Pat, let's not jump to conclusions before we know more than we know at this moment. I sent Gary to Washington to go through those files, see what we have there. And that brings up what we—I—wanted to talk to you about. I don't think it would be wise to mention anything about those files until we have an expert evaluate them for us. Incalculable damage can be done through loose talk before the facts are known. Not that I think you would mention anything confidential to anyone outside this room. And everything in all those files is confidential, of course." He smiled his good television smile.

"Listen, both of you," she said slowly, deliberately, "I've read enough of the documents to understand what Huysman was up to, to understand that he was funded by the government, that there was no supervision throughout, and that he was conducting human experiments. There are over a hundred people, the results of his experiments, being held in a hospital in New Jersey. Many of them are children."

"Now, Pat, are you certain that you are enough of an expert in science to interpret all that data yourself? I say we have to wait for an expert, and then we'll take measures . . ."

"You're right about my science," she admitted. "I already talked it over with an expert. Julianna—"

"Willie Jo's girl?" Randolf burst into laughter and said to William, shaking his head, "She's that tall ugly black girl who skulks around the place. Got some kind of scholarship to some school or other—''

''Radcliffe! And she's a year away from a Ph.D. in physics!'' Pat said indignantly.

''You two girls got together and figured out the whole Huysman scheme all by yourselves?'' William asked, smiling.

Pat set her glass on a table and carefully stood up, determined not to shake, not to throw anything, not to scream at them. ''Good night, Dad. William. Don't hold dinner for me.''

''Now, Pat, don't act like a child,'' Randolf said. ''Don't be petty.''

She walked from the room without a backward glance. She went upstairs and packed her suitcase, recovered the envelope from her desk, and then sat on the edge of her bed and wondered where to go, what to do. She was still there a minute later when there was a soft tap on her door. She crossed the room and stood with her hand on the knob.

''Who is it?''

''Me, Julianna.''

She released the lock and opened the door.

''I heard them,'' Julianna said. ''Bastards.''

Pat nodded. ''Now what? I want to get those papers to a safe place before it occurs to either of them to try to find them and burn them, or whatever.''

''Exactly my thoughts. You know, they're so sure you're a twit and I'm a black twit, that'll favor us, give us a little time. Even so, I think we should get out of here. I mean, what if they got a court order or something for the papers?''

''That can't happen instantly,'' Pat said.

Julianna laughed. ''You've been on that side of the fence too long to know what can happen instantly when powerful people want it to happen.''

''Okay,'' Pat said. ''Let's get out of here and go where we can talk and think. Goddamn it! I don't have my car here. I left it in Washington. Can we use your car?''

''Not a good idea. If they decide you have papers and stuff, they might claim I kidnapped you or something, that I'm holding you for ransom. Wouldn't stick, but they wouldn't want it to anyway, only long enough to stop us, confiscate documents.''

''The staff car,'' Pat said firmly. ''Let them put out a bulletin on the staff car!''

They both laughed. William would not do anything like that, with the certain publicity it would cause.

"I think we'd better go down the back stairs," Julianna said as they left Pat's room. "I doubt your daddy even knows where they are. And they're milling about in the front of the house, waiting for you to come down so they can talk reason to you."

Julianna left Pat in the laundry room and sauntered out to the kitchen to speak to her mother. Strange, Pat thought, waiting for her return, how she trusted these two women now and not her father, not William who had asked her to go to England and France with him. And her father trusted her to be in her room, pouting, sulking. She could visualize the scene with him on one side of her, William on the other, making her see it their way, talking sense to her, explaining. How they explained! Always explaining! Men loved to explain to women, she thought savagely. She had to think of a place to hide the papers, but her thoughts refused to lead in that direction; all she could think of was how much they enjoyed explaining things to her, forcing her to accept their worldview, unable to accept that there could possibly be an alternative worldview. William saw the research as a way to get to Cummings, who had power that William wanted to tap. And her father saw her as a way to get to William, tap into his power through her. What did Julianna want? She could not answer that. She had no idea of what Julianna wanted.

Julianna came back. "Mam's making us some sandwiches and stuff. She's almost done. We think I should stay down in the seat, let you drive out through the servants' driveway, and after that I can direct you to a place we know where they won't come looking today. Is that all right with you?"

Pat nodded. "Tomorrow I can put the papers in a safe deposit box."

"And I'll have time to read them over again and see if they say what I think they do. Okay. We'll go out through the kitchen, pick up our grub, and be on our way."

"I'm already packed, but what about your things?"

Julianna laughed softly. "Mam packed for me when I went up to talk to you."

Late that night they were in a small house owned by a friend of Willie Jo. Frangie Jefferson had looked her over, then welcomed her guests. Julianna had hugged her warmly and had not explained anything. Frangie had asked nothing. There was an extra room with twin beds. She brought out bedding, but did not make up the beds, simply left everything available. Julianna cleared the kitchen table and spread out papers on it, got out her notebook, and became silent.

Pat made the beds and lay down on one of them. She was so tired she was twitchy, the way she had got as a child from too much excitement, too late hours, Christmas, almost anything out of the ordinary. It was too hot to go to sleep, and she was too tired to sit up. Miserably she wished it were morning, that decisions were out of her control. Her father would assume she had gone back to Washington, she knew. She had yo-yoed back and forth so much recently, it was the likeliest thing for her to have done. Also, she had not taken calls for days; they would think little of having the robot answer the telephone. William might send Gary to check on her, but what could he do? There was no doorman, no one to say if she was in or not. She did not believe anyone would break in; there was no reason for them to go that far. She was too biddable; they would count on that.

She believed that the files would vanish now. Gary would clean them out, take them back to Richmond where William would find his expert, and then . . . ? She tried to predict his reactions. Probably he would want a first-hand investigation. Gary again. Someone would have to go to that place and talk to the man in charge now, find out what had come of the experiments, where the children were, if they were normal, and if not what their needs were. A shudder passed through her. Human experiments! Producing children who were not normal! What had they hoped for? She did not believe the papers she had read. They had stated that their intention had been to produce supermen and women. People who had total control of their thought processes and who were in constant and instant communication with each other at all times. She shivered again.

It was another hot morning. Pat had slept fitfully and was not rested. She thought Julianna had not slept at all. Her bed looked untouched.

Frangie had gone to work, leaving the house to her company. Julianna had made coffee, and neither of them wanted more than that immediately.

"We have to decide what to do," Pat said wearily. "I think the safe deposit box is a good idea."

"And then?"

Pat did not know what then. She had not thought beyond making sure the papers were in a safe place.

"I'm going to go talk to Drew," Julianna said after a moment. "I want to know how much of this he's found out already."

Pat bit her lip, then reluctantly told Julianna that searching the files had been Drew's idea. "I think he either knows, or suspects, most of it."

Julianna nodded. "I don't think it's a good idea for anyone to know much about this right now. I don't know who's supporting this research, who's opposed to it. How desperate anyone is to keep it moving, to keep it secret. It could be dangerous."

Pat looked at her with surprise. Dangerous?

"I can't help but wonder," Julianna went on, "if they made progress. If they didn't, why'd anyone keep pouring in the money? This has not been cheap, year after year after year. They must have had something to report that made their sponsors decide they'd get their money's worth."

"It doesn't have to be like that," Pat said. "Sometimes things just keep going because no one stops them, not because they're accomplishing anything in particular."

"God knows I hope that's the case here."

Dangerous, Pat thought again. Drew was mixed up in it, and he had Sherry with him. Did he realize that this could be dangerous? She doubted it. He never explained anything, and he did not believe anyone cared enough about anything to be a menace if threatened with its loss. He would see this as an interesting problem, an intriguing puzzle, and he would more than likely blunder right into the robbers' cave, if there were robbers handy with a cave. And she no longer cared, she reminded herself; he was no longer her problem. But Sherry was.

"Let's go to Princeton," she said to Julianna. "That's where he is. I can put the papers in a bank up there if I have to."

TWENTY-ONE

As Pat drove, her thoughts kept going back to scenes with Drew; she remembered vividly when they first met in Brentano's where he was signing books, his first published book. Exactly nine people had come. Drew and the store manager had both been apologetic and embarrassed. At first he had been drinking coffee, waiting for the customers to flock in; then a stiff scotch and soda had appeared at his elbow and he had been grateful. Another had followed, increasing his gratitude immensely, and he no longer seemed to care if the customers showed up or not.

"Hi," she had said in a soft voice. She had noticed him, watched him, and finally approached him. "Do you think my father would like your book?"

"Is he literate?"

She shook her head.

"Does he have a sense of humor? Does he like people? Would he be interested in learning why a great man was driven to compose great music? Does he like, listen to, understand anything at all about music?"

She continued to shake her head.

He sighed and drank the remainder of his drink that had been served in a Coke container. "He won't like it," he said morosely.

"Would it be good for him?"

"My darling girl, never, but absolutely never give anyone anything simply because you think it might be good for him."

She said later that that had almost driven her away, but he had looked so lonely sitting there surrounded by his books that no one else would buy, she decided to buy two, one for her father, one for herself.

"Why not read one, then give it to him?" he asked. "You won't leave eye tracks on it."

"I thought if you make enough money on two sales, you might be able to buy me a sandwich or something like that for lunch."

As it turned out he did not make enough money on the first book to earn out the advance that had long since been spent. He told her this over lunch and she was sympathetic. Two weeks later they were in bed together, and two weeks after that he met Randolf, who had not read the book, who never got around to reading any of his books. When Randolf learned that they were planning to be married, he offered Drew a job. He had nothing against self-made men, he stated emphatically; he was one himself, but if anyone had offered help along the way he would have been smart enough to accept it. Grown men, he also said, don't spend their time scribbling. That was for ladies and queers.

Randolf tried to get Pat to go to Europe for an extended trip; she would not go. He dangled other bait in front of her; she would not bite. He warned her that Drew was interested in her money; she laughed and said there was plenty for two. There was, and it was hers, left to her by her mother.

Over the years, especially after Sherry was born, Pat had made herself believe he had accepted Drew finally. He was almost insanely devoted to his granddaughter but also blamed Drew for the fact that there was only one grandchild and that one a girl. He saw nothing illogical about his attitude. Then he had had his attack.

Pat knew he had not been seriously ill; perhaps she had known from the start and had not wanted to know. During the few months she had spent with him then, he had found her guilt button, Drew claimed, and pressed it constantly. Guilt over having money, over being pretty, being intelligent. Guilt most of all about not using her mind to accomplish something in her lifetime. That had been the button, she could admit now, and admitting it, she could not deny the guilt. People did have to do something with their lives, leave a mark on earth to show they had been here. Or what was life all about? She had worried the question for one sleepless night after another, searching for a way out of the maze she had found herself in. There was no out. she had to do something for someone other than herself, someone other than her husband and child. That was a given, that one helped family; that did not count. She had to do more than that, and she got only derision from Drew when she tried to talk about it.

She shook her head impatiently, remembering Drew's reaction when she first mentioned this. Do volunteer work at a hospital. Join the Peace Corps. Demonstrate. Join a sit-in. Endow a university chair. Open a clinic in the Bronx. Be a teacher.

"You don't understand! Those are all transitory. When I quit any of those things, they'll just vanish. I want to do something that will have a lasting effect, that will change things." And she had told him about joining William Wiley's staff as an aide, an economic adviser. He had laughed.

"You're a smug idiot!" she had cried. "Do you know what percentage of the population even knows you're alive? What percentage reads the books that you spend three of four years writing? Less than one twentieth of one percent!"

"Fewer."

She had thrown a book at him. He had ducked, and the book hit a lamp that in turn had crashed into the glass-topped end table and wrecked it.

"Are you having a fight?" Sherry had asked from the doorway, dressed in her too-small Strawberry Shortcake pajamas, rubbing her eyes. "Can I watch?"

"May I," Drew said mildly and Pat had run from the room to the bedroom where she locked the door. The next day she had left him.

When she told him she was getting the divorce, she had said, "At least my father and William appreciate me and don't laugh at me for wanting to do something worthwhile."

"I don't think building the big muddy dam is very worthwhile."

"I don't give a damn anymore what you think!"

"I appreciate you, Pat. More than you can know. More than you appreciate yourself. And I love you more than you can know."

She shook her head. "You would be happy as a monk in the Middle Ages, stuck away in a monastery, working all your life on one lousy illuminated manuscript. That would be enough for you.''

''And you would be happy to be Daddy's little girl again? I don't think so, Pat. Not for long.''

It wasn't that, she thought, driving too fast in the August heat. She did not want to be her father's little girl; she wanted to be herself, and somehow life wouldn't let her be that person. She did not even know who that person was or could be. And now her faith in William Wiley had been shaken badly. She had believed, had wanted desperately to believe, that there was salvation in working for a senator, doing things that were important to many people, and now . . . ? She realized she was doing eighty, that Julianna was clearing her throat a lot; she slowed down with a muttered, ''Sorry.''

After she got Sherry out of what could be a difficult if not dangerous situation, she would talk to William, reach an understanding with him about the Huysman affair, *make* him understand, she corrected herself. Make him see that a terrible injustice had been done to real people, that it had to be corrected.

He would see it, she told herself firmly. He would understand and not use what was in the files for only political purposes. He would! In her mind she heard the peculiar hoot that always began Drew's laughter.

The night Pat fled with Julianna, Drew had stayed up late also, mulling over the problems of the fortress on the hill, Lisa, the black boy, the Indian, Sorbies. (And what the hell was he doing up there?) And especially the more than one hundred kids who were being held prisoner in the hospital.

If Pat had not left him, he thought suddenly, he would not even be here. He, Pat, and Sherry would be out camping in some mountains, in Wyoming or Montana or maybe Canada. He remembered with grim pleasure how offended and outraged her father had been the first year they had gone camping. Sherry had been two. ''Someone will get killed,'' Randolf had sputtered. ''There are wild beasts, rock slides, poisonous insects.'' And there were, but the three happy campers had not come across them. Pat never had camped before that time. How worried she had been, and how determined not to show it or show the fears her father had put in her head. He wished that he had punched the senator in the nose, and Randolf too.

Randolf had won in the end, he admitted, and lifted his bourbon in a salute to his former father-in-law. A drip that never lets up wears down the hardest stone, he said to himself. He had his daughter back. But if Pat had not left, he mused, going back to his original thought, he would not be here. No way. He would have been involved with a different book by now, a different person, someone a hell of a lot more interesting than Stanley Huysman had been. He knew his own work methods very well. He finished a book and apparently did nothing for months, even a year sometimes, and then flew into a new work. And it was true that his work was without significance, just as Pat had said many times during the last year, but he went at it as if the entire world were waiting breathlessly for it.

But he was here, and earlier that night Sherry had been aghast when he had suggested that they leave and spend a week or two in Florida. "No way," she had declared. "We have a job to do."

Little big ears, he thought, grinning. She missed nothing. She had more or less adopted Lisa, as had Irma. As he had done also. Suddenly he had a memory so sharp and immediate that he felt jolted by it. Sherry had been five or six and had fallen in the playground at school, cutting her leg in a long ugly gash. The school called and he and Pat had rushed to the emergency room of the hospital to find Sherry screaming in panic. She had seen him, clung to him, her screams stilled, and had cried no more, not even when they administered the deadening shot and stitched her up. Afterward the doctor had tried to unwrap her arms from him and she had been like a leech fastened for life. The doctor had given him a tiny paper cup of water, and he had realized how very near he had been to passing out. His heart raced with the memory and he felt his own terror again, his helplessness, and most of all the overwhelming love that had weakened him. That feeling of love had come at times when he checked her at night, stood gazing at her in the dim light from the hall or, earlier, her own night light. She was a busy sleeper, all over the bed, making a mess of the sheet and covers, scattering all the toys she insisted on sharing her bed—bears, dolls, a book, cars. Sometimes the pile of toys she started with hid her almost. By the time he was ready for bed, stopped in to check on her, they were all on the floor.

He remembered her at eight, in bed with a virus or something, rebelling at having to stay in bed, too ill to be up. She had taken all her miniature cars to bed with her and a hundred dinosaurs—none over two inches long—and blocks. She had built mountains, propping up sheets and the blanket with blocks, her knees, even a water glass, and placed the dinosaurs in the valleys. Then she had run them down with the miniature cars.

Who loved those kids on the hill with an aching intensity? he suddenly thought, and downed the rest of his bourbon in a long gulp.

TWENTY-TWO

Although T.M. had virtually used force the night before to make Michelle go to bed at one, when he woke up at eight her half of the bed was empty. He groaned and staggered into the bathroom, pulled on a kimono, and went downstairs where he found her at the kitchen table, which was covered with papers.

"I found it," she said quietly.

T.M. did not even know what she had lost. He poured coffee and made a clearing in the paper forest. "Not yet," he mumbled, closing his eyes, sipping the steaming coffee.

"Do you remember the scenes in *Dracula* where Mina is hypnotized and tells them where the vampire is? You know, she hears the sound of lapping water, then horses' hooves, things like that."

He took a deep breath but did not open his eyes. "I don't think I want to remember it."

"It's like that with me, T.M. I keep knowing things I don't really know. Getting impressions of places that aren't this place, places I haven't been. I'm scared."

Now he looked at her. She was pale, her eyes shadowed. She looked as if she had not slept at all. He took her hand; it was cold. "Tell me," he said.

"First, there's a long corridor with metal doors, like a prison, something like that. And rooms like dormitory rooms, but not any school I've gone to. There's black water with a few lights shining on it. There's another room that's in an expensive house, antiques everywhere."

He squeezed her hand and got up to pour them both more coffee. He knew she sensed his relief. Little fantasies, he thought, the kind of little fantasies that most people had now and then. Daydreams.

"There was a computer monitor," she said, more deliberately. "It had a word on it: *synchronicity*. That's all. I tried that for the code word and got access to the computer in the hospital."

"Good Christ! Michelle, you'll put us both in jail! What do you think you're doing?" He spilled coffee when he jerked around to confront her. Her eyes were large, fathomless, almost like the eyes of a stranger.

"He's planning a demonstration for Friday," she said, looking past him at the wall. "I have to tell someone, stop him."

"Who? Will you for chrissake tell me what's going on?"

She continued to stare blankly at the wall for what seemed an interminable time. Then she shook herself and came back. He thought of it that way: she came back.

"I can't tell you. I don't know what's going on. As soon as the computer is through copying the files, we have to load it, the discs, everything in the car and go down to Princeton. There's someone down there like me. I have to find that other person, T.M. Something terrible is going to happen. Please believe me even if I can't explain it. Please."

He gazed at her helplessly and believed every word she said.

"Boy, you've done nothing but pace for three hours," Jack Silver Fox complained. "And nothing last night but toss and turn like there was ants in your bed."

"I've got to find Lisa," Franklin said, pacing. "Something's happening, something real bad's going on, and I've got to find her again."

"Them agents set eyes on me and something worse than that's going to go on."

"I know. You stay here. They aren't looking for me. One pretty black face is like another, you know? I'll hitch."

Jack Silver Fox did not argue. He remembered one time when his mother and father had wakened him in the middle of the night. His father had been getting dressed. His mother had been making up a pack, and he had realized with a shock that she was putting bandaging material in it. She filled the canteen with water, and silently his father had left; his mother had watched at the door for a long time. The day had passed, hours into the night had passed, and then his father had returned, riding his horse, leading another horse that bore his mother's brother, wounded. He would have died out on the plains if no one had found him. No one ever talked about the incident. He did not now question Franklin. If the boy said something bad was happening, it was.

"You're right. You'd best not take the truck," he said after a moment. "They'd spot that for sure and stop you. I'll walk to the road with you."

The narrow dirt road that led to the highway was in deep shade and pleasantly cool that August morning. A cardinal made a red streak in passing and chipmunks skittered out of the way, too tame to stay in hiding, too timid not to run. Neither spoke as they walked. Theirs had been an easy companionship from the start, from the first day he had seen the sassy kid on the side of the road, bright eyed and skinny and afraid of nothing. He remembered taking the boy inside his house, saying to his wife, "This is my grandson, Franklin." Maria had looked the boy over carefully and then put another plate on the table, and from then on they had the child both had wanted to replace the three who had died too young. That simple. Life should always be that simple, he was thinking when they reached the highway.

He stayed back in the shadows and watched his slender grandson advance to the edge of the road and raise his hand. A car screeched to a stop, backed up. The passenger door flew open; a pretty girl scrambled out and she and Franklin stared at each other. Jack found himself advancing toward them and stopped again, but Franklin turned and waved to him to come.

The driver of the car pulled it into the dirt road and also got out, looking completely bewildered, maybe even frightened, Jack thought.

"Grandfather," Franklin said formally, "this is my sister. Michelle. This is my grandfather."

She reached out her small hand and said, just as formally, "How do you do, Grandfather?" Her eyes were round and as blue as the sky; her hair was the color of ripening wheat, and she was his grandson's sister.

"I am well, granddaughter," he said.

Michelle introduced T.M. and in a very short time the car

was back on the highway heading for Princeton. Jack Silver Fox watched it out of sight gravely. Some day someone would explain it all. Or maybe not. He turned and went back to the cabin.

Arnie Sorbies had learned to be a chameleon many years ago. Any role he adopted he played out fully, and so far no one had ever questioned that. He was playing the elderly, infirm farmer just as if he were putting on a command performance. He leaned heavily on Mike's arm, the seventeen-year old who had asked him for help. Arnie was no longer in the cast, but he still had a brace on his injured leg, still used a cane.

"Why the hell don't you kids made a break for it?" he growled at Mike.

"Careful. Mr. Bramwell," Mike said, guiding him over the low rock barrier that divided the lawn from the driveway. "Where would we go? There are a hundred thirty-four of us, you know. A few could hide, but most would be caught and that would be worse than ever."

"Anyone in sight?" Arnie asked. There were trees between them and the main building now.

"All clear," Mike said.

Arnie stopped leaning on him and walked straighter. He fished in his pocket and brought out a key, passed it to the boy. "My truck" he said almost harshly. "If you decide to make a run for it, the thing'll hold a couple dozen of you. And it'll crash right through that damn gate down there. Just don't slow down too much and keep moving it. You sure someone knows how to drive?"

Mike looked at the key, then at him, back to the key. "Thanks, Mr. Bramwell. We won't forget this. A lot of us know how to drive. We just haven't had the chance to do it yet."

"Yeah, yeah. Ain't as easy as it looks on TV. Slow down on curves and practice using the brake before you have to use it."

"Take my arm, Mr. Bramwell. Vera's coming."

Arnie leaned on him and slowly continued to move without looking back to check on Vera. If the kid said she was coming, she was.

"Lousy setup," Arnie muttered as they walked. "Tell you

this, Mike, when I get out of here, I'm going to do something about this setup. I don't know what or how, but I'll do something.''

"Did you ask the doctor when that's going to be?"

"Yep. Something's happening this weekend and he doesn't want any complications right now. Next week, he said. And, Mike, I got those names for you. It's Ellie and Pam. They're going off Thursday afternoon, be back Saturday." The boy seemed to go rigid for a moment, then relaxed again. Both girls were twelve or thirteen, little kids, Arnie brooded. What the hell was going on?

"Thanks again," Mike said softly. "That's what we really needed to know. Do you mind if we go back now?"

"Back it is, son."

When they got to the building again, Mike let him in the sunshine, stretched out on a chaise to rest. The kids were everywhere, Arnie knew. They went where they wanted to, when they wanted to, and the interior security was a joke, but they could not, would not leave this place. Unless all of them could go, none of them would. He never had seen kids loyal to each other the way these were, even the older ones to the babies of the group, the adolescent boys to the adolescent girls, all of them to all of them.

It was spooky, he thought, and he scowled because he too was a prisoner, at least for now. Dohemy had made it very clear that no one was leaving yet. And what the hell was Lancaster doing on the scene? His scowl deepened. He had the feeling of a caged animal being observed from behind a one-way glass. The kids knew what was happening, he felt certain; they had wanted only the names of the couple or three who were to be selected for a short trip. Given enough time they could have found out themselves; there weren't any secrets around here, he had realized weeks ago. If one knew something, they all seemed to know it, but it didn't work with the staff, not with him, not with Dohemy or Vera or anyone except themselves. They were prisoners; he was a prisoner, and something was brewing, something not at all good, he knew. He felt it through and through with the same instinct that had kept him out of prison all his life, kept him out of police records altogether. Out of prison until now, he corrected himself bitterly. Now he was stuck just exactly like a fly on sticky paper.

* * *

"Look," Florence Charmody was saying to Drew, "Huysman never thought of those chimps as real, somehow. They were his constructs, creatures he had made. It's all through his notes about them, that attitude. He wasn't cruel or malicious or even especially heartless; he simply thought of them the way you might think of a mold culture you decided to grow in a petri dish."

"And the kids? You think he was like that where they were concerned?"

"Probably. It was just another way of looking at experimental subjects. A scientist has to divorce himself from them, from the things he had to do to them, or no science would get done. If you inject an animal with a deadly virus, you have to be removed emotionally from it. A torturer simply wouldn't make it as a scientist; he couldn't maintain the objectivity he would need."

"Let's stick to the kids. Do you think he subjected them to the same kind of experiments he used on the chimps?" Drew felt fascinated and repelled by this conversation, the way he had felt as a boy turning over a rock after a slow approach, knowing that anything might be under there—a thing that he did not want to see, could not bear to touch, but still intended to view.

Florence shook her head slowly. "I really don't think so. He had proven a lot already, things he did not have to prove again. Remember, he was his own firmest believer. He knew what he was doing, that it worked, and he needed no more proof. There probably were other experiments, psychological experiments. I think that's how he would have carried on with it."

"And Dohemy?"

Her face looked pinched suddenly, chilled. "He would have no hesitation to do anything that occurred to him. Huysman acted out of scientific curiosity to prove this theory with nothing beyond that in mind, I'm sure. But Dohemy? He wants power, wealth, prestige, god knows what all. And he thinks he deserves all that and will do whatever he has to to get it."

Finally Drew asked the question he had put off too long. "Do you think he's dangerous? How far would he go to protect his project, himself?"

"As far as he has to," she said slowly after a minute's thought.

Drew nodded glumly. For most of the night he had worried about Dohemy and his castle on the hill and the children held within it. Bluebeard, he thought, with his hideous secrets. And worrying about it for hours on end had brought him not a single idea about what he could do. He was very afraid there was nothing he could do except make accusations, bring in investigators, make a hell of a stink. And he was reluctant to do that for reasons he had not thought through. Something to do with Lisa; she would be in the middle of it, of course, a freak, an experimental animal produced by the insane genius. He frowned in rebellion at that idea. Any publicity at all, he had decided, was to be avoided if they could avoid it, but what did that leave? A frontal assault? He had an image of himself leading his females up the hill, all of them carrying clubs, spears, stones to throw. Followed by Leon's troops, he added, and saw in his mind's eye the procession that would make, a real invading army. He needed more troops, he decided, before they could think of invasion.

There was a loud knock on the office door then and Sherry stuck her head in and yelled, "Hey, Daddy, Franklin's here with another sister! And Daddy, Mom and Julianna just came in too!"

TWENTY-THREE

Michelle, Lisa, and Franklin were huddled, talking. Sherry was looking at Lisa with woebegone eyes, T.M. looking at Michelle with the same expression. Julianna and Florence were deep in a discussion with notebooks, papers between them on the coffee table in the untouchable living room. Pat stood abandoned, bewildered, more tired than she liked to think about after the race to Princeton, starting at dawn that morning. Drew stood looking at her, thinking that she was still the best-looking woman in the room, and my god, there were a lot of women in the room suddenly.

"Drew, what on earth is going on?" Pat had come to his side, looking at the roomful of people with wide eyes. "Who are all these women?"

He had made the introductions as well as he could. She did not mean that. "How are you?" he asked, seeing now the shadows under her eyes.

"What's going on? I'm going to take Sherry back home until you get untangled from . . . from all this."

They both looked at Sherry, who had edged up to Lisa, was holding her hand possessively.

"She doesn't want to go anywhere," Drew said uneasily. Sherry clearly had a crush on Lisa. And elephant might drag her out, but anything less than that would not be very effective.

"Who is that woman? And that one and that one? What are you doing here?"

"It's a long story," Drew started, and she frowned impatiently at him. "Have you had a chance to look at the files?"

"Yes. They're all confidential, of course."

"Of course." He stopped because Lisa, Franklin, and

Michelle were coming toward him with Sherry like a budding sprout on Lisa.

"Could we talk with you?" Franklin asked.

"Daddy, something awful's going on in the hospital!" Sherry said solemnly. "That doctor up there is going to do something really bad on Friday, and we have to stop him!"

"Drew!" Pat exclaimed, meaning, See what you've done!

"We have half an idea about how to get inside that place," Franklin said. "If there's someplace where we could talk . . ."

"Sherry, come with me. We have to go now," Pat said, reaching for her daughter.

"You don't understand," Sherry cried. "Someone might even die! I can't leave!"

Pat shot a baleful glance at Drew, saying without words: Do something.

"You'd better go with Pat, honey," he said. "We'll take care of things here. I promise. And later I'll tell you all about it."

"No! They might hurt Lisa!"

"What does Lisa have to do with that place?" Pat demanded. "What do any of you have to do with it?"

There was a long silence. Finally Michelle said, "We'd better all sit down, I guess, and talk about this."

In the doorway Irma Huysman held on to the frame to steady herself and nodded. She joined the group in the living room silently and sat down in one of the brocade chairs.

"Mrs. Huysman," Drew said after they all had talked and talked. "You asked me to find out if your husband had done something shameful, as you put it. You be the judge."

Her skin was like parchment, so pale and brittle looking now that she was a caricature of herself. Her gaze kept going back to the three young people: Lisa, Michelle, and Franklin. She moistened her lips. "Thank you, Mr. Lancaster. What is to be done about this . . . this travesty of science? If you learned all this so easily, I fear that the secret is not buried very deeply."

Drew glanced at Florence, who said, "There were special circumstances, Mrs. Huysman. The scientific community isn't at all likely to stumble onto any of it. Even if someone did, they would discount it because the decision has already been made that what he did can't work. No one believes in it."

"No one in physics would touch it," Julianna said with assurance.

"What are you all doing?" Pat cried. "We can't just sit back reassured that no one else is going to learn anything about this! There are children up there, young people, being experimented on, their lives in shambles! Drew!"

Drew was watching Irma Huysman who was collecting herself again; a little color had returned to her cheeks and she looked as indignant as Pat.

"I did your bidding," he said gently. "Do you want me to take all these people away now? You weren't involved; no one holds you responsible."

"Of course I have responsibility," she said sharply. "I shall have my attorneys look into the matter of ownership of that . . . that place. There is no such church. The Church of Inner and Outer Harmony; the name itself is an abomination. Those children shall not be held prisoner a day longer than it takes to wrest control from that loathsome man, Claude Dohemy. Drew, will you continue? I have only one request, please: no publicity. It would harm everyone, the children, the memory of my husband, everyone."

"No publicity," Drew echoed fervently. "God no! Think of the press getting hold of these kids! But it isn't enough just to get Dohemy out of there. If the government's been funding this project all these years, they must expect a payoff eventually, something in return. And Friday Dohemy's planning something, I think a demonstration. Probably to reaffirm that he's capable of carrying on alone. We have to discredit him and the project so thoroughly that what reports get back to Washington will make everyone back off. We don't want them taking Dohemy out only to put in someone else, someone more capable than he is."

Irma rose from her chair without a trace of the care and hesitation she had shown only a week ago. She said, "Technically those children were fathered by my husband, they are not government issue. They must be cared for properly. If that man has a plan, and if it's in your power to foil him, do so. Meanwhile, you must all consider yourselves my guests. Whatever I can do, please ask. I feel that this is war, Drew, and I want to win it no matter at what cost. They cannot have my children!"

*   *   *

Later Drew considered them all. Michelle, Lisa, and Franklin had to do whatever they had to do. They were driven, called, and could only obey. Mrs. Huysman had her answer about her husband and now had the responsibility of a family. He shook his head over the size of her new family, then shrugged. She could afford it. Pat was a crusade looking for a cause and now had found it. She was happy. Julianna and Florence had been clobbered right in the middle of the cortex; and, intellectually stunned, they would follow this up no matter where it led, in disbelief, wonder, opening new frontiers in science, delighted and dismayed at once. Even if they never told a soul, they were in all the way, he knew. And poor T.M. would follow Michelle into the flames just as long as he held her hand. And that, he said to himself then, left only him.

He did not know why he was here, why he was breaking the law, conspiring to break it again, and probably more than just once. He had no mission, no crusade. He was very fond of Lisa, but was that enough? Sherry was fonder of her, but was that? He would not write Stanley Huysman's biography. No one would. This was his legacy, and it was a secret so monumental, so shattering that no one ever would learn about it if it could be avoided. No one in this house would ever tell, he knew. He gave up trying to unravel his motives for being here, for going through with this, because he was going to go through with it, that was certain.

He thought again of the twin studies. Mary marries John A and Martha marries John B and they have two children each on the same days and name them the same names and have their tonsils out on the same day and smash their cars on the same day. And John A and John B and doctors here and there, and other drivers and parents and teachers and deliverymen and telephone men were all involved in seeing to it that the parallels were maintained. A chill crept up his back, down his arms.

He could leave this minute, he thought. He could get up, kiss Sherry good-bye and walk out the door, get in his car and drive to California.

He remembered what Florence had told him about the chimps. Huysman gave one a jolt and watched how the other reacted. When he sacrificed one, the other died also, very soon afterward.

He was gazing absently at the room without noticing the others in it until Sherry said, "If there aren't enough rooms to go around, Lisa can stay in my room." She was gazing at Lisa adoringly.

He imagined her stiffening suddenly with the pain of an electric shock that came from nowhere. He imagined her weakening, going into the hospital where they sought a cause and found nothing, and let her die because they could not keep her alive.

Leon Lauder held the phone some distance from his ear and listened to his wife. Sell the house immediately, take the condemnation money and put it in the condo, now. He could hear his grandson screaming in the background and, closer, his granddaughter yelling for money because the ice cream man was coming. He closed his eyes. In his mind he saw his new Ambassador rose, in bloom this year for the first time, and the trellis he had made over winter for the Black Velvet climber, roses so dark red that they did indeed look like black velvet. State Fair roses, that was what he had, the best roses to be found outside a nursery. Not a spot on them, not a speck of mildew or black spot, not a bug-chewed leaf. Picture-book yard. Dream yard. And now a goddamn road would run through the middle of it, and the road would carry fat cats to the airport in ten minutes less than it would take using the main highway already in place.

"I'm telling you," Mildred said shrilly, "I'm fed up with fighting it. We can't win. You never win a lawsuit like that. When it's condemned, it's gone. Why won't you face it?"

"I have to go now," he said quietly. "Business. We'll talk about it when I get home."

Gently he cradled the phone. Bob Samson was concentrating on the view out the window of the motel parking lot. Neither spoke for a long time.

Princeton was a bust, he had decided. Lancaster really was researching a book on the scientist. Lauder knew his superiors would not agree to keep the army he had in the area much longer. Too expensive, too nebulous a lead. They wanted something real to justify expenses. His instincts, intuition, just plain old-fashioned faith in himself meant nothing. His boss tended to look on the bill that had turned up in Atlantic City as a fluke, one that had been out there a while, in someone's bureau drawer; just now put in circulation by an innocent bystander. The fact that it had been finished by someone other than the Artist impressed no one. Just went to prove the theory that the original counterfeiter was out of the picture now, probably for good. Oh sure, they would catch him eventually, they always did, but there was no urgency about it, no need to spend the entire budget on this case.

And now Lancaster was throwing a party in the Huysman house. So what? Get pictures, he had snapped at Bob Samson. He would continue to treat this seriously until they actually yanked him off, and that meant pictures of everyone going into that house, everyone connected with Lancaster just as long as there was even a suspicion that he might be in touch with Sorbies. Bob Samson was still at the window, and he was still staring broodingly at the telephone when the pictures were brought in. The third one Lauder examined showed the kid that Jack Silver Fox claimed was his grandson. The kid had entered the Huysman house.

Irma Huysman spoke into the telephone with authority. "I shall come this afternoon, Dr. Dohemy. At three." She did not wait for a response but hung up decisively. It was Wednesday morning.

Drew nodded approval. Pat had taken Sherry and Lisa out shopping for a camera. As soon as they returned, Drew and his photographer were to leave for the hospital. You don't have to know how to use it, he had told Lisa. Pretend.

They had to spend at least two hours up there, give Franklin time to make contact, talk with some of the kids. Two hours. He grinned at Irma Huysman, who looked as excited as a girl. T.M. came into the room then, decked out in a chauffeur's uniform, spiffy as hell. They all went out to the garage.

Franklin got in the back of the Continental, arranged himself on the floor. Drew put a brown rug over him. Irma Huysman got in and carefully positioned her feet so she would not mash him, and sat bolt upright, as imperious as a queen. With T.M. behind the wheel the picture was complete. Drew looked in, even put his head partway inside trying to see Franklin. He could tell something was there, but who would dare get this close? It would do, he decided, and held his thumb up to T.M.

"Bon voyage," he said to them. "We'll follow in half an hour or so. Luck."

Michelle leaned in to kiss T.M. and they gazed at each other soulfully for a moment, then she withdrew. Everyone moved out of the garage; the door opened and the car glided out.

Step one, Drew thought. When Pat returned with Sherry and Lisa, step two began. He watched Lisa go through the motions of taking pictures; she looked professional enough to fool him. Then he and Pat went to his room for a talk. It was the first time they had been alone since her arrival.

"I can't let Sherry stay," she said in a low voice. "I'm worried about all this. It could become dangerous, and she's a child."

"I know. Take her home with you. This will be over in a day or two, or we'll have to blow the whistle on the good Dr. Dohemy. One way or the other, it'll end."

She was shaking her head. "I don't want to leave until it's finished. Maybe there will be something else I can do. Like today."

"Pat, you can't have it both ways. Are suggesting I take her out of here?"

"I'm worried," she said. "I don't know what I'm suggest- ing. You're really mixed up in all this, aren't you? How did that happen? I don't understand."

He shrugged. "Me neither. But I am. Where will you and Sherry spend the afternoon?"

"Here," she said after a moment. "I don't think I could pry her away. Remember how she used to fight when she was a baby and didn't want to do something? It would be a different kind of fight but a good one."

They were standing in his room, arm's length apart. He closed the space between them and held her, then kissed her. "Later, when we get back," he whispered in her hair, "we can sneak off and go to a motel. Show you my picture postcards."

"Be serious, Drew. Please."

"Baby, am I ever serious. I've been surrounded by volup- tuous women for days. Believe me, I am serious. I'll throw in ice cream and chocolates."

She laughed. "Idiot! Get going. And be careful. We'll be here."

"Daddy, really can't I go?" Sherry asked once more when Drew and Pat went downstairs again.

"Nope. That would look suspicious, since I already found out that I can't take a harem inside with me."

Pat made a strangled, snorting sound.

"Since Mrs. Huysman insisted on pictures of herself in the place where her husband toiled, Dr. Dohemy is rather stuck with the idea of a photographer, but he probably would draw the line at a brat. And I don't blame him a bit. I'd draw the line myself if it wasn't years too late."

Sherry grinned feebly but gave in and hugged him, and hugged Lisa longer.

"See you for high tea," Drew said, and he and Lisa left the house.

This time they were admitted through the gate with hardly any delay. Lisa was very pale by the time Drew stopped the car at the front entrance of the hospital. Her hands fumbled with the camera equipment—a very expensive Hasselblad, Drew noted with amusement. Pat bought only the best.

"Are you okay?" he asked softly.

"I will be. It's . . . a little overwhelming."

"Here comes Dohemy. Walk back from the joint and take some long distance shots, give yourself time to relax a little. Okay?"

She nodded and opened the car door.

"Lisa, don't forget the lens cover."

She flushed and walked away quickly before Dohemy had reached the car. Drew got out his side and watched her for a moment, then said to Dohemy, "Pretty, isn't she? I always use pretty photographers." Lisa was looking through the camera, her face hidden. Behind her under some trees was the Continental with T.M. polishing it.

"You're late," Dohemy said. "I interrupted a rather busy schedule, Mr. Lancaster. If we could get on with it."

"Late? Really? We only stopped a minute or two. We'll want some pictures of you, naturally, inside and out, if that's all right." He saw Sorbies and his wheelchair behind Dohemy on the wide top step of the hospital.

"Lisa, can you get some of the doctor on the steps here? I'll just go and help the old geezer get out of the frame."

Dohemy frowned at him and tried to smile for Lisa simultaneously, and Drew ran up the steps two at a time and took the handles of the wheelchair, turned it around, pushed it back inside.

"What the hell are you doing here?" Sorbies asked. "Never mind. Here's a letter. Read it carefully, Lancaster. It's important. And it's the real thing."

Drew stuck the envelope in his pocket. "Do you want out of here? We're going to blow the whistle on the doctor; there may be cops and such. Can you leave?"

"Not without help."

"Do you want out?"

"Hell yes!"

"I'll be in touch. Gotta run."

He sauntered back to the step and watched Lisa pose Dohemy with the sun in his eyes.

It was not a good afternoon for the poor doctor, he thought an hour later. Mrs. Huysman was difficult, insisting on examining every room her husband had ever entered, every office he had worked in, sat in, looked in. She went over the laboratories inch by inch as if searching for dust. She shooed people at work out of her way with a flick of her hand. She did not like the way Lisa posed Dohemy and had all the pictures taken over again. His smile became fixed, then turned into a grimace. His lips twitched.

"Where are the computers?" Irma Huysman asked finally. "Stanley used to talk about the computers at his command."

"I'm afraid that area is, ah, off limits," Dohemy said with his forced grimace of a smile, his lip twitching.

"Nonsense! Take us to them. I have an appointment. This is taking much, much longer than I anticipated. I trusted you to cooperate, Dr. Dohemy, not to delay these tedious proceedings."

Drew wrote in his notebook and hardly even noticed the murderous look Dohemy directed at him. They went to the office that housed the computer system. It was impressive.

"Don't you have real files?" Drew asked plaintively. "Real paper I could go through sometime?"

"No," Dohemy snapped.

"But Stanley worked with those machines? How dreadful. I've seen enough. Mr. Lancaster, do you have all the pictures you need? I am quite fatigued."

"Yes, ma'am. I guess we're all through here. Thank you, Doctor. You've been helpful."

Drew went ahead to tell her driver to bring the car around, and she leaned heavily on the arm of Dr. Dohemy and walked agonizingly slowly all the way. He grimaced and twitched. Mrs. Huysman had taken up two hours and forty-five minutes of his time.

Drew handed her inside the Continental, where she positioned her feet carefully and leaned back in exhaustion. The car moved out of sight with hardly even a whisper.

"Listen, Lancaster," Dohemy said when it was gone, "this is the end. I don't have anything else for you and I'm a busy man. I can't afford to waste another hour for your project. Do you understand?"

"Indeed I do. You've been very patient. Come, Lisa, onward. I saw a nice looking tavern a few miles down the road where I bet the beer is icy. What do you say?"

"Mr. Lancaster! You know I don't drink!"

"I'll teach you. Bye, bye, Doctor. Thanks a million and all that."

They got in his car and followed the Continental.

TWENTY-FOUR

They had all gathered on an airy sun porch where Marion had brought trays of sandwiches. Irma was glowing, spots of color firing her cheeks, her eyes sparkling with excitement; she was drinking scotch with very little water. Drew raised his bourbon to her in silent salute and she bowed slightly, acknowledging his congratulations on her performance.

"What did you find out?" he asked Franklin.

Franklin swallowed and gulped juice, then said, "Boy! Those kids know everything going on in that place! But there wasn't any way they could see to get out of this test coming up on Friday. There've been other tests when Dr. Huysman was still in charge, and they could handle them all okay, but not the kind Dohemy is planning for them this time. He's got this chair all wired up and everything, and he's going to let the observers give the kid in the chair a jolt now and then and watch the other kids' reactions. Two kids will be in a motel out of Princeton, and one in a different room up in the hospital."

Pat looked sick, and Irma closed her eyes and drank her scotch down. Lisa and Michelle exchanged glances; both were pale. T.M. held Michelle's hand in a tight grasp. On the far side of the room Florence and Julianna watched impassively. Sherry was missing. Pat had sent her upstairs until further notice. Drew caught a glimpse of her bright head behind a rattan sofa and sighed.

"'Come on out and sit down," he ordered. "Hop to it!"

Pat exclaimed, "Sherry!" and the child looked mildly embarrassed for a split second, then said, "I have something to report, too."

"Let's have it," Drew said.

"There are a lot more cars with agents by now. I went for a walk up and down the street and saw them."

"Okay. We'll have to keep that in mind. Anyone else?"

Pat cleared her throat. "I called William Wiley today and suggested that I observe what's going on at the hospital Friday. He agreed. He is making the arrangements with Dohemy."

She did not add that he had agreed because he trusted her, still trusted her, and because he was afraid Senator Cummings would gain an advantage in secret. When she looked at Drew his eyes were warm and shining as he regarded her.

"Are you sure you want to do that?"

"Yes. And Julianna—Dr. Jones, that is—will go to the motel and be our observer there. He doesn't have a clue that Julianna is Dr. Jones, of course."

Drew nodded. "We don't want merely to upset his test on Friday. We want to discredit him entirely, the whole project. Agreed?" There were nods.

"I can erase his files," Michelle said excitedly. "All of them."

"I don't think so. He would be able to prove a case of sabotage."

"Not erase," Florence said thoughtfully. "Edit. I can turn those files into the most godawful garbage anyone every tried to unravel and make it look legitimate. But it will take time." She glanced at Michelle who was nodding.

"And I've got to get back inside the castle keep tomorrow night," Franklin said. "I have a list of stuff to take in with me, insulating wire, resistors, stuff like that. I can fix the chair, the system he's got set up. His monitors will work just fine Friday, everything will look like it's working just fine, but the kid won't feel anything but a tickle."

Drew studied him. He started to ask if the experiment would succeed otherwise, but there was no need. It would. "Good." He looked at Michelle. "Can you turn off the electricity in the fence with your computer here?" She nodded. "Okay. So we'll have a timetable and a way to get you up there. There's a guy I want out of that place before anything starts on Friday. Any suggestions?"

There was a long silence. Franklin stared at his feet. "Let me read part of a letter from him," Drew said. He pulled the letter from his pocket and read, " 'You know I don't lie, and

I'm telling you these kids are in prison here. It's not a hospital, it's a jail, and they don't deserve it. It's my neck, I know that, but call the cops and raid this joint, Lancaster. Bring in the whole damn army if you have to. Something's coming up real soon and it might be too late if you don't do it now. I can't get out to do it myself, or so help me God I would! Make a stink. Call reporters. Get publicity. That's the last thing Dohemy wants now, so do it that way.' " He looked up from the letter. "It goes on a bit more, but it's like that. I want him out. He isn't lying. If he's caught, it's prison for him."

Franklin took a deep breath. "If I can talk Jack into helping, we can lower him down the cliff and let Jack meet him with our rowboat and take him somewhere. If I can talk him into it."

Drew began to laugh.

The Indian Leon was looking for! The Indian and the paperhanger getting together after all these years! He thought Jack Silver Fox was in for a surprise. They were all watching him warily.

"Mr. Lancaster," T.M. asked suddenly, "why are all those police out there? Are they after you?"

"Secret Service," he said. "They think I'm in cahoots with a counterfeiter."

Michelle's face blanched, then turned scarlet. She and T.M. clutched each other's hand harder, but did not look at one another.

Drew remembered his little fantasy of leading the agents up the hill to storm the castle. He mused aloud, "If only I could get my hands on some funny money." To his infinite surprise Michelle opened her mouth to say something.

He put his finger to her lips. "Let me talk to you later." He did not want to make anyone an accomplice to a crime before, during, or after the fact, especially his wife—ex-wife—and child. He felt just a little dizzy.

Julianna spoke for the first time. "I know how we can get Franklin out of here without a tail, that is, unless they're tailing everyone who comes and goes. Guess we should test that first. Why don't you put together a shopping list and we'll see if anyone follows me to a shopping mall and back."

"I'll go too, and we'll take Sherry," Pat said. "That will

give us an excuse to have to come back to the house, to bring her back with us.''

Drew watched them, thinking: conspirators all. It came naturally. Even, or maybe especially, Sherry and Pat in there conspiring with zest and skill. He decided he was proud of his two females.

Drew wormed the story out of Michelle and T.M. who both looked guilty as hell. He hoped they would not arouse suspicion just by the expression on their faces. ''I'm not going to pass them,'' he said gently. ''I want bait. Unfinished is fine, maybe even better, less criminal maybe.''

''The man up there in the hospital,'' T.M. said then, ''can hide in our house, if he wants. It isn't far from the hospital.''

Pat, Sherry, and Julianna returned. Drew stared at Julianna in disbelief. She was wearing a large, blousy top, printed, garish in reds and yellows, and a flared, shiny black skirt. Earrings dangled from her ears, beads glittered at her neck.

''You are a sight!'' he said fervently. ''Going to a party?''

Julianna grinned and did a slow pirouette. She had low-heeled gold sandals and black hose.

Pat was studying Julianna; she said absently, ''We rented a car for her. No one followed us, by the way. Maybe they think I'm above suspicion.''

''They're going to deliver the car to the motel,'' Sherry said. She was glowing with excitement. ''We bought rope and tools and wire and stuff like that. Isn't she great, Daddy?''

''Indeed she is. Julianna, will you stop dancing and tell me what this is all about?''

She winked at him and raised both hands to her head and removed the Afro hairdo, a wig. Her own hair was in short tight curls next to her scalp. Silently she crossed the room, approached Franklin, and positioned the wig on him. The change was miraculous; his eyes seemed to widen, his lips curled slightly, and without a missed beat he began to mimic her movements and they danced in a languorous rhythm exactly in step. She led him toward the door where she picked up a large shopping bag, and together they vanished down the hallway.

Leon Lauder tried to puzzle it out. He did not want to move in on Lancaster in that house. Mrs. Huysman would make trouble for sure. And now that Lancaster's ex-wife and her black companion—maid?—had appeared, it complicated everything even more. And she was here in a staff car—on business? And who were all those others? First the blond girl and now the couple who had arrived with Franklin Silver Fox. All part of a gang? He did not believe that. Silver Fox had worked with the Artist, he had always known it, but he did not believe anyone else ever had. The Artist was a loner, not involved with a gang. That's why he had been able to elude them all these years. Alone and low profile, that had been his strength from day one.

He studied the picture of the good-looking kids, carrying in boxes of computer stuff. Helping Lancaster? Students? Whiz kids with computers? He gnawed his lower lip. Not yet, he decided abruptly. Give them rope. They had the license number of the car the kids had come in; they could find them when they wanted them. He wanted the black boy and he wanted to keep Lancaster in sight, his two prime goals right now. Let the others come and go, let kids drift in and out, just as long as they didn't let Lancaster and the kid slip through their fingers again.

Later, when Bob Samson reported that the ex-wife and the maid had departed, he nodded, unhappy, uneasy, but not enough to change the standing orders. He knew where to find her if ever he needed to, he thought, trying to ignore the subliminal buzz that was making his head ache.

Drew and Sherry had walked to the car with Pat and Franklin, who was decked out in Julianna's new clothes. Sherry waved to the agents in the parked car across the street. They ignored her, and Pat drove off without a follower. Drew took Sherry's hand and they started up the walk back to the house. Franklin was on his way.

Drew started to hum. Will you come back after a while? he had asked Pat, and she said yes. Later. He danced a little jig and Sherry copied him. Dancing, they went up the stairs, turned, bowed together, and entered the house.

After Drew Lancaster and his photographer had left, Claude Dohemy stormed down to the basement offices where he found Vera and Joe Bramwell watching television.

"I told you to stay the hell out of the offices!" he yelled at the old man.

Bramwell started to roll his wheelchair through the doorway.

"Cool it, for heaven's sake," Vera said. "We were just watching a sh—"

"Shut up, and come with me. We have work to do. Those fools finally have gone. Come on!"

Vera sighed and turned off the set. When they went out into the wide corridor, the old man and his wheelchair were already out of sight.

"He's lonesome," Vera said in a placating voice. "That's all. He's not used to a place like this. And, I admit, it's not the most exciting joint I've spent time in."

"Will you just shut up. I told you this phase ends very soon now. After this test, another couple of weeks, we'll be out of here. What I think will happen is that they'll want us to put on some more tests down in Washington for the real bigwigs. How'd you like that, Vera? A hotel suite, maybe even in the Watergate? A few weeks like that will make up for a lot. Now, let's get on with this."

"Sure, sure. What're we doing now?"

They entered a laboratory, one that he had not shown to the old bitch Huysman and Lancaster. On a desk was a floor plan; he went to it, beckoning her to follow.

"Here's the layout. The bedrooms are over here, but this is the room where we've got the TV camera set up. I want you to pay particular attention to where the kids are at all times. I put a line down where they cross out of range. See to it that they don't cross that line. You understand?"

"Claude, will you stop! You're acting as if I can't be trusted, all at once. It isn't as if we've never done anything like this before."

"We've never done anything like this before," he muttered.

"Well, the setup's the same, no matter what you do at your end here. I know how to run it, honestly."

He made her examine the room plan with him. It was a large motel sitting room with two couches, several chairs, a round table and wooden chairs. There would be coffee and pastries delivered, he told her again. The kids could have a sweet roll and milk if they wanted it. They would have assorted toys: dolls, crayons, paper, books. By nine sharp they were to be seated at the round table at play, and her observers were to be on the couches and chairs across the room.

"And you don't do a damn thing except wait," he said harshly. "Don't explain anything, don't predict anything. If they have questions, tell them we'll cover them all at the conference that will follow the tests, up here. As soon as it's all over, send them on their way and get those kids back up here. They might be upset, frightened, or something. You and Johnson get them back here, pronto."

"They'd better be able to walk."

He gave her a sharp look; her expression was unreadable. "I'll make this up to you," he said. "I promise." He reached for her, but she shrugged out of his grasp. "For god's sake," he snapped, "no one is going to be permanently damaged."

Her eyes had become opaque, iced over. "If I were you," she said distinctly, "I'd change the locks on the dorm wings just before dawn on Friday."

"I'm doubling security," he said in a rasping voice. "Albert's going to be here personally, and the kids don't know a thing about any of this yet. Unless you've told them."

"They know what they want to know. Do you have a clue yet about which ones they've selected to share this little experience? Just don't kid yourself, Claude. Don't underestimate them."

Even as he glared at her with malevolence, he could feel cold sweat prickling his arms and back; his hands were clammy.

"Albert is bringing in his own security people and medical personnel," he said in a sudden rage. "Don't come on now like an avenging angel, Vera. Not now, after all these years!"

"Years under Huysman weren't like this and you know it! Did you bother to read his predictions and the corresponding results over the years? Did you? My God, they were almost precisely the same! He knew exactly what he was doing all the time. Exactly!"

"You're turning chicken on me," he said.

"Because you're like a kid playing with matches in a munitions factory!"

"I told you we planned this together; he would have done it last year—"

Her expression of frank disbelief made him stop.

"So," she said very coldly. "Is there anything else?"

"No. Get out. I'll talk to you later."

She left him alone in the laboratory. He put away the floor plan and moved one of the observers' chairs an inch or two, then went to the window of one-way glass and gazed at the chair in the other room. On a table under the window was a dial. Slowly he turned the knob to the halfway mark, and more slowly the rest of the way to the highest setting. Then, with a jerk, he turned it down again. Sweat was running down his face, burning his eyes.

TWENTY-FIVE

When Franklin entered the cabin in his garish clothes, Jack Silver Fox blinked but made no comment. Franklin stripped down to his shorts in the living room.

"Whew!" he said. "That's better."

"Are you in bigger trouble than I am?" Jack asked then. "Or is your trouble my trouble?"

"Oh, it's mine, I reckon, and I reckon it could get big even if it isn't right now. Tomorrow sometime a woman's going to come and pick up that car and take it away with her."

Jack nodded. Franklin would tell him when the time was right. He knew this because he knew Franklin did not have to tell him and the boy knew that too. That made it easier. "Hungry?" he asked.

"You wouldn't believe how hungry."

Jack went to the kitchen and rummaged in the refrigerator. The boy was always hungry and ate like a hand who didn't know for sure there would be food tomorrow. And not an ounce of fat to show for it. Sinewy muscles and bone and skin, no matter what they fed him or how often. Maria had tried one whole year to fatten him up with pies, cakes, cream sauces, gravies; Jack had gained fifteen pounds, none of it wanted, and she had given up. Franklin had followed him to the tiny kitchen and moved out of the way when Jack brought out pork chops and leftover beans. He waited, knowing there was more that Franklin had on his mind.

"There's something you could do," he said finally. "If you're of a mind to."

Jack laid two chops in the skillet and for a moment had a surge of real-time memory, the kind that makes dreams and the real word merge until you can't tell which is which. There

had been several times in his life when things had happened
that you don't talk about to others, especially whites. He
could have talked about them to his mother but no one else.
Some of them had wrapped themselves around her, had been
shared with her at the time of happening. She would have
nodded over the other things, accepting without question.
Now he had this memory that he did not like, coming up in
front of his closed eyes. He recalled his grandfather, very old,
never feeble until he died, and crazy. Real crazy, alcohol
crazy, white jail crazy, paranoid crazy. There are circles, he
had told Jack, all through your life, circles, and when you
start one it's got to be closed or you're not through with it.
Eventually you close them or you die unfinished with business. You understand what I'm telling you? Jack had nodded
but had not understood, not then. Over the years he had come
to understand little by little. He felt now that he was going to
close one of those circles that had been left open many years.

In the unwelcome memory he was in Dallas in a tavern that
had girls dancing and wiggling like worms. The paperhanger
had come to sit down next to him.

"You're not drinking."

"Nope." He had not drunk then or later, not one of his
many faults. Alcohol was poison to him and he knew it.

"I've seen you around. Want to talk?"

Nothing had come of it that night or for the next half dozen
nights that they had talked. But then he had dreamed of the
stranger, the paperhanger, and he had known that a circle was
opening, that he was going to be part of it. In the dream he
was rowing the paperhanger on black water, taking him somewhere in the night. That was all. When the paperhanger got to
the point he had been edging up to for a couple of weeks,
Jack was already committed, already his accomplice.

When Franklin got around to telling him what they wanted
him to do, he grunted. He was already committed, already an
accomplice. The two ends of the loop were to join now, the
circle completed.

"I haven't changed," Drew said to Pat in his bedroom in
the Huysman house.

"You seem changed."

"Something's happening and I got sucked into it, not my
doing."

"You could have walked away from it."

"I don't think so."

He was at the door; she had crossed the bedroom to stand at the dresser where she was picking up and putting down his hairbrush. She pulled some hairs from it and looked for a wastebasket, deposited the hairs. "I think it's ostentatious to build a cultural center and name it after yourself," she said in a low voice, not looking at him, apparently looking instead for something else to tidy up. "And the big muddy dam is a boondoggle. I didn't think so at first, but . . ." She shrugged. She ran her hand over the bedspread which was already unwrinkled. "You're making it awfully hard, Drew."

"I don't know my role."

"I'm trying to say I was wrong. It isn't very easy. I was wrong." In a rush she went on. "And I was wrong about your books. It's important that you write them even if hardly anyone reads them."

He let out a whoop of laughter. She looked startled, then embarrassed.

"I didn't mean it the way it sounded."

"You know what I think?" She shook her head. "Too much talking gets in the way of sex. Can we go to bed now?"

"That's all you think of."

"Damn right." He pulled her to him and kissed her thoroughly. He undressed her the way he had always done and kissed each breast, lingered over the hard nipples, kissed her navel, not the deep pit it had once been, but deformed a little by pregnancy, quirky now. He found and kissed the two stretch marks and she gave up trying to get his clothes off him. The way she always had to.

They reexamined each other's body and murmured their findings.

"I'm sorry that you've lost weight."

"And you're perfect. You could sell skin like this."

"Eight . . . nine . . . ten . . ." she counted his ribs. "You're just as thin as you were when we met. Remember how you looked me over the first time?"

"No pig in a poke for me. Ah, what a hot little box!"

She caught her breath and closed her eyes. A moment later she discovered a gray hair in his bush of pubic hair and yanked it out.

He yowled and she giggled. "Don't yell! They'll think I'm killing you."

"And you are. Enough of this nonsense. Now you get it!" She said, "Sh. Don't talk."

And he didn't.

Later, drifting away, she thought this was how it had always been with them. They played, then got serious; their orgasms were explosive, and then they fell asleep wrapped in each other's arms. She thought of William, who believed she was frigid because she had dodged his bed for the last two months. That was all right, he had told her solemnly. He understood and would not make demands. He was romantic, not an animal, he had told her. She giggled softly, remembering something Drew had said very early, before they were married. This is the way I like to fall asleep, he had whispered, warm, wet, and stinky.

"What?" he asked sleepily.

"Nothing. I love you. I've always loved you and always will love you, even when we fight."

"Those are my lines."

"I know. They sounded so good I thought you should hear them, too. Good night, Drew."

On Thursday T.M. and Michelle arrived very early, and T.M. handed Drew a bulging envelope and looked relieved as soon as it was out of his hand. Irma was going out, T.M. driving her again, this time to deliver Julianna to the dirt road that led to the cabin Franklin and Jack Silver Fox were staying in, where she would collect the rented car. And Sherry was bursting with joy, Drew thought, eyeing his daughter who knew too much. She had taken one look at him, then a long look at her mother, and had flung herself into his arms laughing. Pat said she had better run around the block and burn off a little energy, but she said it with a soft smile. Julianna came down, ready to hide under Irma Huysman's feet in the Continental. She would retrieve Franklin's disguise and the car he had escaped in.

"You look like an Ethiopian princess," Drew said to her. Her hair, in tight curls close to her skull, made her facial bones more prominent looking than ever. She smiled broadly at him, and he added, "At least until you show your teeth."

She roared with laughter. "This man's fixing to get himself

strung up yet," she warned Pat. "I'd gag him if he was mine."

Pat was wearing her I-can't-do-a-thing-with-him expression.

Drew watched the Continental leave again and crossed his fingers. He knew Leon Lauder was in the area, and there were enough agents to raid Fort Knox, but what were they all doing? What was Lauder waiting for? Lisa volunteered to take Sherry out for a couple of hours, shopping, a movie in the mall, lunch. They left in Drew's car. Florence and Michelle were hard at work with the files. And Pat was doing something with Huysman's financial files at Mrs. Huysman's request. That left only Drew, he thought glumly, with nothing useful to keep busy with. At eleven Lauder came to visit.

"Leon," he said with genuine pleasure. "I'm glad to see you. Coffee? We might even have some ice cream. I could ask the cook."

"Nothing, thanks. I'd like a word with the kid who came here yesterday, if he's handy. Franklin Silver Fox."

Drew shook his head. "You must mean the hitchhiker Michelle and T.M. picked up. I think he left."

"Hitchhiker," Lauder said slowly. "Is that what he was?"

"That's right. Do you want to ask Michelle about him? She's working in the office. I'll call her."

"No need. I'll just go with you."

They went to the office. Michelle was at the computer; Florence was reading a printout that was many pages long, still joined at the folds. At a card table Pat was reading a separate printout, making notes as she worked.

"Busy little bees, aren't they?" Drew commented. "Michelle, this is Mr. Lauder of the Secret Service. He wants to know about the hitchhiker you picked up yesterday." Bless her, he thought; she hardly even flinched.

"What about him?" she asked, her hands on the keyboard out of sight.

"Where did you pick him up, miss?"

"I'm sorry," Drew murmured. "It's Mrs. Michelle Mathews and this is Ms. Stevens and Dr. Charmody. Mr. Leon Lauder, ladies."

Leon was feeling more and more uncomfortable, but the buzz that was not audible kept going on in his head. He looked them over, noticed the reams of papers, printouts, open files. They were working, that was evident. But Stevens? What was she working on here? She worked for Senator Wiley. He felt as if he had been dumped into a swamp. He cleared his throat and repeated his question to Michelle. "Where did you pick him up, Mrs. Mathews?"

"I don't know exactly. On the road between our house in Harmony and here."

So why was she so nervous, Leon Lauder wondered. She was young, sometimes that was reason enough. He sighed. "What did he say when you stopped for him?"

"Just could we give him a lift."

"Where was he going?"

"He didn't say."

"Why did you bring him here, then?"

"We thought there might be jobs for all of us."

"He was looking for a job? Doing what?"

"I don't know."

He chewed on his lower lip, studying her. He could take her in, and he would get something out of her, find out what was making her so nervous, but then what? Abruptly he said to Drew," I don't have a search warrant, but I could get one. Would it be possible to have a look around the house?"

Drew shook his head regretfully. "Leon, as much as I want to help you, that is not possible. It isn't my house, you know. I can't let just anyone come in and look around. You'll have to ask Mrs. Huysman."

"Mind if I wait for her, then?"

"Not a bit," Drew said cheerfully. "But not in here. The ladies have work to do and we're in the way. Let's go out on the sun porch and have that coffee. I want some even if you don't."

Lauder asked a few more questions. What time had Franklin left? No one had noticed. Did he say where he was going? No. He followed Drew to the porch. He paused long enough in the kitchen to ask the cook the same questions. She was more hostile than anyone else had been, with the same information.

"You know," he said, settling himself, "it really doesn't make much sense. A strange black kid comes in and no one pays any attention to him? No one notices when he leaves. You'd think with a house full of expensive stuff like this, they'd be more careful." Even the porch had expensive vases and pots, all with blooming plants. He doubted if all the dishes in his house cost as much as a single vase here.

"I certainly would be," Drew said emphatically. "Ah, Marion, thank you. Do you have any ice cream? Vanilla or mocha or chocolate. For Mr. Lauder."

"Ice cream?"

"Yes. Just not strawberry. He puts it in his coffee."

"That's all right," Leon Lauder said hastily. "That looks fine just the way it is. Thanks."

"Ice cream!" Marion cast a searching glance over him and then marched away, shaking her head.

"Thanks," Lauder said sourly to Drew.

Drew grinned and poured for them both.

After a minute of silence, Lauder said, "Pretty porch, isn't it? Nice geraniums."

"Very nice. You like flowers?"

Leon Lauder started to talk about his roses. Last night he had made a list of people he could give his rose bushes to, and there had not been many. "Not many people care about flowers anymore," he said to Drew. "A shame. Would help people who have stress, tension. It's therapeutic to work with plants."

"Not much room in most city apartments," Drew commented, puzzled and pleased by this side of his old friend Leon Lauder.

"That's the problem right there," Leon agreed. "And people get too busy, those with yards. Call in the professional landscaper, get whatever takes the least amount of care and be done with it. A shame."

They chatted until Irma Huysman returned with T.M. She looked at Leon Lauder as if he might be carrying a loathsome disease.

"He's a what?" she asked Drew.

"A Secret Service agent, ma'am. He's looking for someone."

"On my porch? How ridiculous." She turned away to leave them.

"Mrs. Huysman," Leon Lauder said politely, "we know the man entered your house, and we did not see him leave it again. Franklin Silver Fox, a black man aged twenty-four or so."

"He left at about the same time I did yesterday," she said haughtily. "I saw him go. He is no longer here, Mr. Lauder.

And of course I shall not give permission for anyone to search my house. If you have further questions, my attorney is Malcolm Letterman. Good day, sir.''

When she was gone, Drew shrugged with sympathy. "Sorry."

"Yeah. Way it goes. What a woman! Think anyone on God's earth would dare cross her?"

"Not me," Drew said promptly.

"I'll be on my way. See you around, Mr. Lancaster."

"Drew, please. Leon, I feel that we're becoming friends, all this coffee that's flowed between us should mean something."

Suddenly Leon Lauder grinned and held out his hand. "Drew," he said pleasantly, shaking hands with him, "nothing would please me more than to nail you on a counterfeiting charge. Know what I mean? Good day, sir."

They both laughed, but Drew had an uneasy feeling that Leon was telling him the absolute truth, which, considering the treatment everyone in the house had given him, was incredible.

When Julianna returned late that afternoon dressed in her flamboyant clothes and Afro, she had a message from Franklin. He wanted Pat to deliver a few things to the castle the next morning. "He wants the funny money, some of it anyway. And half a dozen reefers. I told him I would bring them, if I'm the one going to the hospital, but I'm not the one going up there. You are, honey." he looked at Pat with an unreadable expression.

Pat paled a little and nodded. "Where can we get the marijuana?"

Julianna showed her teeth again in a broad smile. "Florence and I will handle that. In a college town that shouldn't be any trouble at all. Not at all."

TWENTY-SIX

Drew looked from Michelle to Lisa uneasily. Michelle was at the computer, Lisa in a chair at her side with her eyes closed. It was twenty minutes after ten on Thursday night. Michelle's gaze was riveted on the monitor.

Pat moved closer to Drew, reached for his hand, and held it tightly.

Lisa did not move, apparently was oblivious of everyone in the office. She was "with" Franklin in a small rowboat at the bottom of the bluff that prevented entry to the castle on two sides. In the hospital Claude Dohemy was reviewing data, his plans for the experiment coming up in the morning. He had been at it for nearly an hour.

Florence and Julianna were watching both young women with absorption. Suddenly the printer made its throat-clearing noise and started to print.

"He's making six copies," Michelle said. "A handout for tomorrow. I'll make one for us."

The printer zipped back and forth, one page, two, three. It stopped. Drew thought of all the computers out there, accessible, open to anyone with the knowhow to enter, mutable data, no secrets, shared information without anyone's knowing with whom it was being shared or for what purpose. His gaze did not leave Lisa, who had not yet moved. And these young people, he thought with disquietude, what were they? How had they been changed, for what purpose? Stanley Huysman had expressed no purpose beyond proving that he could do it, but Dohemy? Huysman had used his own sperm to impregnate women up until twelve years ago, and since then there had not been any new altered children? Why not? The information Michelle had gotten from the files indicated that Dohemy

had tried repeatedly to replicate Huysman's work and failed.
He was still trying and failing. Huysman's experiments with
the children as they grew up had been subtle, and according
to Julianna and Florence, indisputable. He had proven his
theory. Dohemy's planned experiment was not at all subtle,
could not be as subtle as those of the past because this time he
was out to convince nonscientists of the validity of the work.
A dramatic demonstration was needed for his purposes.

"He's through," Michelle said quietly.

Drew watched Lisa. She did not move, but seemed somehow to withdraw even more. Her hands were closed in her
lap. Slowly they opened and relaxed.

"Franklin's starting up the cliff," she said. No one else
spoke. "Now," she said after several minutes.

Michelle's hands moved over the keyboard. "The power's
off. I think."

"He's at the fence. Touched it with a tool, nothing. He's
cutting it. Going through. Okay."

Michelle nodded and touched the keys again. Power had
been restored.

Drew wiped his forehead. He could feel sweat trickling
down his back, under his arms. Pat was staring at Lisa; her
hand clutching Drew's was so tight her nails were cutting
him. He did not try to release it.

Every day since this trio had first met, this . . . bond,
whatever it was, had strengthened, deepened. It was uncanny
and frightening, he thought, and he knew what Dohemy had
to sell. If they could do this, merge this way, and if they
could be controlled, forced to perform on command . . . He
thought of the phrase Dohemy had used in one of his reports:
They are ready to be utilized.

Jack Silver Fox watched Franklin vanish into the darkness
at the top of the bluff. More and more over the past two
weeks his thoughts had roamed in and out of the past. He
recalled the stories his mother had told when he was a boy,
many of them to do with abilities the people had once had and
lost. She had not called them powers and neither did he.
Abilities. Franklin had abilities, he had decided days ago. His
true grandson, after all. As a child he had believed all her
stories, as a young man none of them, and here he was
coming full cycle, he thought. He was an old man, getting

senile, ready to believe in magic again, welcoming magic into
his life, not questioning a thing. He nodded in the darkness.
Not questioning a thing. Franklin asked him to do a job, and,
old man or not, he would do it, and one day he would have
an explanation.

He sat without movement, waiting for the man who would
be lowered down the cliff. He would take him to a safe place,
make certain he was delivered there, and then come back and
wait for Franklin. A faint smile creased his face. It pleased
him that Franklin had asked for his help, that Franklin had not
doubted that he could do what was asked of him. He waited.

In the office the group waited. No one knew how long Lisa
could stay with Franklin. None of these three had tried this
before. She looked asleep. Not strained, not wet with sweat
as Drew was, just relaxed with her eyes closed, resting. They
could not leave the power off for an extended period; the
guards checked it periodically.

Drew was getting cramped from sitting without movement.
He eased his legs outs, stretching. Behind him, out of his line
of sight, he heard T.M. move. A wave of pity swept him.
T.M. was married to one of them, crazy with love for her;
what was the thinking of this new union that was so much
deeper than anything he could share with Michelle?

"Now," Lisa said without opening her eyes.

Michelle's hands moved over the keyboard.

Sorbies was out, Drew thought. On his way down the
cliff, dangling over the water, helpless. He wished he could
see the expression on Arnie Sorbies's face when he got a
glimpse of his benefactor tonight.

Now Franklin had his job to do inside the laboratory:
rewire the experimental equipment, rewire the monitors.

The kids could have got out of that place at any time, he
thought, but the time had not been right until now. They had
waited to get out in a certain way, not as fugitives to be
hunted down, at risk for years to come. They wanted this
phase over with, wanted to get on with the next phase, and he
did not have a glimmer about what that next phase would be.
He studied Lisa, then Michelle, trying to fathom what it was
like to be them, failing to come up with anything. They were
both pretty, all-American girl types, to all appearances their

heads filled with marshmallow cream, and yet what he had just seen them do had made him break out in a cold sweat.

Lisa glanced at him and smiled her lovely, helpless, little girl smile. "We can all relax," she said. "It's going to take him a couple of hours to get everything fixed. The others up there will watch our for the guards and the doctor."

"I want a drink," Drew said, getting to his feet. "Orders being taken now."

Drinks, coffee, cookies, cheese, it was like halftime at a ball game, he thought, making mental notes of what they all wanted. Pat was at the door.

"I'll help you," she said.

In the hallway she stopped and faced him. "Drew, I'm frightened. Are we doing the right thing? What did he do to those children?"

He took her into his arms and held her. "We're doing what we have to do," he murmured, and he did not even pretend to know at this moment if it was the right thing or not.

Arnie Sorbies had been in his room reading when Rachel, one of the older teenaged girls, came for him. "It's time for you to leave here," she said, smiling.

"Right."

"Mr. Lancaster has a way to get you out," she said. "Come on."

Lancaster? Slowly he got to his feet. She helped him, handed him his cane.

"We have to be quiet," she said. She looked up and down the hallway, then motioned for him. They left the building without seeing anyone, and outside Mike joined them. And now they were going to smuggle him out of prison. They stopped in the deep shadows of trees when the guard on patrol passed, and then continued. They went to the fence where an opening had been cut. He scowled.

"You kids know I'm not in much shape for mountain climbing," he whispered hoarsely.

Suddenly, kids seemed to appear out of nowhere. They got a rope under his arms, his good foot in a loop, and over the side he went. He bumped into the cliff until he managed to ward himself from it with one hand, clinging to the rope with the other. And then he was· down, and strong hands were guiding him into a boat; the rope came down around him, and the other man in the boat began to row. There was a strange rumbling sound that he only gradually realized was quiet laughter.

"I'll be goddamned!" he said under his breath. "Jack Silver Fox! I'll be damned." He began to laugh.

"This is all so grandiose," Florence said, pointing to the handout Dohemy had printed, "that without a corroborative demonstration, he will just look crazy. No scientist would swallow any of these claims. It's exactly what Huysman was claiming years ago with the chimps. They laughed at him then; they'll laugh at Dohemy now."

Drew glanced at Julianna, who nodded vigorously. "I don't believe a word of it myself," she said with a shrug. "Not even after what I've been seeing."

"You've got the files fixed?" he asked.

Julianna grinned at Florence, who said gravely, "The files are fixed."

Drew said, "You're showing your teeth again," and Julianna began to laugh.

"You wouldn't believe what a mess he's going to find in those files. Michelle is one clever little girl. She planted a time bomb. As soon as the file is activated, it turns into garbage, starting Friday morning. This morning. And every time his name is mentioned, it's expanded until it takes almost a whole line all by itself. It's beautiful."

Florence raised her eyebrows, as if to say she knew nothing about any of that. He decided he did not want these women out for his scalp.

Nothing was happening at the moment in the office. Lisa was waiting for Franklin to leave the castle. Michelle was at the computer, also waiting. T.M. was at her side, holding her hand. The others had scattered to the kitchen, the bathrooms. It was after two in the morning.

"Drew, after all this is over, then what?" Julianna asked. "I want to work with those kids, if they'll let me."

"What about your degree?"

She snorted. "I may write a new physics book one day. I don't think I'll miss much by not going back right now. I want to stay with those kids."

"Me too," Florence said. "They're going to need help, no

matter what they're capable of. And no more outsiders if we can keep them out.''

This too? he wondered: Was all this part of the plan? To have helpers demanding access to them, volunteering to give up what lives they had to do this? Thank God, he thought, he was not a scientist.

Pat came to the door to say Lisa was with Franklin again, he was leaving the hospital. They all returned to the office, but this part did not take long. Very soon Lisa opened her eyes and said that Franklin was across the river. She yawned and stretched.

"I'm going to bed. Good heavens! It's after two. I told Sherry I'd take her swimming today."

Drew watched her closely. She looked no different than any other girl, he thought again. Prettier than most. And Sherry loved her madly. He felt as if the Lisa he had met that day by the road was gone forever; a stranger had taken her place here. She waved good night to them all and went upstairs. Tonight she was sleeping in Sherry's room; tonight everyone was staying, sleeping all over the house, even on the rollable rug in the living room. At least, he corrected himself, on the couch very near the rollable rug. He remembered his invitation to Florence to test the softness of the rug, and he sighed.

When he and Pat went to bed, they did not talk, but made love with an intensity that was startling, and he knew it was because she was afraid. And he was afraid. They were all aliens, he thought, every one of them.

TWENTY-SEVEN

And now, Drew thought a few hours later, the last act was about to begin. He hugged Julianna and kissed her forehead. "Give 'em hell, tiger," he murmured. She was sober this morning. He turned to Pat, who was pale and determined.

"You'll be careful," he said, not quite turning it into a question.

She nodded. "And you." She was studying his face, as if memorizing it. "If anything goes wrong . . ."

"I'll end up in the pokey," he finished. "But it won't. With any luck I'll see you in the castle in a couple of hours." He kissed her, and the kiss turned out to be hard and fierce and demanding. She caught her breath when it ended.

"I love you," she whispered. "Later."

"Later."

Pat drove the staff car. It was a bright hot morning with no wind. The forecast was for afternoon thundershowers, but there was no sign of a weather disturbance now. She caught herself speeding and made an effort to keep under the limit. It would not do, she kept thinking, to be stopped for anything this morning. She was carrying counterfeit money in one envelope, and a dozen marijuana cigarettes in another. What would her father say if she was hauled in and searched? And William. What would he say? She wanted to laugh and recognized that as a sign of her nervousness.

What she did not want to do, she realized, was think too hard about what Lisa had done the night before. She shivered and adjusted the air-conditioning, knowing it had nothing to do with her chill. She could not quite think how she had become involved with all this. She had come to Princeton to collect Sherry and to do what? It seemed so long ago that the memory had blurred. When she had gone through those files in William's office, she had not planned on telling Drew, she remembered. She had been shocked at the extent of the human experimentation William's father had backed and perhaps even more shocked that William saw it as a political weapon. And then she had become so involved that this morning she was carrying funny money and dope and had no idea what the kids up there would do with either.

She and Drew would leave as soon as all this ended, she told herself resolutely. They would leave, she said again under her breath.

It was fifteen minutes before nine when she was admitted to the hospital grounds. She drove to the front entrance and parked and was met by Claude Dohemy.

"Ms. Stevens, how good to have you with us this morning. It is gratifying that Senator Wiley is interested in this project. I trust you will find our little demonstration edifying. I'm Claude Dohemy."

He talked her out of the car and took her hand in his for what turned out to be slightly too long a time. She withdrew her hand with a jerk, and he said, "Forgive me. I was not expecting a senatorial aide to be so . . . so young and pretty. Won't you come in?"

The grounds looked deserted; no children were in sight, no help of any sort. Dohemy led her into a large comfortable office with leather couches and chairs. There was coffee service on a long conference table with a platter of pastries under a plastic cover.

"Are you alone here?" she asked then.

"Of course not. We have a staff of twenty just to run the hospital itself, and the kitchen help and grounds keepers, they add up to another twenty-five. In the summer, naturally, we don't hold classes for the children. They need a vacation too."

"You have assistants for the scientific work you're conducting here?"

He cocked his head, listening. "Ah, another car is coming now. That will be Walkman Perry and . . . Mr. Brown, I believe. If you'll excuse me, I'll just greet them. Please help yourself to coffee."

She poured coffee and walked around the office, looking

out the various windows. There was a tennis court, a swimming pool. All empty. Like a summer camp waiting for the first busload of campers. Just like Drew said, a summer camp. Dohemy entered with Walkman Perry, whom she knew, and a man she did not know. Military, she thought. Too stiff not to be military.

"Pat! Good to see you," Perry said, but he did not look at all pleased to see her. His handshake was limp. "This is Wayne Brown. Another observer. Ms. Stevens from Senator Wiley's staff." Wayne Brown shook hands as if they had agreed to a contest. She pulled her hand free a second time.

"I was just asking Dr. Dohemy about his help," she said. "Are they all scientists, doctors, nurses? What?"

"I have a few graduate students," he said. "This is rather like an internship for them. And a few medical people on a regular basis. You'll met several of them shortly. Gentlemen, please help yourselves to coffee, a snack. Before we begin I should brief you on what to expect."

He mentioned Huysman a few times, then it was "we" and that ended very soon, and it was "I." Pat kept her gaze on the windows, listening to him.

"I saw immediately what this would mean militarily. Industrially. At the bargaining table between any adversaries. Imagine, if you can, gentlemen, and, ah, Ms. Stevens, experiencing what someone else is feeling, having every image in your head accessible instantly to another human being no matter how distant! That is what I will demonstrate in just a few minutes."

A head popped into sight outside the window. A young boy stuck out his tongue at the group in the room. Dohemy's back was to the window, but Walkman Perry and Mr. Brown and Pat were all facing it. She glanced at Walkman Perry and raised her eyebrows. He scowled. The boy at the window began to lick the glass.

"What we'll do is let one of you administer the shock at random intervals, just when you feel like it," Dohemy said. He laughed. "And we'll watch the second subject in the observation room, and meanwhile your colleagues in the motel outside of Princeton will watch the subjects there. They will be visible to us through closed circuit television. That's all, just watch them and see what happens." He laughed again. He was nervous, Pat thought, and decided it was time to ask a few more questions.

"I looked up this hospital," she said briskly. "It is described as a home for mentally disturbed youngsters. How disturbed are they?" A second person had appeared at the window, a teenaged girl who was pulling the hair of the boy, who contorted his face in an expression of agony. He turned and bit her and she began to pummel him; they both sank out of sight.

"They are the best adjusted young people I've ever seen," Dohemy said in a tone that was sepulchral. "What we did to them has turned them into perhaps the first really sane people, that is, since Adam and Eve." He glanced swiftly from Brown to Perry, as if to gauge their religious proclivities.

"Sane!" Pat exclaimed and shook her head. Through the windows she could see a young man in his early twenties, she thought, stark naked, pissing against a tree.

Deliberately she turned away from the window. "I think you need more attendants in this institution."

Dohemy swiveled and started; he jerked out of his chair, all color gone from his face. He looked as if he had been hit in the solar plexus. He ran to the door, remembered his guests and muttered something, dashed out. Moments later he appeared outside the window with a burly man at his side. The man took the naked youth by the arm and vanished with him. Pat's lips tightened.

"Sane," she muttered to Perry. "Do you suppose the doctor is sane?"

Perry looked disquieted. Brown was stiffer than ever and frowning thoughtfully. Dohemy returned and said in a rather strained voice, "I don't know what's come over them. They must sense something important is about to happen. If you agree, I think we should get on with it." A tic spasmed in his cheek.

Drew smiled genially at Leon Lauder in his motel headquarters. "But, Leon," he said, "I thought this was exactly what you wanted me to do at the first sign of hanky-panky with money. I found it, or rather Pat found it, in my pocket and I came straight over here. Or came as soon as I could."

Leon Lauder, felt his stomach tightening, felt his breakfast turn leaden when all efforts at digestion stopped. The two bills on his table were incomplete, no serial numbers. They had come from the Artist's press.

"Tell me again," he said mildly, denying the knot that had formed in his stomach, the fury that was lodged just behind his eyes.

"When I was at the hospital the other day one of the kids ran up to me and whispered for me to get him some dope. He was all over me, you know the way kids can do that, hands everywhere at once. I got rid of him and never gave it another thought until this morning when Pat was going through my pockets and found the bills. I was putting them in an envelope to send back to the doctor at the hospital when I saw that there was something suspicious about them, and I instantly thought of you."

He was lying. Leon Lauder knew it without a doubt. But why? Now what was he up to? He had to follow it up, he knew, and that was the cause of the anger that was twisting his brain, a headache in the making.

"And Ms. Stevens didn't notice that they were counterfeit?"

"I don't think she even looked at them. They were wadded up, for one thing, not a lot, but enough that the numbers or lack of numbers wouldn't have been noticeable."

If those bills had been wadded up even one day, let alone two or three, he'd eat them, Lauder thought, and studied Drew Lancaster's face, wondering why he was lying, why he was risking a federal rap. Pat Stevens would not have anything to do with counterfeiting, he knew, and Mrs. Huysman? It was a laugh, he had told Bob Samson. It was. But Lancaster? He would get mixed up with it for no other reason than that he was bored. But why this now? He got to his feet. "What's going on up there this morning?"

"The hospital? Damned if I know. Pat said something about a demonstration. Dohemy is up for new funding or something like that, I think. That place must be expensive as hell to run."

"Let's go see what they're doing."

"Me too?"

"Someone has to point out the kid who stuck the money in your pocket. Isn't that right?"

Drew sighed. "I suppose."

And Leon Lauder had the sinking feeling that this was exactly what Lancaster had been counting on.

TWENTY-EIGHT

Claude Dohemy had decided that it was time for the project to come under government sponsorship openly. Under certain conditions. He would administer the whole thing. No more lab work, no more drudgery trying to modify sperm in the way that Huysman had done. He wanted to direct an army of bright young biddable scientists. It would go on record as being the Dohemy Project, naturally, and one of those new scientists would find the method Huysman had developed, and they would be off and running.

He was nervous; something was already going wrong, and he had not even taken his observers to the laboratories yet. How the hell had those kids gotten outside? They were supposed to be locked in the dorm wing. Ever since Huysman's stroke the kids had been different. He was uneasy now when they were in the same room with him; he felt as if they were watching him, measuring him in a way that made him want to look over his shoulder often. Not just uneasy, he admitted, frightened, scared to death of them. They were inhuman in a way he could not fathom. They knew things they could not have learned in any way he could discover, yet they knew. And, worse of all, they knew he feared them. They showed him none of the acceptance they had granted Huysman, but then, he thought savagely, Huysman had been a fool. He had not seen any use for them; he just wanted to produce them, and when he stopped producing them, he was content to watch them and plan new and elaborate psychological tests for them. And, paranoid fool that he had been, Huysman had trusted no one with the details of the methods he used to alter the sperm. What few notes he had made were garbage, undecipherable.

That did not matter, he had decided. There was living proof that Huysman had accomplished his goal, and that proof was enough. It was all scientists needed: the knowledge that something was possible. If the Russians had done this and word got back to the United States government, there would be a new Manhattan Project, and damn the expense. That was what he wanted: his own Manhattan Project, his own army of scientists working around the clock, searching for the answer. After he got that much, he thought often, he would never have to see those kids again as long as he lived. He wanted that more than almost anything else.

It pleased him that Senator Wiley had sent an observer also. Let the two senators compete for the honor of sponsorship. That could do nothing but help his cause. He led his small group down the stairs to the basement laboratories. Ms. Stevens spotted the women's room and excused herself, the others went into the men's room, and finally everyone was ready to settle down and start.

"Periodically," Dohemy said then, "I have taken the children out on field trips. Always to something very unique. Then we tested all of them and again and again came up with the same imagery from those who had not gone on the trip. We repeated this experiment many times, too many possibly. It became very difficult to find new things." He laughed nervously again. "In fact, it is very hard to test them at all, since the older ones by now know so much and what they know is accessible to the younger ones. The test I have devised for today is new for them. They are naive subjects for today, but by tomorrow . . . Well, I have to be creatively inventive, as you can understand."

Pat yawned and looked at her watch pointedly. "Perhaps we could have documentation about those 'very unique' tests and the results?" She had left the bogus money and the marijuana in the rest room, as Franklin had instructed, but she did not see how any of the inmates here could retrieve them.

"Of course. I'll have some printouts made while we conduct our little test in here." He lifted a telephone and asked someone to run off copies of test files one and two.

"Now, as you'll notice, we have two windows in the room, to your left and to the right," he said after hanging up. He raised the blinds by pushing a button on his desk. "The windows are one-way glass, standard in testing procedures, as

you all know. In the room on the right there is a television set
and a joystick. Our subject will play a video game in there.
And in the room to the left there is a table with drawing
materials. In there a subject will be asked to draw whatever
comes into his head.'' He looked from one to the other of the
observers intently. ''The children are accustomed to testing
and will consider this just a routine day, believe me. Now,
here is a dial calibrated from one to ten. When this dial is
activated an electric current will flow through the joystick and
give our subject a mild shock. I ask you to direct your
attention at the time to the subject in the other room. We will
have electrodes attached to his head and arm, so we can
record his reactions precisely—heartbeat, respiration, blood
pressure, that sort of thing. That data will be made available
to you also. But the evidence of your own eyes will be the
most important data you will receive today. You'll be able to
see the medical reports being recorded in the oscilloscope
here.'' He pointed to the monitor that was not yet turned on.

''How high up are we supposed to turn this thing?'' Walkman
Perry asked, touching the dial for the electric shock.

''One or two will be quite sufficient.''

''Then why is it calibrated that high?'' Pat demanded. ''Is
it dangerous?''

''Ms. Stevens, scientists are not in the habit of damaging
their subjects, I assure you.''

''Then why is it set to go to ten?''

''It's the same dial we use for a number of other experiments where we need higher numbers. I saw no point in
having a new piece of equipment made for this one.'' He said
this with the kind of slickness that Pat had come to recognize
as the way certain men talked to women about things they
were thought incapable of understanding.

''I'll just turn on the television monitor here. Ah, there
they are—''

He stopped abruptly. Two little girls were visible on the
screen in the motel room. One was on her hands and knees,
crying; the other was sitting on the floor, her legs straight out.
She was staring at the wall. A very pretty dark-haired woman
was pulling at the crying child, trying to make her stand up.

''What the hell . . . ?'' Dohemy muttered and picked up
the phone, started to dial.

Pat walked to the door. ''I think I've seen all I want.''

Dohemy banged down the phone and turned off the monitor angrily. "I don't know what happened at that end," he said in a furious voice. "But it doesn't really matter. The real experiment is here. Let's get on with it."

He pressed another button on his desk. The doors to the other two rooms opened and a little girl was led to the room with the television set. At her side was a woman in a white lab coat.

"She's just a child!" Pat cried indignantly. "You can't give a little child electric shocks!"

"It won't hurt her, Ms. Stevens," Dohemy said, sounding almost desperate now.

The little girl was slouching, dragging her feet. She was sucking her thumb. In the other room a male attendant had led another child, a boy, to the table with the papers and crayon and markers. The boy began to throw them.

"Goddamn it!" Dohemy muttered. "Excuse me a moment, please" He left his observers and entered the room with the boy, who shrank back from him fearfully.

"I've had just about enough," Pat said in a flat hard tone. "That man is insane and those kids are sick. This is the ugliest thing I've ever seen."

Perry nodded. He looked disgusted. Wayne Brown had said nothing, still said nothing, but he looked stiffer and more military than ever. Now, when he glanced at Perry, his lips were practically invisible.

Dohemy got the boy seated, the materials in place in front of him, and attached the electrode wires to a plug. He returned to the observation room.

"It's like I said," he muttered. "It gets harder and harder to test them. I'll turn on his monitor now and we can start. You can see that Janey is starting to play the video game."

He turned on the monitor and the lines peaked wildly.

"Christ!" He adjusted knobs. The lines continued to peak.

"He's terrified!" Pat said, moving closer to the window.

Janey was lethargically moving a clown on the television monitor. A bear was chasing the clown. It caught the clown over and over. Janey did not seem to mind.

With a grunt Brown suddenly reached out and turned the dial to two. Janey dropped her hand from the joystick and stuck her thumb in her mouth again. The boy was drawing something, holding a crayon the way an infant does in his fist. His lines on the oscilloscope continued to peak, possibly somewhat less wildly than before. Pat glanced at Dohemy, who was looking from one child to the other in disbelief. The woman with Janey forced her hand on the joystick again.

Dohemy nodded to Brown who turned the dial again, this time to three. Janey cried out and flung the joystick away from her. The boy kept on making childish heavy marks with no apparent control. His lines on the monitor did not change.

"They got wind of this somehow," Dohemy said savagely. "They're putting on an act." Sweat was beading on his forehead; a trickle ran erratically down one cheek.

He reached for the dial and as soon as the woman with Janey got her hand on the stick again, he twisted the dial up to six, seven, then ten. Janey screamed and arched her back, screaming. No sound reached the observers, and that somehow made it even worse.

Pat ran to the door. "This is insane! You're torturing that child! I'll see that this place is shut down from one end to the other! I insist that you stop this torture this minute of I'll call the police and stop it myself!"

Beyond the men in the room she could see through the window where the little boy was drawing. He had not reacted to anything.

"I tell you they're pretending! They're faking it, putting on an act! They found out about the test somehow and they're putting on an act!"

She wrenched the door open and stamped out into the hall, closely followed by Walkman Perry. At the far end of the corridor she saw Drew with three other men. She let out a long breath.

They waited in the large comfortable office where fresh coffee had been served and their printouts were waiting for them. An agent stood by the window. Pat studiously avoided looking at Dohemy. She was busy writing in a notebook. Drew was reading a thick book on physiology. Perry and Brown had looked over the printouts of earlier experiments. Perry's face had turned red; Brown had carefully folded his paper and put it in his breast pocket, all without a glance at Dohemy. They had had a whispered consultation, and now they were both silent, brooding. Dohemy's face was like wax, shiny and white; his gaze was wild.

Finally Leon Lauder entered the room with Bob Samson. He sat down at the desk and surveyed them all. He sighed.

"Dr. Dohemy, are your patients ever allowed to leave here unaccompanied?"

"No. Never."

"I see. What about company? Do they have visitors? Family? Relatives?"

"No. They are all orphans. They have no family or friends."

"Are they allowed in the offices?"

Dohemy shook his head emphatically.

Leon Lauder sighed again. "This little demonstration you had set up today. Will you tell me exactly what you and your guests did? I don't mean the demonstration itself. Your physical movements, actions from the time you arrived."

Dohemy moistened his lips. "I really don't understand what this is all about, Mr. Lauder. I want to cooperate, but perhaps I should contact my attorney first."

Drew stood up suddenly. "That's what you were doing? Demonstrating your discovery? Leon, this man is one of the really original thinkers. He told me about this discovery, and to be truthful, I doubted him. An enzyme that allows people to digest grass! Isn't that remarkable? Was that the demonstration?"

"That was a joke!" Dohemy practically screamed. "I told him that to get rid of him," he said, turning to Perry Walkman, Wayne Brown, allowing his gaze to remain finally on Pat, pleading. "You can see that this man is irresponsible. I wouldn't tell him anything about my actual work. I just wanted to get rid of him."

"Oh dear," Drew murmured. "I've done it, haven't I? Let the cat out of the bag for sure. I said I wouldn't reveal his discovery. I'm sure these people will all go along with that, Doctor," he said.

"What are you doing here? How did you get in again? I want an attorney."

"I'll tell you what I did," Pat said sharply. "He met me at my car and brought me to this office. I had coffee. Then Mr. Perry and Mr. Brown came and we all went downstairs to the laboratories. I used the ladies' room in the basement. I was just leaving the laboratory when you arrived."

Lauder nodded and glanced at Walkman Perry who hastened to describe his movements. Brown did also. Lauder asked both men to give their names and addresses to his assistant and said they could leave afterward. He nodded to Pat. "You also, Ms. Stevens. We have your address. I may ask all of you for a statement a little later."

Drew stood up, Lauder waved him down again. Pat nodded to all of them in the room and walked out stiffly, Perry and Brown followed. None of them looked at Dohemy.

"Will someone please tell me what in hell is going on?" Dohemy demanded as soon as the three observers had left.

Lauder reached out his hand and his assistant gave him a large manila envelope. Lauder emptied it onto the desk. There were twenty-dollar bills, and there were marijuana joints. He surveyed them moodily. Without looking at Dohemy he said, "I have a few questions to ask you, Doctor. Is there someplace where Mr. Lancaster can wait in comfort?"

After Drew had been escorted out to the terrace, Lauder said, "Dr. Dohemy, you may, of course, call your attorney. But tell me, could any of these visitors, say in the past ten days or so, have mingled with your patients? Lancaster, for instance?"

For a moment Dohemy's face lighted with hope. Would anyone back him up if he said yes? Not unless he could have a word with them first. Vera? His lips tightened. After her betrayal today, after the way she had fouled up in the motel . . . He suddenly remembered the other observers who were on their way now to the hospital.

"Dr. Dohemy!" Lancaster said sharply. "Lancaster told me you keep your patients totally isolated, quarantined practically. Is that right?"

"Yes. Yes. It's the treatment—" He thought of the kids fighting under the windows, Jud out there in plain sight naked. How had they got out? How? Albert, he realized with rage. Albert must have conspired with them, was out to undermine him, get him off the project. And Vera! They were in it together, Albert and Vera! With a great effort he reined in his chaotic thoughts and tried to concentrate on the question this agent had asked. The congressional aides had seen the kids; would one of them add that to the report? He moistened his lips. "Sometimes one or another of them goes out of bounds, but only for a few seconds at the very most. They're under constant supervision. As are all guests."

Lauder sighed. "Will you show me where you and your observers were this morning, please?"

"My lawyer first," Dohemy said, almost pleading. Lauder nodded and he used the telephone and spoke briefly. He then led Lauder to the basement where he watched the agent examine the doors, feel the walls, and all at once he knew he had been right during the test. The kids had staged everything. They had known exactly how to fake everything. They could go wherever they wanted, do what they wanted. They had known his plans, the test procedures. Watching him, plotting. If Albert had helped them, and now he doubted that, it was because they had forced his help.

"They didn't need outside help," he muttered. "They did it themselves."

"Who, Doctor? Did what?"

"They're dangerous! Listen to me, they are dangerous. Oh, my god! The files!"

"Dr. Dohemy, are you all right? What are you talking about?"

"They've been at the files. They knew about the dial," he whispered. "That has to be it." His face became more ashen; he looked about wildly. "They can go anywhere they want, do anything!"

One of Lauder's men appeared; there was a phone call from the gate. Other congressional aides were there, and a woman from the hospital with two children.

"Where's a phone down here?" Lauder snapped.

Dohemy pointed, and Lauder went into the room the observers had used.

"I'll be in my office next door," Dohemy said and walked away stiffly, thinking, they knew about the test, knew about the dial, the joystick, the settings: high enough to convulse Janey, to induce electroshock trauma in her as well as the other three children, maybe a few of them in the dorm wing. No one had known; this test would have told them. It wouldn't have damaged anyone, he said under his breath. Not really. Not with any permanent damage. No one would have cranked the dial up all the way, not if things had been working properly. He turned his computer monitor on, called one of the files onto the screen, and when he saw it, he moaned. They knew! They had got into the files somehow! How had they learned to do that? They could go wherever they wanted, whenever they wanted . . .

Drew sat on the terrace in the back of the building and watched the kids in the swimming pool. When he had come out, none of them had been around; then they appeared as if on cue. They were all good-looking, well built, healthy. A boy went off the high dive in a graceful back flip and made hardly a ripple when he landed in the water. Drew closed his eyes.

He roused from a doze when he heard a sharp report. He started from his chair, then became motionless. Half a dozen of the kids were also motionless with a stiffness that looked unnatural. Suddenly they all began to move again, some going back into the pool, two of them walking away in conversation. One who remained looked directly at Drew. His expression was remote and cold, and he no longer looked like a boy but like someone who had lived for a very long time, had seen too much of everything. His expression was wise and chillingly remorseless. Slowly Drew leaned back in his chair; the boy turned away.

Hours later when Lauder came for him, he was there with his eyes closed, but no longer dozing, no longer in any danger of falling asleep for even a second.

"I'll take you back to town," Lauder said woodenly. "You know about Dohemy?"

"I head the shot, all the commotion. Was that . . . ?"

"We were in the basement office. Crazy business. He went in the john and blew off the top of his head. Who would have thought he'd have a gun? For what?" He looked tired and old, as if he already had accepted the responsibility, the consequences. "Let's go."

They did not need him here, Lauder knew. The local police were handling Dohemy's death, and no one would ever learn a damn thing about the money or the dope. He knew this as if he had read the script for the next few months. Samson could take care of things here. He wanted to go back to his motel, put his feet up, have a couple of drinks in a cool room. As he walked to his car with Lancaster, he was thinking what a pretty place this could be if anyone had cared enough to do it and then maintain it.

"I should have gone into landscaping," he said. "Good

life, out in the open air, making things grow, pretty things. Not a bad life.''

"You couldn't have stopped him," Drew said. He felt sick.

"I know. If not then, later. When they want to do it enough, they do it. I misjudged him. I didn't think he was the type. Crazy, I guess. He acted crazy. Thought the kids were out to get him. Said there wasn't anywhere to go far enough away from them. Crazy. I'd put pink roses along the driveway there. Tea roses.''

They got to his car. He drove. At the gate house one of his men was now on duty. He spoke to him briefly, then drove on with Drew. For a long time they were both silent.

"What really pisses me," Lauder muttered, "is the feeling that I've been used.'' He lapsed into silence again.

Drew nodded. Lauder had been a necessary part. Lauder and his agents had been the final touch in the discreditation of the whole project; necessary, used. The senators would duck out fast—dope, funny money, scandal, child abuse, god knew what all . . . The discreditation was total, irrefutable. Those kids could have broken out at any time, but they would have been fugitives. This way there were no questions hanging over them, over the project. No loose ends. Irma would step in, take charge, everything open, above suspicion, the project dead, a boondoggle of breathtaking magnitude, best buried and forgotten as soon as possible. The youngsters would be free to leave, disperse, scatter. No questions asked, not ever again.

But without Sorbies and the play money, there would have been no Secret Service involvement. Sorbies had been necessary, too. Bait for Lauder. The whole goddamn agency, he thought with wonder and added, plus the IRS. He felt dazed. Michelle and T.M. had been necessary, had been maneuvered step by step through audits, losing both jobs, the play money . . . They had been brought here, just as surely as Lauder. Sorbies, as he had been.

He could trace his own steps, each one apparently independent of the rest but with a pattern, he admitted reluctantly. He had had to be alone and that meant the separation and divorce—and Pat's father's illness? Necessary. Necessary. What else could have been used as a wedge between them?

Franklin, the Indian, Lisa . . . Even Irma's fortune, her father's wisdom . . . More than fifty years ago, he thought with a chill that raised hairs on his arms.

If the universal clock had been started eons ago, he thought then, someone or something had recently made an adjustment, reset the time.

"I'm very much afraid we're the new dinosaurs," he murmured without realizing he was speaking aloud.

Lauder glared at him. "What's that supposed to mean?"

"Nothing, Leon. Nothing at all. You know about gerbils?"

"Christ!"

"They say—people who know about things like this—that if even a few are released, free to scatter, scatter their seed, eventually they'll replace the native rodents. Would that be so awful, do you suppose?"

"Knock it off, will you!" Lauder snapped. He took a breath, then said in a quiet voice, "You'll have to go back once more. Today's not a good day, but you'll have to point out the kid who gave you that paper."

"I didn't really see him," Drew said. "I doubt that I'd recognize him."

Lauder grunted. "Way it goes. We'll try."

Drew could not rid himself of the image of the kids, frozen, the one remote and icy gaze. Had they done it? Could they do something like that? Or had they simply known? He could not answer his own question. He wondered if Leon believed in God, in fate, in hidden variables.

"You really going to write Huysman's biography?" Lauder asked.

"No."

Drew remembered what Sorbies had said a long time ago, that he was interested in world changers, people who made a difference. He was, but not this one. No one would ever write his biography, no one.

At the Huysman house Lauder turned off the motor. "You and Ms. Stevens getting back together?"

"Yes."

"That's nice, Nice lady. Think if I ask her, she'd tell me what the demonstration today was all about?"

"I don't know."

"Yeah. I've been thinking. If I wanted to discredit someone, I'd wait until he was having an important demonstration with bigwigs and then I'd lead the cops in on a bum rap. He thought the kids were behind it. I don't think that."

Drew looked at him steadily. "Leon, there are things in life that no one ever knows. Haven't you found that to be true?"

Lauder sighed more heavily than before and turned the key in the ignition. "I'll be in touch. We're not through with each other, Mr. Lancaster. Not yet."

"Drew. Call me Drew. Leon, maybe some day you can tell me what it's been like, being a Secret Service agent all these years, your adventures, disappointments, successes. Would you do that? I'll pay for lunch and dinner, whatever."

Lauder made a strangled sound deep in his throat. "Get out! I'll call you in a day or two. Beat it!"

But he would do it, Drew thought, leaving the car. Leon's life was a fascinating book idea, and he had both sides he could work with. The same story from both sides. That always made for interesting material. And they would talk about God and fate, he decided.

Pat met him at the door. He nodded silently and then kissed her. Through the doorway he could see into the living room where Lisa was on the floor with Sherry, looking at a scrapbook, evidently one of Irma's. She was on a brocade chair beaming at them both.

Lisa looked up and smiled at Drew, her wonderful, beautiful, helpless-little-girl smile. And he felt the recurring chill.

What had he done? What would they do? What could they do?

He tightened his hand on Pat's shoulder and they entered the living room, as he thought: and now it begins.